INTO THE GAME

C.A.A. ALLEN

I0618250

FANTASTIC SCIENCE
FANTASY ADVENTURES
PRESS

This is a work of fiction. All characters within are the products of the authors imagination. Any resemblance to actual persons, living or dead, is entirely coincidental and all incidents are pure invention.

ISBN-13: 978-0-578-43263-2

ISBN-10: 0-578-43263-3

Published by

Fantastic Science Fantasy Adventures Press

New York • San Diego • Toronto • Nottingham • Sydney

First Edition: April 2019

Book designed by Master IAM of Zwolle Ltd, St Ives Plc

Ϯ Ҡ

Cover, maps, & illustrations by Darko Tomic

For Charlotte Rose Arrington.

DUNGEON CRAWL QUEST

A BRUTAL LAND IS AHEAD...

WIZARD WARRIOR QUEST

CHAPTER 1

I pat the top of my computer monitor for luck. *Do me right this time. No cemetery.* I palm my computer's mouse and move the party of six adventurers forward, down a dark stone-lined tunnel.

My screen is a clunky CRT, awarded to me my senior year of high school for being the top achiever in technology club. That was three years ago, and the color representation is still true, albeit a bit pixelated.

I guide the party through scattered bones, down a flight of stairs, and into a hazy corridor with a thick layer of sludge on the floor. Slime drips from above as I take them through the muck, up a couple steps, then down a long hall. Their steps leave wet imprints as they run to a small room with an arched, glowing door. It is made of heavy dark wood with iron bands and has a small square peek-hatch in its upper middle surrounded by four ring knockers, one at each corner.

A prompt appears at the bottom of my screen.

>*WELCOME TO THE MONSTER ALLOCATION CHAMBER*

"Okay." I gulp down the last sip of my Frag Fuel—The Energy Drink by Gamers, for Gamers— and take a deep breath. This is the first time I've made it this far with my full party alive. And we are all maxed-out on hit points and armor class. Today has to be the day I kill this sorry overpowered SOB.

I scoot closer to my desk. First things first—got to take down the force shield with Hawkwind's Cadence. I click on the lead character, and his fist pounds the door using the pattern it took me three months to find. It was a long grind in the East Dungeon, and an epic battle with a Medusa Demon to get that knock—three quick, three slow, and one loud pound.

I back the party up a little and watch the glow around the door dissipate from top to bottom. Good. Now for step two.

The bottom right knocker morphs into a grotesque ghoul head with a long nose and large brass ring in its mouth. *And there it is.* I move my cursor over the head, click, and watch my lead character raise and slam the ring down.

SCHLIK! The door peek-hatch snaps open.

I lean in, my nose practically touching the screen. *Okay, here we go.*

The bloodshot cat-eye of a goblin—*the* goblin—appears, peering through the grill. "Provide a password, flee, or fight." His voice croaks through my computer speakers.

>F) ORWARD R) IGHT L) EFT K) ICK U) SE ITEM E) NTER PASSWORD

I survey my options. Rumor has it the password is a myth, and I am not one to flee. So, I open my possessions menu.

>EQUIP CHARACTER *Jareth Goblinmasher.*

What combination should I go with this time? I can't mess this up. Not again. Not with the prize money at stake. The prestige. The—

Focus. I scroll down the list, surveying every item, and choose.

>BOMBARDMENT BOOTS.

I reach the bottom of the list and finish with:

>BLADE CUSINART.

I am going to scream if this doesn't do the trick.

I rest my left index finger gently on top of the 'K' key and grip the mouse. "Here's a password for you, deez nuts." I press the key down and push my mouse forward, left and right. Jareth kicks the door down, jumps, and thrusts his blade across the mammoth greater goblin's left knee.

The blade snaps in two against his bone and blood sprays across the room.

"Buh-wooo!" The beast shrieks, then stiff-arms Jareth in the chest, blasting him backward into the trailing party members. They go flying like pins hit by a bowling ball.

The goblin stumbles backward and dark smoke billows into the chamber. "Bwahaaa!" He grumbles.

My screen turns black. Then I see it.

>Jareth Goblinmasher... DEAD
>Runner Treborbunk... DEAD
>Richter Ufgood ... DEAD
>Vin Brandywater... DEAD
>Camille D'Voidoffunk... DEAD
>Madd Overlord... DEAD
>YOUR ENTIRE PARTY HAS BEEN SLAUGHTERED
>PRESS THE RETURN ↵ KEY TO LEAVE THE CEMETERY AND START AGAIN

"No!" I pick up my keyboard at both ends and slam it down, sending several of the keys bouncing to the floor.

I growl, then hang my head in my hands. So much for the prize money and prestige. But that isn't the main reason I play. The very existence of my favorite game is at stake. "Damn that goblin. I'll never get past him." I lean back in my chair and wince at the screen. *Back to the temple for resurrection once again.*

My bedroom door slams into the back of my chair, barely missing cracking my skull open.

"Ah-ha-ha-ha. Wipeout!" My younger brother barges into the small room, as unwelcome as the graveyard scene on my screen.

"Hey," I snap. "I'm pretty sure I locked that door, Mack." My brother has the worst timing. He's only one year younger than me, but it might as well be ten. Agreeing to let him be my dorm mate often feels more like a babysitting job...that doesn't pay.

"Oh, you did lock it." Mack shakes the back of my chair. "But there's not a lock I can't pick, or a computer I can't hack."

"Leave me alone." I shove him. Why does he goof around so much? "This is serious, okay?"

"Ol' boy whooped you again, huh?" My window curtain gusts open, blown aside by a hot morning breeze. "It's a glitch, Riff. There's no way to kill the goblin, and everyone knows it."

I lift my head and squint up at Mack. His rat nest of dreadlocks hangs in his face. "There is a way. And I'm going to be the one who finds it." I've spent countless hours of my life playing this game. I refuse to write them off as wasted time. Solving this puzzle is going to make me a legend in the gaming industry.

"You ain't finding nothing." Mack twists a lock and shakes his head. "The dude who developed that game is dead. If there is a way to kill the goblin, he took that secret with him to the massively multiplayer online game in the sky." For Mack, the self-proclaimed "best computer hacker ever" to say this revealed how truly low he'd let himself sink. No faith whatsoever. No stamina.

4

"I got this, Mack. All I need to do is double my efforts like Commander Jerjerrod."

"Commander who?" Mack picks up a small green circuit board from the top of my desk. "You do know that the side-channel power analysis and glitching capabilities of this board suck, right?"

I snatch the board from him and put it back on my desktop. "The goblin's chamber is just one in a series of puzzles that needs to be unlocked. Step one is the force shield cadence. Step two is using the Bombardment Boots to get the door open." I curve in the fingers of my right hand, blow on the nails, and rub them on my chest. "I was the first to discover that move."

Mack rolls his eyes. "You're still stuck and unable to kill the goblin like everyone else."

I raise a finger. "There's a difference between them and me. *They* enter the chamber and get slaughtered. *I* have found a way to hurt the beast and draw the killer smoke. It's the goblin that kills them. It's the smoke that kills me. I'm one step *ahead* of everybody else."

Mack picks up my guitar from its long-standing spot against the wall. It's an acoustic model with a mahogany top and maple neck. In the battle between guitar lessons and gaming, the computer wins the bulk of my time. But I keep the guitar around because girls like it, and because my name is Riff. I can actually strum the chords of Bob Marley's 'Three little birds' with some accuracy.

Mack blows dust off the guitar's tuners and runs his fingers across the strings. "You've been stuck at that same spot for the last five months."

"Stop playing with my stuff." He doesn't understand. I'm a natural at this game. I have leveled up faster and advanced further than anyone. "I know I'm on to something by targeting the goblin's left knee. I just need to find the correct weapon to exploit it. A weapon that won't snap in two upon impact."

Mack replaces the guitar and picks a crumpled computer key out from under his shoe. "Give up, bro. People don't even play Dungeon Crawl Quest anymore." He flicks the key onto my desk. "Nobody wants to invest their time trying to achieve an impossible goal. You're not going to be able to kill the goblin, because it can't be done. It's the greater goblin glitch."

"For the last time, it's *not* a glitch." I snatch up the keyboard key and snap it back into place with a little too much force. "It's a puzzle begging to be unlocked."

"Wake up and smell the Red Bull, Riff. DCQ is dead as Toontown Online. It's a game that will end up right next to those Atari E.T. cartridges in that New Mexico landfill. I mean, how in the name of Gul'dan's butthole did the publisher release this game? If the developer was still alive, he'd be trampled by a gang of frustrated gamers."

If Kurht Knaud was still alive," I let out a wishful sigh, "everything would be different. He could give clues. He could affirm it's not a glitch." But he was dead, and the online newspapers had barely covered his passing last week. All he'd gotten was a two paragraph obituary.

I look back at my screen and the six tombstones with my party's names on them. "So you need to watch your mouth," I warn Mack, as I hit the return key to leave the cemetery screen. "DCQ is the greatest, deepest, and most ingenious game of all time." I am also the top-ranked player, and the only person to ever cap-out at level ten. But I stop myself from reminding him. This is an age-old argument between us. That's why he is getting a degree in productivity software development, and I am getting one in interactive media and game development. We both love gaming, but we come at it from different angles.

I spin around in my chair and stand, careful to avoid the dirty clothes and crumpled potato chip bags. "I've got a large, loving faction of dedicated gamers counting on me to figure this out. My closest competitor is a butt-ugly mage named Madmartigan, who is only at level eight. But if he catches up to me at level ten, he'll be able to equip with any weapon he finds, and I truly believe that finding the right weapon is the key to killing the goblin and unlocking this—"

"Glitch."

"—*puzzle*."

Mack peeks into the crumpled potato chip bag and fishes out one lone, old chip piece. "It's a glitch, Riff. Can't you get that through your big tossed-salad, hairdo-havin', cantaloupe head?" He pops the chip piece into his mouth. There's not even a crunch as he chews, it's so stale.

"No. Because it's a doorway to unlocking a whole other world in DCQ. And when I do, I will be the king of the MMORPG gaming world." And I would get the cash prize being offered, which I need badly. But Mack doesn't need to know that.

"Yeah, right." Mack steps out of my door into the living room. "You know it's almost 9:00 a.m., and you're a mess. Don't you have a breakfast date?"

I look down at my pajamas and almost laugh. I always lose track of time playing this game. And now it is time to play, "How quick can I get dressed?"

Three bangs on the front door echo through the room.

"Speak of the devil." Mack races to answer it. "Let me get this for you."

Oh man, I can't believe this. "Hold up. Wait a minute," I plead.

Mack grabs the doorknob and looks back at me. "Let me put some pimpin' in it." He swings the door open wide.

"Excuse me, Mack." Mileena—my always-sexy, but often-angry girlfriend—takes a couple steps in and straightens her white silk blouse. Her long legs, flawless lipstick, and magazine-cover hair look comically out of place in the center of our grimy bachelor pad.

She picks her way around a coffee table weighed down by day-old Chinese food containers and empty soda bottles. "You ready?" She gains her footing and looks me over. "You're not ready."

"Mileena." I turn my computer monitor off and close the bedroom door behind me. "Is it 9:00 already?"

She puts a hand on her hip. "You are unbelievable. I told you this was your last chance. Clearly you didn't think I meant it."

I run a hand through my hair, hoping it'll result in something other than un-showered bed-head. "No, you see, I was really close to a breakthrough in my game last night."

"Riff, save it!" She strides to the bathroom door, pushes it open, twists the ring off her finger, and looks down into the open toilet. "Hm, someone forgot to flush." She flicks the ring into the bowl. "That's what I think of your promises and your promise ring."

I grit my teeth. The ring is real gold, and—I thought—something special to both of us. At least she said it was when I gave it to her. Good thing the toilet is broken, so I know it's not going anywhere. "Mileena, don't overreact. I can be ready in just a few…"

She looks down at my plush hobbit-foot slippers. "I should have known not to make a date with someone whose dream vacation would be in Hobbit Town. You and your dreams are going nowhere."

"It's Hobbiton not *Hobbit Town,* and it's actually a really nice resort in New Zealand. I think you might like it."

"Whatever." She spins around, steps out our door, and snatches a pink piece of paper taped to the front of it. "This note is from the financial aid department. It says you must vacate the dorm and campus in five days, due to nonpayment." She crushes the paper in her fist and throws it at my chest. "Broke-ass. You ain't nothing but a broke-ass. I quit you." She slams the door.

I grab ahold of the knob to rush after her and…pause. If I could only make her understand why this game is so important to me. I give the knob a quarter turn, then stop. What can I do to make this better?

"Bye, Felicia," Mack laughs. "You need a gamer girl in your life, Riff, not whatever that is. I mean, I'm sorry playa, but your princess in another castle."

"Shut up, toad." *I have to go after Mileena. Maybe I can make her understand.*

"What ya gonna do?" Mack says, with a conniving smile.

"I'm gonna chase her down in my hobbit slippers." My declaration is a bit half-hearted, and then I notice something. There is a toaster-sized parcel on the kitchen table, wrapped in brown paper and tied in twine.

I hover by the door for a moment longer, then release the knob and step toward it. "When did that get here?" I ask.

CHAPTER 2

Mack picks up the wadded pink slip from the floor and shrugs. "I don't know. I think it was outside the door when I came back from class this morning. Which reminds me, thanks for the tips on that systems analysis test." He smooths out the pink paper and hands it to me. "This is bad news. If you get kicked out of school, I don't know what I'm going to do without my study partner."

"Well, not all of us got a full-ride scholarship. Some of us got to pay for this education the hard way, and the Beef and Bun is cutting hours." That reminds me: I have to be at work at noon. I'm in no mood to flip burgers today, especially for just a two-hour shift, but it's the only job I've managed to scrape up. And with the pink paper of pending eviction staring up at me, I'd best ditch the hobbit slippers and don the apron.

"Don't hate on me," Mack shoots back. "I'm not the one who got caught bypassing the I.T. department's block, got kicked out of technology club, and lost all my awards and scholarships."

Bypassing my high school's firewall was the biggest mistake I had ever made in my life. But who could blame me? All I'd had at home was an outdated, sluggish computer that got me killed in every game I played. I couldn't take one more day of the stuttering, lag, or long moments of complete frame freeze.

My plan had been simple. Use the superior power of my school's new computer and my own hacking abilities to trick games into giving me virtual currency I could sell at discounted prices on eBay for real money. It would be a win-win situation for me and my fellow gamers. And I was only going to do it until I had enough money for a new computer. I had only needed three hundred more dollars when the network administrator had called me into her office. I still don't know how she found out that I had bypassed her security measures. But the hammer had been solidly dropped on all my scholarships.

I'll never let myself do something that stupid again. And the worst part of it was, I had to repeat my twelfth-grade year and graduate in the same class as my little brother.

I run my hand across the top of the parcel. "This just may contain what I need to win Blizivision's prize money and make my dorm payment." I might have graduated late from high school, but I am determined not to repeat that for college.

"Good," Mack says. "Because we're in this together. All of it. College and the great beyond."

I know what he means. We have agreed to apply to all the major software companies as a design *team* after graduation. Mack might be annoying, but we work well together.

I tug on the package's twine, but it barely stretches.

Mack slides me a pair of scissors. "I would say you should go after Mileena, but I've never liked her, and you know it. She's all wrong for you."

My heart is pounding through my chest, but not for Mileena. Mack is kinda right about her. She may be one of the prettiest girls on campus, but she doesn't treat people well. I think, deep down, I'd been hoping she'd break up with me so I didn't have to break up with her.

"You heard her." I shrug. "She quit me." And said my dreams are going nowhere. That's the wrong thing to say to me. I was raised not to let anyone talk down my dreams. I'll be damned if I let that start now.

I stare down at the label on the package and the New York postmark. I won't have much time for a girlfriend after I open it anyway. This package is from Kurht Knaud himself. Only the first four players to reach level nine were slated to receive it. And now that Kurht is dead, I'm probably the only player to get one.

"This might have a clue to unlock the goblin chamber puzzle," I tell Mack.

"You mean the goblin chamber *glitch*?" Mack opens the door to our mini-fridge and looks over the contents. The fridge sits on top of an old end table in the spot a regular-sized refrigerator stood before it stopped running. Lucky for us, a neighboring student had an extra mini we could borrow.

I hack at the twine. The scissors are about as effective as a butter knife. The blade finally cuts through and whacks into my finger. Blood bubbles from the cut and drops onto the table. "Awwww, damn. Where did you find these dull-ass scissors?" I fling them across the room where they lodge into the wall.

Mack covers his mouth, but it doesn't stop his laughter. Drink spews from behind his hand. "You might need a tetanus shot with that cut."

"Shut up, fool." I dress my wound in paper towels, secure it with clear tape, and return to the package. "Okay, here we go." I tear off the paper and rip the top open. Packing peanuts barely cover the piled items and glittering swag filling the box. A deadly calm fills me—as though my body isn't sure how to process the potential of this moment. "Look at all the stuff in here. It's the deluxe fan package."

Mack digs a hand in and pulls out a round gold disk. "A pocket watch? Or is this the Golden Compass?"

So, it's true. I grab the disk from Mack's hand. "This is not an Alethiometer. *This* is a Grimoire." I push a small button on the top with my thumb.

The lid flips open, and a screen lights up with a red dot in the middle.

GRIMOIRE BETA - SERIAL NUMBER 05
SYNC INTO A DCQ PLAYERS DEN COMPUTER TO START
TOUCH HERE TO BEGIN

●

I thought these things were just a rumor. But they're real, and I have one in my hand.

Mack pushes my shoulder. "What does it do? Touch the red dot."

"This is the DCQ developer's latest gaming peripheral. Not only does it hold my player stats, but it also contains access to new abilities, weapons, equipment, and items. Magical items. Things I know can help me unlock the puzzle." This is a dream come true. "Mack, I've been chosen as a Grimoire beta-tester. All I have to do is sync this thing into one of the developers optimized computers to unlock the goods."

I'm a tester for a new element of my favorite game. The one game I'm really good at, which also happens to be offering a cash prize that could pay for my dorm room and school.

I close the Grimoire and slide it into my pocket, not willing to part with something so important. It takes all my willpower not to throw on real shoes and sprint to the DCQ Players Den then and there.

A folded piece of paper protrudes from the top corner of the peanuts. "What's this?" I pull out the sheet and unfold it. It's the DCQ game map—The Kingdom of Fear. The map's layout is burned into my brain, but I never tire of looking at it. The Kingdom's topography is laid out like a giant quintuple fidget spinner. The City of Cittadella is in the center, and five points of interest are located at the end of each prong around it—The East Dungeon, The North Caves, The West Labyrinth, The Town of Chittor to the Southwest, and Parts Unknown to the Southeast.

"A map? Lame." Mack flicks a packing peanut off the kitchen table. "They come in every game box."

I rub a corner of the map with my thumb. "But the one that comes in the box is regular paper. This is vellum."

I look the map up and down. "There's some weird hand-written annotations on this map," I point them out to Mack. Two notes written in green ink: *A-Sampir* and *B-Taguban*. "They could have been added by the developer himself." I can't wait to fire up the game and check these map points out. I re-fold the map and put it in my back pocket.

Mack pulls a bronze coin from the box. It has a three-legged frog on its face. "This is cool. Can I have it?"

"Hell no, you can't!" I smack the top of his hand, pinch the coin, and rip it away. "This is DCQ swag. You don't want to get glitch on you, remember?"

"Oh, I remember." Mack pulls his hand back. "I just like the coin."

"This coin, along with a secret password, gains entrance to a private room called The DCQ Players Den in Los Angeles. The entrance to the room is hidden in a LAN gaming center called The Spirit & Game." This is my chance to see the den, sync the Grimoire into one of the optimized computers, and obtain information I need to unlock the puzzle. I pull out my phone, open Google Maps, and enter the starting point: *University of California, San Diego.*

Now, where am I going? I dig into the box and pull out a strip of blue raffle tickets with The Spirit & Games address on it, enter the info into my phone, and get the route information. It's just a two hour and twenty-minute drive. But how to get there? Man, I hate not having a car.

"Good luck with all that." Mack heads to his room.

Wait. Mack has a car. Not a reliable one, but a car nonetheless. I have to talk him into taking me. "We should go. It's just a short drive from here to The Spirit & Game. We can be there in just, uh, an hour or so," I lie.

"Nah." Mack slurps his drink. "I have zero interest in some geeky club house. And why go all the way to LA? This is the digital age. Everything is on the internet. We shouldn't even have to leave this room."

"It's not a club house. The DCQ Players Den is a private gaming suite." How does this not intrigue him? "Not only does the den contain the developer's special optimized computers, but word is it has a corkboard filled with hand written notes by him, and—get this—it also contains the DCQ world server. It would be an honor to get in there and see all that stuff!"

Mack crushes the can in his hand and shakes his head. "As much as I love server architecture, I don't want to see the world's glitchiest one. Besides, you only have one coin, I won't be able to get into this den."

"But you will be able to get into the gaming center. And once we're in the center, we'll finagle you into the DCQ den. You know how *we* do it." I look over the raffle tickets and my eyes widen. "Hey, these are food and drink tickets." I hold up the strip and dangle it in his face. "And each one includes an hour of free gaming. Never mind about The DCQ Den. We are going to be in a state-of-the-art fiber LAN gaming center with free food, drinks and game play. They even have a bar there. You just turned twenty-one last month, and we haven't really celebrated yet. If you drive fast enough, I'll even treat you to some Roscoe's on the way. That Carol C. Special got one succulent breast, and for sure one delicious waffle."

"Free drinks and Scoe's? Let's go." Mack struts into his bedroom. "But you have to drive back, cause I'm gonna be drinking. And you gotta pay for the gas. And there better be some naughty nerdettes there."

I pump my fist and scramble to change out of my hobbit slippers.

"Wait, don't you gotta work today?" Mack calls.

"I got the work thing handled. Just get ready." My boss has given me an ultimatum: next time I show up late, I'm fired. But I can't pass up this opportunity. It's way more important than burger flipping.

I walk past the bathroom on my way to my room and remember the ring. If I leave it in there, I might forget it. I step into the bathroom and look in the toilet bowl. A swirling brown vortex has what looks like a burnt corndog spinning in the middle.

"Ugh." Somewhere in this slurry lies a gold-plated, limited edition, Tengwar inscribed ring that took me six long months to run down. I feel like Frodo at Mount Doom. How could Mileena do this to the pseudo One Ring?

I return to the kitchen and rummage through the cupboards. Surely, we have something I can use to fish out that ring. Would salad tongs be too much to ask for? Or even a slotted spoon? I dig through a drawer filled with sticky ketchup and soy sauce packets and pull out a set of nine-inch disposable chopsticks.

They just might work.

I return to the bathroom, roll up a sleeve and position the two sticks between my fingers. *I don't care how long this takes. I am getting my ring out of this pu pu platter.*

CHAPTER 3

My head flings forward. I open my eyes and grab the back of my neck. "What the—"

"Wake up." Mack turns the radio knob to max volume. "This is my song. I love LA radio stations."

I squint at the road in front of me. "Where are we?"

"Between Normandie and Western." Mack pulls down the sun visor, accelerates, and cuts into the right lane. "And deep in LA traffic. I decided to pass on Roscoe's and go straight for our drinking destination. We should be at your Spirit & Game place in just a few minutes."

A few minutes. Yes! I don't really have Roscoe's money, anyway. I pull the Grimoire from my pocket and run my finger along the embossed spiral pattern. With this, and snooping around The DCQ Den, I will be that much closer to unlocking the goblin chamber puzzle.

"So, what's the password?" Mack asks, exiting the freeway.

"The password to what?" I flip the disk over and try to decipher the fine script on the back.

Mack weaves into the left lane, floors it around a trash truck, and then cuts back to the right. "What's the password to enter the private DCQ den?"

"Oh, it's 'Kurht sent me.'" I pull the disk in close, finally making out the fine print, despite the rattling of Mack's rickety car. *UNIT 5 of 7.* Five-of-seven? I don't get it. Only the first four players to reach level nine were supposed to get one of these, and I got number five. Who has the first four? Was the developer able to send out six and seven before he died?

"That's not exactly a brilliant password," Mack slams on the breaks, shifts into reverse, and backs into a parking spot between two cars.

I slide the Grimoire back in my pocket. "Doctor Kurht Knaud was not only DCQ's developer, programmer, designer, and director, he was also an accomplished neurologist."

Mack twists his key up and down in the ignition several times. "Argh, come on." He yanks and the key comes free. "And yet Doctor Kurht made a glitchy game," he adds, goading me.

I ignore him, get out of the car, and look over the storefront. A polished metal sign, with the words *The Spirit & Game* punched out, is mounted on a red brick wall above the door in front of me. Two blackened square windows on either side have bright neon signs in them. The one to the right says *Southfarthing Frogmorton Ginger Beer*. The left says *Internet Bar & LAN Gaming Center- Free Wi-Fi*.

This looks like something Kurht would do. A vintage brick front with modern metal and neon highlights. The old meets the new.

"Word online is Kurht lodged a Javanese dagger into the ceiling above the bar here," I tell Mack. "The last person to touch the thing was a freakishly tall girl. She had to have it, after drinking a few cocktails, to cut her steak dinner. The girl couldn't pull the dagger out of the ceiling but was able to write down some numbers she saw engraved on the pommel. Those numbers gave her a small lotto win the next day."

Mack jumps up on the curb and stretches out his arms. "Lotto win, my eye."

19

"Check it out, Mack. I believe the password to enter the goblin's chamber without triggering the killer smoke is actually the numbers engraved on that pommel. I told you, I'm in Kurht's head."

"Out of your mind is more like it." Mack opens the bar door and waves me in. "After you, head doctor."

The deep but narrow room is dim and cool with blue neon lighting. The left side has a long bar with beer taps and liquor bottles behind it. The right has a row of computer gaming stations with oversized high-back leather chairs running the length of the room. Several players are seated on the computer side wearing headphones with boom mics. A large flat panel TV on the back wall has a giant red and blue spinning logo. *NGL - The best of professional eSports live!*

This is my kind of place.

I'm so entranced by the call of the nerd that I almost run straight into a vacant hostess podium.

Mack breezes past me to the bar. "No girls," he grumbles, "but at least I can drink."

I jog to catch up, not wanting *him* to be the first to step into *my* domain. "Look around, Mack, this is awesome. They got all the best games here."

I look over the chairs at the first two gaming stations. The first one is occupied by a hooded gamer slumped over his keyboard, eyes closed. Empty candy wrappers and several energy drink cans litter the floor around him.

I pump my fist and smile. Finally, I get to meet some gamers just like me: people who play their favorite games so long they pass out right on the keyboard.

I look back at Mack and whisper, "This guy is knocked out for real." I got to get one of these stations for the dorm. The game play must be amazing.

I hover over the second player in the computer rows and accidentally bump his chair. He looks up at me, scowls, and scoots in closer to his monitor. I recognize the online game menus, the grassy terrain, the wide-eyed characters.

I step back and grab Mack by both shoulders. "This guy is playing Mabinogi. A girl in China lived in an internet café for ten years playing it."

Mack shakes off my hands. "It better not take me ten years to get my free drink. My mouth is as dry as a saltine birthday cake." He plops down at the first bar stool. "I notice the gaming station with DCQ is unoccupied. I told you, nobody plays that game anymore."

"Unoccupied? I'm going to go play right now." I take one step toward the station and stop in my tracks. I'm itching to visit the new map points, but I've got a dagger to see, a den to enter, a Grimoire to sync, and most importantly a puzzle to unlock. I turn, sit next to Mack, and scan the ceiling. Where is that dagger? I got to have those pommel numbers.

A guy about my age, with black spiked hair and round purple shaded goggles on the top of his forehead, walks behind us to a crowded table at the back of the room. He sneaks up on the occupants and pops his head over one of their shoulders. "Boo! I made it." He points at the giant TV. "What time does the next match start? My money's on Team Kaliber."

Several people at the table stand and greet him with fist bumps.

I look closely at him and tap Mack on the shoulder. "Hey, I think that's Antonio 'Ant-Bot' Taylor, the Let's Play YouTuber."

Mack leans back, looks over at the table, and returns his attention to the bottles behind the bar. "Who?"

I roll my eyes. Mack doesn't keep track of anything in the gaming world. How can he live like that? "Ant-Bot Taylor makes gameplay commentary videos, reviews games, and plays eSports. I'm pretty sure he live-streams form the bar here on Thursdays." And today is a Thursday.

Mack twists a dread and takes another look at the table. "I remember you talking about that dude. Isn't he the one that blasts DCQ all the time? I'm surprised you haven't gone over there and punched him in his face."

I kind of want to. Ant-Bot is a big part of the reason my game gets badmouthed. His show is cool though, so he gets a pass. Besides, I can't hold it against the little folk for not being able to enter the goblin's chamber. Their bitterness comes from their own stunted stamina. I turn my attention to a monitor behind the bar showing a live League of Legends eSports gaming match.

A thin man with box-frame eyeglasses drops two napkins in front of me and Mack. "Welcome to The Spirit & Game. My name is Anton T., at your service. What will it be, guys?"

Mack points to a row of taps and licks his lips. "An IPA would be wonderful."

I look over at a shelf of gaming supplements and spy my favorite. "Frag Fuel for me." I pull the drink tickets from my pocket. "We have these."

Anton scrunches his lips and mumbles, "Kurht continues to drive me out of business."

"Did you know him?" I blurt, ripping off two tickets. Time to start gathering information.

He snatches the tickets from my hand. "Kurht was my best friend and business partner. We co-owned this place. Then he died three days ago and left me in a whole lot of debt." Anton cracks open a can and pours the fizzy light blue liquid in a glass over ice. He then pours a draught beer and sets the drinks in front of us. "Debt that would have been paid, if he didn't give away drinks or make glitch-ridden games."

"Ha!" Mack nudges my arm and smiles from ear to ear. "Did you here that? Glitch-ridden. I told you."

I wave Mack off and wrap my hand around the ice-cold glass. "Don't you get any royalties from DCQ, though?" I ask.

Anton turns, rises on his toes, and pulls a skinny glass bottle down from the top shelf. Its label is embellished with an elegant cathedral, topped with several gold onion domes. He fills a shot glass with the crystal-clear liquid and holds it up, staring at the glass.

"Not a dime." He pounds it back, then slams the glass down on the bar. "Because unfortunately, the game's publisher, Blizivision Studios, put a clause in the DCQ contract that suspends all royalties until any occurring error is fixed. So, please don't tell me you're a fan of that chain around my neck."

Mack scratches his head and sucks air through gritted teeth. "Here we go. Don't go off on him to hard, bro."

I down half of my beverage and plunk the glass to the bar. "I'm DCQ's biggest fan. I love it." A couple sitting farther down the bar looks at me, then returns to their drinks, chuckling. "It's not a glitch, error, or programming fault. It's a puzzle that needs to be unlocked."

Anton refills his glass with the clear liquor and then fills up another one right beside it. "You're going to need one of these, then." He slides the extra shot to me. "You see, if nobody advances past the Monster Allocation Chamber by midnight tonight, the DCQ servers will be shut down indefinitely. Apparently, subscription numbers have dropped below five-hundred and Blizivision is cashing out."

I just sit there. Numb. Surely, I misheard.

"Damn." Mack takes a sip off the top of his beer and makes a sour face. "They're not even giving the game a proper MMO apocalypse?"

"Nope." Anton swallows his shot and sets the glass down. "One of the main servers is located right here in the bar. If you hang around until midnight, you just might get to see the publisher's goons come in, shut it down, and remove the hardware."

Midnight? *Midnight?* That is barely twelve hours away.

Anton scoots his glasses up the bridge of his nose. "Once the server is shut down, all the game rights, revenue, technology, and properties revert to Kurht's very unreasonable development partner. A man that has vowed—and I quote—to terminate everything that has to do with the DCQ money pit. My bar here is one of DCQ's properties. This place goes down with the DCQ ship."

"They can't do that," I say, my stomach in my throat. This can't happen. My game and character will be gone forever. I gave up my girlfriend and my job for this. I practically gave up my life, if you added up all the hours I'd spent. I have to do something. "I can unlock the puzzle by midnight," I say, pulling the bronze coin from my pocket and holding it up. "Kurht sent me."

Anton grabs my wrist and pulls the coin in close. "What did you say?"

"Kurht sent me." I try and pull my hand back, but he tightens his grip. "That *is* the password, right?" I stammer.

"That is the password." Anton cocks a smile. "I like to follow the progress of the top, um, seven or so characters in DCQ. I have a hunch about who you are." He looks at me with fixed eyes. "Jareth Goblinmasher?"

"Yeah, I mean, that's my main character. My name is Riff Jenkins, and this is my brother, Mack."

Anton releases my wrist. "Do you have a Grimoire?"

24

I pull the Grimoire from my pocket, flash it to him, and drop it back down.

"Well, well, well." The bartender rubs his chin. "Nice to meet you, Riff and Mack Jenkins. Riff, you have a coin, a Grimoire, and know the password. That makes you one of only seven individuals with the ability to enter The DCQ Den. Maybe you *can* unlock the puzzle."

Only seven? I had no idea the den was such an exclusive club. "Okay. Let's do it. Show me to the den."

"You're not ready." Anton pushes the shot glass closer to me. "Drink up. You're gonna need it."

I wrap my hand around the shot. "I'm the designated driver." I look at Mack. "Do you want this?"

"Just go on and take it to the head," he says. "But you're cut off after that." He leans into the bar and takes another sip of his beer. "Blaah. Is there even any alcohol content in this watered-down swill? Anton, I asked for an IPA, not this sewer water. And where is that lotto-dagger I've heard so much about? Riff needs it."

"No IPA with free drink tickets," Anton growls. "The dagger is lodged safely in a high ceiling beam inside of The DCQ Den. But it's never had anything to do with the lottery."

Mack pushes his beer back. "I knew that whole story was bogus."

I dump the shot down my throat, pause, and then pat my chest to ease the burn. Lotto or not, I need to get a look at that dagger and read its pommel numbers. They have to be a clue to cracking the game.

Anton flips up a small section of the bar. "Okay, gamer. Come on back and follow me."

I leap up so fast, my bar stool clatters to the floor behind me. I'm about to enter my own personal Mecca.

Mack snatches his beer and swallows it down with three loud gulps. "Ahh, nasty." He stands, picks up my fallen bar stool, and claps his hands three times. "Yup, let's go see this den."

"No." Anton holds out a hand. "No coin, no entrance. That's the rule."

Three young girls dressed in halter-tops and mini-skirts pull out bar stools alongside Mack and sit. They giggle amongst themselves, but neither Mack nor I miss the flirtatious sidelong glances they send his way.

"Besides," Anton raises his eyebrows, "someone needs to keep these ladies company while I take Riff back."

The girl closest to Mack stands and looks at him with crisp cat-like eyes. She has light skin, waist-length purple hair and fiery blood-red contacts. "Can you help us settle a bet?" she purrs. "Do I look more like Sylvanas Windrunner, Nika, or Nova Terra?"

Mack sits back down on his stool and looks the girl over. "Anton, I think I'm going to need another drink."

The girl spins around and strikes a pose. "Well? What do you think?"

Mack sits up straight. "Well, your eyes say Sylvanas, but you sure got Nova's hips. If you want to add some Nika into your look, I can make some suggestions."

I trail behind Anton to a narrow metal door at the far end of the bar. The closer we get, the more the bar-noise buzz fades. To the right of the metal door is a single shelf holding a myriad of old dusty trinkets and used game parts. A red velvet cloth covers several lumps in the center of the shelf.

It is on this cloth that Anton rests his hand. "Take out your coin."

I obey, gripping the coin tight in my fist. Anton glances around in all directions before snatching the cloth off. A cast iron statue of seven bright yellow and black frogs sitting in a row is on the shelf. Four of the frogs have their mouths open, three closed.

Anton inserts an iron skeleton key into the statue's base. "These are the Chachu. Put your coin into one of the open mouths but be careful. Its bite can paralyze."

I look at Anton to judge if he is kidding about the paralysis thing. Not a twitch of humor crosses his face. Why is he trying to psych me out?

He winds the key several times. "Go on, put it in."

It doesn't seem to matter which frog I choose, so I place it in the mouth of the end frog, carefully balancing it on the frog's tongue. Its head snaps back and the coin drops down its throat. "Hey, my coin." I grab the frog's mouth with both hands and try to pry it open.

Anton pushes my hands away. "Your coin has been swallowed. It's gone for good. This is a one-time entry situation."

Click! The metal door opens a half-inch, a cool draft hitting me through it.

Anton takes a step back. "Do me a favor while you're in there. Remind your fellow den members of the deadline. If none of you get past the goblin by midnight, Blizivision pulls the plug."

"Plug pulling is not gonna happen," I assure him…and myself. "Just watch out for my brother while I'm in here."

Anton nods. "I'll keep him in good spirits. You just concentrate on the task at hand." He turns and walks back toward Mack waving one finger in the air. "You've just been upgraded to IPA, my friend."

I wrap my hand around the cold metal doorknob. Does this room contain the answers I need? What are the other den members going to be like? I open the door and take a few steps into a dim room. "Hello?"

Click.

The door closes shut behind me, removing what little bit of light I had. I reach for a knob but there isn't one—just a smooth, cold metal surface.

"Hey." I turn back to the room, blinking away the echo of light in my eyes. I guess there's no going back until I solve Kuhrt's puzzle.

As my vision adjusts to the dark, I make out a rectangular room about the size of my dorm living room. To the left, a server rack covers the wall from top to bottom and left to right. Its computer's fans and electronics fill the room with an ambient buzz, and its multicolored lights give the room a dim glow.

I run a finger across the DCQ world server. I'll be damned if I'll let anyone shut this baby down.

In the middle of the rack, I notice a square glass box with a glowing green stone inside of it, held between three metal prongs. I've never seen a hardware component like this before. What the hell was Kurht into? I reach out and touch the glass, and suddenly the stone's glow changes from green to purple. "Whoa." I jerk my hand back.

Now that my eyes have fully adjusted to the dim lighting, I make out a single door across the way, and six gaming stations against the wall to my left. All the monitors have brown and gold *Dungeon Crawl Quest* logo screen savers spinning on 24-inch curved displays. They call to me. Optimism matches the pulsing in my chest. I'm gonna do it. I'm gonna solve this game. These are the DCQ optimized game stations– six of them. But where are the gamers?

I walk along the game stations from left to right. The first one has a blue and black zebra pattern sport wheelchair in front of it. The chair's seat back and frame have assorted NGL eSports, Overwatch, Dota 2, and skull stickers all over it. The wheelchair looks familiar, but I can't remember where I've seen it.

The other five stations all have high-back gaming chairs, and each computer has a backlit keyboard, mouse, and a half-moon shaped docking cradle in front it.

I pick up a cradle from the station in front of me and look closer at the others. Three of them are loaded with Grimoires. But where are the gamers who synced them? Maybe I caught everyone on a lunch break or something. That just means fewer distractions as I jump back into the game.

I sit at one of the non-synced stations and wrap my hand around the mouse. There's no way I'm waiting another minute to try this out. I give the mouse a shake and the screen changes.

>*WELCOME TO THE WORLD OF DUNGEON CRAWL QUEST!*
>*YOU CANNOT PLAY WITHOUT SYNCING A GRIMOIRE.*
>*S) YNC GRIMOIRE*
>*B) EGIN GAME*

I'm so excited I let out a whoop of joy. If only those suckers in technology club could see me now. I pull the Grimoire from my pocket, drop it in the cradle, press 'S' on the keyboard, and feast my eyes on the screen.

>GRIMOIRE UPDATE IN PROGRESS
>PLEASE WAIT…

A loading bar pops up and the filler is barely visible, it's updating so slow. "Argh!" I grab onto the chair armrests with a death grip. I can't stand updates. Especially when the clock is ticking nearer and nearer the destruction of all that I hold dear. Okay, maybe that's a bit much, I flop my head back on the gaming chair and try not to count the seconds.

That's when I notice a large beam bisecting the ceiling with a dark object jutting from the center, high above my head. The legendary dagger.

I roll my chair under the spot and step onto the seat. With one hand on the seat back, I stretch out my other arm. I'm close, but I can't quite reach. How in the heck did that one girl reach the thing without help? She must have been half-elf.

I let go of the seat back, rise on my tiptoes, and stretch both hands up. I'm still an inch or so from the handle. I look around, but don't see anything that could help me get a leg up. The room is full of expensive and easily breakable technology, but little else. I'm going to have to jump or give up. And I'm not giving up.

I steady the chair, bend my legs, and push off, grabbing the dagger's handle with one hand. To my surprise, it doesn't come loose. It holds my weight and my legs flail, kicking the chair out from under me, so I'm left hanging from the ceiling by my one-handed grip on the knife.

The chair rolls into the server-wall, bounces off, and tips over.

"Come on, you." I wiggle my body and jerk it sideways, trying to work the blade loose from the wood before my arm gives out. "Come on!"

With a satisfying creak, the dagger slips from the beam, and I crash to the floor.

CHAPTER 4

"Hey there, are you all right?" A sweet female voice floats out of the darkness.

Have I been asleep? Or did I hit my head? I don't remember.

I open my eyes to slits, but the sun overhead blinds me. Wait…*sun?* A hazy hourglass-shaped figure stands over me. I angle my face so the figure blocks the direct ray of the sun. I try to speak but only manage a cough. It feels like there's dirt in my mouth.

A larger shadow falls over me and a grumpy male voice says, "Who's the lanky stiff?" He jabs me in the ribs with a boot. "Hey stiff, get up before I slit your throat."

"He's with me, Castilian." The sweet voice turns harsh. "Now, back off."

"I don't allow unregistered questers in my stronghold." The man moves away. "So, get him to the tavern before I send my people to apply some unpleasantries."

Quester? Stronghold? Tavern? I sit up and shade my eyes with a hand. It feels like the devil is banging on my skull with a war hammer. Where am I? How long was I out? And who was that rude bastard jabbing me in the ribs?

A slender girl, who looks to be about my age, kneels beside me. Her brown hair is in a loose bun, but the curls framing her face are dyed red. She wears curvy leather corset armor, a leather skirt with studded tassels, and has a nasty

31

looking dagger in her double-strapped thigh scabbard. "Sorry about the rude awakening. Castilian doesn't like afternoon arrivals in the Marketplace. Announced and early morning is the only way to avoid his grumpiness. Anyway, welcome in."

I look around. Not only am I no longer in the gaming Den, but I'm apparently no longer indoors at all. I sit in the middle of a dusty road in what seems to be an ancient village marketplace. Buildings and small booths of different sizes and shapes are situated in a large circle with lots of people walking between them.

"What...where...?" My pocket pops and vibrates wildly. "Whoa." I grind my palms into the gravel and crawl backward in a frenzy. "What the—" The Grimoire flips out of my pocket and pulsates across the ground. "I-I put that in the cradle. What...*what's going on?*"

Is all this just a dream? An elaborate hoax? Did Anton put something in my drink?

"Paperwork." The girl points to the bouncing gold disk. "Check it for your paperwork."

"Paperwork?" I corral the Grimoire, open it, and tap the red dot.

The girl snatches it from my hand. "Here, let me see."

"Hey, that's mine." I try to grab it back but miss by a mile.

She looks at the screen and perks up. "Well what do you know? Jareth Goblinmasher has entered the game. And with a nice abilities number too."

"Who are you?" I try to stand, but my head pounds when I do.

She smiles a wide, dimpled smile. "My gamer name is Madmartigan."

This is the Madmartigan who's been riding my coattails in DCQ? "You don't look like a Madmartigan," I tell her. She is not what I expected. Not at all. For one thing, she's a *she*. "How did you get to level eight?"

32

"Actually,"—her eyes narrow—"I've been at level nine for ages now. And I made it into The DCQ Players Den long before you did, didn't I? And I look exactly like a Madmartigan, because that's who I am."

At this point, I look down and notice my clothes. I am wearing a long-sleeved tunic, leather breastplate, brown trousers, low leather boots, and a thick belt with several empty sheaths and a small attached pull string bag.

"My real name is Bella, if you must kno—"

"Did you change my clothes?" I blurt.

"Not a chance." She runs her finger down my Grimoire's screen. "You're a fighter, Jareth. And that is entry-level fighter's garb." She seems to place an extra emphasis on the words *entry-level*.

I stand, take a deep breath, and crack my neck left and right. "Better." I loosen the strings on my belt's bag, dip in a hand, and pull out a fist full of silver and gold coins. I drop the coins back in and look at Bella. "What is going on?"

Bella closes my Grimoire and examines its back. "You'll find a spot for this on your belt." She tosses it to me.

I catch the Grimoire and find a sheath on my belt that fits it perfectly, just like she said. As I put it away, a small shock courses through my body, and I flinch.

"That jolt is how the Grimoire lets you know you're synced," Bella explains. "Your player stats will now appear in your forward vision."

Before she even finishes talking, stats and blurry words swim in front of my eyes in a translucent neon blue. It's hard to focus on them. And hard not to.

"You'll get used to it," she says. "It takes a few hours to acclimate."

"Um, thanks," I say. "And my real name is Riff. So, we're actually in the game?" I don't care if the question is stupid. Everything is pointing toward that weird reality, and I just want to hear a solid *Yes*.

Yes, my dreams have come true.

Yes, this is as cool as it seems.

Yes, I'm about to be my own hero. "I'm in DCQ?"

Bella holds both arms wide and spreads her fingers. "Welcome to the stronghold of Chittor, in the Southwest region of the Kingdom of Fear. You're in the middle of what you know as the Dungeon Crawl Quest Market Place."

I look around. The pixelated game world I've spent so many hours staring at through a computer monitor clicks into place. A real-life 3D, to-scale scene that no longer looks foreign. A high granite block wall lined with battlements and watchtowers circles the area. The dusty road beneath my feet leads from where we stand to a lowered metal portcullis between two flanking towers. Three goats tied to a nearby stake bleat harshly, and I can smell their musky odor. It isn't pleasant.

"It's perfect." I embrace the moment. I don't know how I've gotten here, but the place looks exactly like the starting point in DCQ. The inn, the tavern, the trading post, and even the temple are all here, exactly as they should be.

I run my fingers through my hair and hit a throbbing bump. Maybe I'm still unconscious from my fall, but I'm going to enjoy this delusion as long as I can. Even with the clock counting down to midnight, I might unlock something in my subconscious that will allow me to beat the goblin once I exit this game-world or dream-world. Whichever it was.

"How did I get here, though?" I ask Bella.

"Probably the same way I did." She drops her arms. "By putting your Grimoire into one of the den game stations." She puts a hand on my shoulder and stares at me with beautiful green eyes. "That started the process of inserting you into DCQ. The technical term, of course, is Virtual Reality Massively Multiplayer Online Role-Playing Game. You've taken a full dive inside."

"A VRMMORPG?" Is that even possible? I mean, there were theories and rumors and attempts to engineer something like this, but the concept never made it past the alpha testing stage. I step back and pinch my left bicep hard. There is no way I am standing inside my favorite game with a gorgeous girl gamer. "You're serious?"

"Deadly serious, Riff. Your body, mind, consciousness—everything that makes you who you are—is now inside the game." Bella bends over and picks something up from the ground, then stares ahead in what looks like a daze. Her eyes flick back and forth and, for a moment, I wonder if she's having some sort of episode. Then I realize she must be looking at her virtual iris screen.

"Are you okay?" I wave my hand in front of her face.

She shakes her head and blinks. "As a mage I can't equip with this."

"You can't do what?"

Bella holds out a piece of ebony wood with a slight pistol-grip curve. It's carved into the shape of a man with a bulging rear and belly. "This came into the game with you. Do you know what it is?"

I take it from her hand and instantly recognize it by the feel. "This is Kurht's dagger. But where's the blade?" There's a slot in the handle where the tang of the blade used to be. But it's gone. "I pulled this out of a beam in The DCQ Den ceiling just before I blacked out. The blade must still be there, and all I got was the handle."

"You brought in the Keris of Knaud." Bella frowns. "Or, at least, the sooang part."

"The Keris of what part of who?"

"The Keris of Knaud has three parts," Bella says, as if talking to a first grader. "The sooang, the sampir, and the taguban."

I don't like that she knows more DCQ intel than me, but hey, I'll swallow my pride if it keeps her talking. We are on the same team: save DCQ, no matter who kills the goblin in the end. And the more information I can gather, the better.

I recognize two of the words she said. Sampir, and taguban are the hand-annotated points on my map. *Do I still have my map?* I quickly pat myself down and feel the soft velum edges in my back left pocket.

"In layman's terms," Bella goes on, "sooang, sampir, and taguban mean hilt, blade, and scabbard. If compatible with its owner, a completed Keris of Knaud is said to grant supernatural power and extraordinary ability to its wielder. If you find the two other parts, you can put that theory to the test."

I study both sides of the hilt. "Extraordinary ability does sounds nice." There are no numbers here, not a one. And I'm sure I need those numbers to stop the goblin's death smoke. Maybe the numbers are on one of the other two parts. But are the other two parts even in the game? Or are they back in the Den? This whole situation makes no sense.

Bella points to my waist. "Put it in your bag and watch what happens."

I drop the hilt into my belt bag, and my Grimoire vibrates.

"Get ready to see your character sheet," Bella says. "You should also get a message about a new primary weapon."

A shock runs through my body and a transparent rectangle the size of a sheet of letter paper hovers in front of my face in 3D. "Whoa, I see it!"

NEW PRIMARY WEAPON: **Keris of Knaud –2 (Sooang)**

Damage: 0-0. Range: N/A. Frequency: Error. Quality: Incomplete.

Melee Weapon Attack: Piercing damage.

Soulbound to 'Jareth Goblinmasher' - Item cannot be traded or sold.

NEW TASK: **Complete the Keris of Knaud II**

Acquire the sampir, and taguban to unlock the Keris of Knaud's true power.

NAME: *Jareth Goblinmasher*   **AGE:** *22*

LEVEL: *2*   **EXPERIENCE POINTS:** *1,724*

HIT POINTS: *30/30*

ABILITIES: *50*

ARMOR CLASS: *3/20*

Leather Armor

GOLD COINS: *18*

SILVER PENNIES: *18*

SPELLS: *N/A*

PRIMARY WEAPON: *Keris of Knaud –2 (Sooang) (Soulbound)*

POSSESSIONS: *Ring, Grimoire (5 of 7), Map+3, Heavynessless Bag, Perfect Placement Belt.*

RACE: *Human*   **CLASS:** *Fighter*   **ALIGNMENT:** *Good*

TASKS: *Complete the Keris of Knaud II*

35:40:09 hours until DCQ server shut down

Bella waves a hand in front of my face. "It's a trip, I know. The DCQ interface uses a combination of the holographic vision screen, and the touch screen on your Grimoire."

"Well, it's awesome." This whole setup is the best gaming experience I've ever had, and it's a DCQ exclusive. "But something is wrong." I reach out, trying to touch the words hovering in front of my face, but my fingers pass through them. "These aren't my stats. I have a much better character than this. I should have more gold, better armor, and weapons. What I see here shows me at level two, like a complete newb, when I should be at level ten. What the hell?"

"You lose a lot of stats in the transfer to this live scenario." Bella looks down and adjusts her belt. "I had a much better character too. Do you see the final stat line?"

"You mean the countdown clock for the server shut down? Anton wanted me to warn the other players, but I guess you already know. But wait, I thought we only had until midnight. This gives us an extra day." I shake my head and the holographic sheet disappears.

"Yep, an extra day." Bella takes my hand and pulls me toward a clump of buildings crowded with people. "Time works differently in the game."

I drag my feet a little as I walk alongside her. I have more questions. I'm not ready to dive right in.

She pulls harder. "Here's the deal, Riff. We have until midnight tomorrow night to find a way back home—that's a day and a half in-game time. If we don't get back to The DCQ Players Den before the servers are shut down, we die in here."

I stop and pull my hand away from her. "By 'die in here' do you mean like dead-for-real-die? Or like video game, respawn, get another life dead?"

"This is full immersion virtual reality in its worst form, Riff. I mean dead-for-real-die.

"How in the world do you know that?" I ask. "Do you have proof? I mean, how did you learn that?"

"The hard way," Bella says. "You'll feel the very real pain, and then get a message explaining how it works when you take your first damage. Shortly after arriving here, I led a party into the valley and got this." Bella spreads the tassels of her skirt and peels back a strap of leg armor. A long stitched black and blue gash runs along her thigh. "Just so you know, the fighting skills of the non-player characters in here suck. Well, at least the skills of the ones I hired did."

The wound looks nasty, but I can't help admiring Bella's athletic physique. She's in amazing shape for a gamer. "So, you can get injured in here for real. Good to know. Did that hurt?"

Bella winces as she re-straps the armor. "At least a hundred times worse than breaking my arm on the monkey bars in elementary. It took me from a 40-hit-point-high to 6 hit points, poisoned, and struggling to live low. I was slashed to the bone, it was squirting blood, and I lost an additional hit point every fifteen minutes."

"Yikes." Damage-over-time injuries, spells, and poisons have killed my character Jareth, numerous times. So, I'm not surprised they exist in this real version as well.

"Tell me about it," Bella says. "By the time I crawled up the steps of the Temple, I had only one hit point remaining. Once inside, it was murmur, chant, prayer, success. That healing unpoisoned me, and a lengthy stay at the Inn brought me back up to 25 hit points, but the whole ordeal cost me all but three of my gold coins."

I look over to the Temple. It's a square, stone building surrounded by tall grooved pillars. A short man in a brown robe scratches the ring of hair around his head and waves to all who pass by. Two acolytes in chain mail stand a few steps behind him. They both have shields on their backs and maces on their hips.

Bella glares at the Temple. "Death here happens just like it does in DCQ, but you don't get to start over after the graveyard. Here, if you die, we're digging a hole six feet deep for you to lie in. It's dead-for-real-die and don't forget it. Thankfully, over at the Temple, they can cure any ailment. For a price. I heard the high priest can turn stone to flesh, if you can afford an exorbitant tithe."

She points to a long two-story building with three smoking chimneys on its roof. "An overnight stay at the Inn will restore hit points you've lost in combat, for a hefty price. There are also magic users that can help heal you, but you'll find they are way stingy with their power."

I knew this was too good to be true. "So, how do we get back home?" As much as I would love to stay and explore all the buildings and the DCQ marketplace, the dead-for-real stuff is too high stakes for me. I'm a gamer, not an idiot.

"To get home, we need to solve the greater goblin glitch," Bella says.

If one more person calls the puzzle a glitch, I'm going to scream. "You mean unlock the puzzle?" I correct her.

"Yes." She takes my hand and pulls in close to me. "I know how."

"You do?" This girl knows all the right things to say. "How?"

Bella lets go of my hand and takes a deep breath. "I received a scroll from an old lady NPC just after I arrived. She told me she was mandated to give it to the first person she met with a Grimoire. The scroll had one cryptic passage."

40

"What did it say?" A direct message to anyone with a Grimoire has got to be the goods.

Bella scratches her head and says:

The first of your kind to enter with a Grimoire deserves a gift,
Information about a mod granting portal your spirits will lift.

It will take you to the den of seven at the phantom and mainframe,
And will grant you special info so that your character will never be the same.

Down and up, through ooze, and past the luminosity,
Where you must go is on the opposite side of a quad-looped monstrosity.

"Easy!" Quad-looped must refer to the four ring knockers on the goblin's door. "The Monster Allocation Chamber."

"Right," Bella holds up a finger. "My interpretation is that there is a portal inside the goblins chamber that will take us back to The DCQ Players Den. At least, that's the only thing that makes sense. The problem is we have to kill the goblin in order to access it. If we kill the goblin, we save ourselves and the game. The scroll must have been slipped into the game as some kind of Easter egg."

I love when developers hide stuff in game for us hardcore fans, especially when it comes with an award. But this is incredible. "Let me see the scroll. If it's from the developer, I might be able to decipher it further."

Bella shakes her head. "The scroll self-destructed like a mission impossible tape after I read it. When I looked up the old lady was gone too." She takes slow steps toward the village buildings. "I know a lot about this world, Riff.

Remember, you're late getting here. First thing we need to do is assemble a team of six to enter the valley. It's time to recruit some NPCs. There's also another real gamer in here. A guy who claims to be the top ranked player in Germany. I suppose you'll have to meet. Just don't count on him joining us. He's a loser."

"There's another gamer in here?" I stay put and raise my arms in a silent cheer. Gamers with Grimoires are the best of the best. With three of us in the game, our chances of success tripled.

"Yes. Now come on already." Bella continues ahead without looking back.

I run to catch up with her and pass several youngsters in tunics hitting pells with wooden blades. Old men stand around shouting instructions and obscenities at them. I know this area. This must be the training grounds where new players create their initial character in the game. I still can't believe I'm in the freaking game.

"Whoa." I shuffle my feet just in time to miss a pile of fly-covered dung. This interface has every detail. Even the stench makes me gag as though the steamy aroma were real. I catch up to Bella in front of a three-story, timber-frame building with a steep roof clad in red tiles. A large board with the depiction of a menacing buck smashing into a docile hen overhangs the entrance.

I look up at the structure and pause. The Stag and Hen Tavern. I have assembled quite a few parties in this place on my dorm room computer. I can't wait to get inside.

"Don't get it twisted, Riff." Bella stomps up the building's front steps to an oversized red door and grabs its iron handle, looking back at me. "Just like in the game, it can be deadly in here. These NPCs will stab you in the back over a penny. It's best to just forget you're in a game and start treating this like real life." She swings the door open and disappears inside.

CHAPTER 5

Flickering torches, massive pillar candles, and a blazing hearth light up the tavern. Smoke fills the main area spiraling off a giant forest hog roasting over a rotisserie fire, and patrons burst into laughter around beat-up wood tables. I breathe in the aroma of roast meat and frothy ale, then choke on a wall of body odor.

"Do it already." A stocky wrinkle-faced dwarf with a scraggly beard backs up to a wall. "Go on." He opens his mouth wide and tilts back his head.

A younger dwarf, with a beard twisted into two thick braids, emerges from the crowd. He licks a finger and touches the air. "Mutton's a fly, old man." He cocks back his arm and launches a small chunk of juicy roasted meat across the room.

SPLAT! The brown hunk spins directly into the wrinkle-faced dwarf's eye. He peels off the hunk, stuffs it into his mouth, and storms back to the crowd chewing. "You couldn't hit an anvil with a sledgehammer, ya cockeyed pheasantshoer. Now, pay me what you owe."

I take a few slow steps in and get cut off by a dainty girl scantily clad in strategically placed green leaves. She whisks by me, does three cartwheels, drops to a knee, and fires a dart dead center into a target board on the wall. She then stands, turns, and bows to cheers from some onlookers.

Nice shot. Her pointy ears decorated with glittering gold rings are a dead giveaway that she's an elf, or maybe a half-elf. While I'm staring at her, a body bumps me from behind and I stumble forward.

"Step aside." A diminutive man—part hobbit?—in a smart burgundy coat saunters around me.

"The word is 'excuse me', Bilbo," I mutter.

The little man looks back at me and tilts his head. "Thirsty halfling in desperate need of a pint." He weaves into the crowd.

I just mocked a hobbit. Then again, who would have thought they were so rude?

A skinny old man in rags drops to his knees in front of me. "The end is near, mon capitaine, so I am selling off. I will trade you my most excellent dagger for a coin of any type." Shaking, he slowly raises a palm to present a short, thin, knife with gaping nicks in its blade.

It's a far cry from Excalibur, but something is better than nothing. I don't feel comfortable not having a weapon in this place. "You've got a deal." I pull a silver penny from my bag and exchange it for the weapon. A skinny rectangle text box pops into the upper left corner of my vision.

SUBTRACT: 1 silver penny to Jolly Wompis. New silver penny balance: 17

Okay, one silver penny won't break me.

"Thank you, mon capitaine." Jolly clutches the coin and rises wobbling to his feet. His eyes darting from left to right. "If you need a quester for your party, my name is Jolly, and I am at your service."

If this is the best NPC this place has to offer, we'll never put together a party capable of surviving the valley, much less the goblin's labyrinth.

A sheath appears at my belt, morphing into the shape of my new weapon. Nice! There are so many advantages to having a perfect placement belt. I insert the dagger and get a shock.

NEW PRIMARY WEAPON: **Feasting Knife**

Damage: 1-2. Range: N/A. Frequency: Common. Quality: Defective.

Melee Weapon Attack: Piercing damage.

Cutlery? My first weapon in the game may be a steak knife, but it sure feels good to have something that can inflict damage. I stretch out my back and stand up straight. Now, where did Bella run off to? I scan the packed crowd but can't see over the raised tankards of a group of men that sing and sway from side to side. Did she ditch me?

A short man in a green suit with buckled shoes hops on a nearby table. "I have a savage trick," he says in a thick Irish accent. "Take a gander."

He tosses a shiny apple, a slatternly turkey leg, and a dagger up in the air one after another and juggles them. This man consists of pure sinew and skill. He could be a good quester. "Throw in one more item. Anything. Just one silver penny for the show."

This is truly the Stag and Hen Tavern, just like the one in the game. "I'm not here for tricks, friend," I say. "But if you're a quester for hire, I may consider you."

A sharp yank on my shoulder interrupts my fascination with the juggler.

I whip around, grab a man by his throat, and back him against the tavern wall. I am *not* about to let someone pick my pocket. He is hefty with plate mail armor and a curved dagger at his waist. "Who the hell are you?" I demand, forcing myself to come off tougher than I feel.

"Calm down outsider," he rasps. "I'm The Master of Chittor."

I recognize this guy's voice. "Hey, you kicked me in the ribs!" I snatch my feasting knife from my belt and press it against his throat.

"Riff." Bella appears behind me and rests a calming hand on my shoulder. "He's not a threat. Castilian is just trying to register you as a questing captain."

Two men-at-arms wearing black tunics with red bucks on them draw their swords and approach me from the side.

I let Castilian go and sheath my weapon. "Kick me in the ribs again and see what happens."

Castilian waves off the men. "You Compass-Keepers are reckless, and I don't like it. Next time you enter my stronghold, check in with me at the gate well before my first bread and beer. Madmartigan didn't check in when she arrived either. Don't let her get you an axe blade upside the cranium." He adjusts his armor and looks around. "Do you plan to form a party, or are you just here to take in all this good ambiance?"

"My name is Jareth Goblinmasher," I say. "And I sure enough came here to form a party." My teeth buzz.

NEW TASK: **Assemble a party at Chittor.**

Assemble a party of six adventurers in order to enter the Valley of Fear.

Okay, I'm starting to get the hang of this shock and message thing. I will the message box away and it disappears. But I'm thankful for the update. The Grimoire is awesome.

Castilian looks me up and down. "Okay, Goblinmasher, consider yourself registered. If you live long enough to get a party together, I'll see you at the gate." He shoves several patrons aside and pushes out the front door.

"So, Riff," Bella scratches her nose and forces a smile. "My funds have dropped below the amount that allows a person to be captain." She rises up on her toes. "Don't you have something to ask me?"

"I do. What is a Compass-Keeper?"

"That's what the NPCs call anyone with a Grimoire. Don't you have something else to ask me? You are now an official questing captain in need of a party."

"Oh, right, yes, I do have something to ask." Okay, I get it. You need at least ten gold coins to captain a party. Bella must be super broke. Let me make this good. "Ms. Madmartigan, I am looking to assemble a balanced party of compatibly aligned questers to enter the Valley of Fear. Would you do me the honor of joining my party?"

She bows her head slightly and straightens. "I thought you'd never ask. Your offer is accepted."

I get a shock and a small icon of Bella's face appears in the upper right corner of my vision. I focus in on it and the small transparent square once again pops up to the left.

---

*ADD: **Madmartigan Galladoorn, Mage.***

Mage: Trained in fighting and casting spells. May use only light weaponry and armor. Primary abilities: Intelligence.

AGE: 21   LEVEL: 3   ABILITIES: 35 ALIGNMENT: Neutral
Spellcasting: 4/3/2

WEAPONS: Flail: Melee Weapon Attack: Bludgeoning damage.
Dagger: Melee or Ranged Weapon Attack: Piercing damage.

This is cool. Now that Bella is in my party, I can see a partial version of her character sheet. I raise an eyebrow and glance at her. "I would have thought you had a 'good' alignment."

"I'm a good girl gone bad. If you don't dead-for-real-die and play your cards right, you might find that out for yourself." She scans the tavern's interior. "We need to add the three best NPCs we can afford."

"Just three NPCs? That only gives us a party of five. We need six to enter the valley."

"And that brings me to the other gamer I told you about." Bella blows out a long breath. "Let's go see him." She pushes through chairs, making a path between tables. "This guy dropped into the game shortly after I did. For being an all-powerful cleric, he's been pretty worthless. I included him in the party I captained after arriving. We got ganked in our first encounter, and he left me for dead."

"Oh, man." A lot of players in the game have this attitude—every man for himself. It's hard to imagine someone being like that in a real life, dead-for-real-die scenario. It's no wonder she has a beef with this guy. "Why not just leave him and find a fourth NPC?" We don't need some back-stabber in our party. I don't care if he is in our elite fraternity of best of the best Grimoire holders.

"If we don't get Hans to join us, our run is going to be a struggle. We need a cleric's abilities to help us fight and, more importantly, to help us heal from potential injuries. Also, he's real, like you and me. And the only way out of this game is through the portal in the goblin's chamber. As much as I dislike him, we can't just leave him here."

Three hooded figures sit at the back of a dimly lit table. The one in the middle flips through pages of a thick book with worn leather binding. I lean into Bella as we approach. "Is that him in the middle? What's that he's reading?"

"It's a spell book of sorts. They're unique to the real version of the game. I don't quite know what to make of them. They show up on random bookshelves around town and contain non-deadly spells that only sporadically work. The best spell I've learned from them enables me to create a flame on the tip of my thumb."

"Really? Show me a little something." I love magic.

"Not now." Bella steps to the table and stops. "Riff, I'd like to introduce you to Johannes and his coterie of flunkies." She slaps both hands onto the table, hard. "Hello, Griefer. This is Riff, the third gamer to enter Chittor. We need you to join our party for a run at the goblin's chamber."

"My name is Hans." The figure in the middle pulls back his hood. He has pale skin, bloodshot eyes, and dry strands of blond hair running down his face. "I don't mean to offend," he says, "but that is not going to happen. Why would I risk death when I can hang out here with my good friends? My acolytes love me."

"Because," Bella growls, "If we don't defeat the goblin by midnight tomorrow, we'll all be dead *anyway*."

Hans gives no indication that he's heard her. He glances down at the book and raises his left hand. "*Partum a malum magia dracone*." With a snap of his fingers, a white cloud of smoke puffs up on the left side of the table. A small, transparent purple dragon tiptoes out of the smoke and looks around with big dove-like eyes. It has a potbelly, an enormous grin, and stands on wobbly hind legs.

The two men flanking Hans simultaneously pull their hoods back. One points at the dragon with a shaky finger. "M-m-magnificent."

The other man's jaw drops. "Look what he has conjured. We are in the presence of a magical genius."

Bella rolls her eyes and whispers in my ear, "You would think these guys were looking at a Hungarian Horntail, or the Ender Dragon, or Smaug or something." Then she waves her hand through the apparition. "Can you get Puff the Magic Dragon out of here? We have serious questing business to talk about."

The dragon prances across the table where it trips and tumbles off the end but grabs onto the edge and hangs swinging by a single talon.

A little girl with high rainbow pigtails and a loaded weapons belt runs to the table. "Oh, what a cute baby dragon."

"Get out of here, kid." Hans snaps his fingers and the spectacle fades into a purple mist. "See that?" He turns his back on the girl and faces us once more. "My dragons are very impressive. I'm a star in here."

The girl grips the table. "Ahhh." Her bottom lip quivers. "Where did it go?"

"Get. Go on." Hans shakes the table and stares the girl down. She runs off with tears in her eyes.

I watch the little NPC quester girl go. Then I turn and stare at Hans. "Really?" Who does that?

He points at Bella. "The two of us were already on a run together. It didn't go well. Why should I risk my life again?"

Bella reaches over the table and shuts the book. "Have you checked your character sheet lately? The DCQ servers are being shut down, and we will be shut down with them. Shut down dead."

Hans leans back. "I'm not worried about the servers." He shakes his head. "This place is its own realm, and it's real. If the servers go down, we might not be able to get back home, but we will live on—in this place—in the cloud."

Woah. If I didn't have Mack to get back to, that would tempt me too. What if Hans was right?

"That's not how it works, Hans." Bella's fists ball up. "You saw the hardware in The DCQ Den with your own two eyes. There is no magical realm-cloud that keeps games living. These things don't go on indefinitely. They shut down and go dark. It's Goodnight, Groddle. Do you even remember City of Heroes, Star Wars Galaxies, or The Matrix Online? Probably not, because they are gone and nowhere to be found."

Good point, Bella. My momentary awe vanishes. It looks like Bella needs some help convincing him. "Hans, we are in a deadly situation here. But I am uniquely qualified to help us get out of it. In real life, not only am I a game development major, but I've also spent every second of my spare time—and then some—playing this game. I may be at level two now, but at home I am a level ten DCQ guru. I know the route to the goblin's chamber like the back of my hand. We can do this."

"In real life." A smirk crosses Hans's face. "Not only am I on pace to graduate at the top of my class with a chemical engineering degree, but I'm also a top one-hundred ranked NGL gamer, a member of my university's League of Legends varsity team, and a frequent contributor on Checkpoint radio's eSports and gaming show. So, don't tell me what we can do. What you don't know is that the valley here is more difficult than the one you play at home." He reopens his book. "Get with me when you have a party together. If it's good enough, maybe I'll join you. If you're lucky."

I look closely at Hans. With all that fame and prestige he's claiming, why don't I recognize him?

Bella slams the book shut again, from both ends, and dust shoots up into Hans's face. "You've lost sight of reality, you over-immersed cleric of little dragons. You'll join us or die in here." She pivots on her heel and strides the opposite direction.

I follow a few steps behind. "So, Bella." I catch up to her and she stops. "Other than Hans, what's our recruitment strategy? You've been in the valley already. What type of adventurer are we looking for?"

"The good news is that I'm a mage and Hans is a cleric. We don't have a lot of spell points between us, but if we're careful, we should be able to supply all the magic we need."

"That works for the budget. I have only eighteen gold and seventeen silver." Magic users always command a lot of gold. Not having to hire one will help us stretch our funds.

"Well, the bad news is that we need to add three randoms to get Castilian to open the gate out of town, and one of them is required to be a thief. Thieves demand a lot of gold."

"Wait, we can't add just random NPCs," I point out. "We're questing into the goblin's chamber. We gotta hire some major beef. No offense to you magic users, but I could use a few really good fighters to defend us."

"Hmm." Bella nods in the direction of the tavern's kitchen. "I've never seen that guy in here before. He's built like a tank. Let's go meet him."

A mountain of a man stands stone-faced and looking straight ahead. He has a bald head, a long, braided goatee with beads woven into it, chain mail armor, and a shield strapped on his back. He looks like the perfect meathead for the front of a marching line.

As we get closer, I notice a long wooden shaft with a bulky metal head hanging low from a hook on his belt. One could inflict some heavy damage with a mace like that.

Bella walks boldly up to him, even though he towers over her. "Are you available for hire?"

The man keeps a steady gaze forward, then says, "Not for a weak wench with no gold, I'm not."

CHAPTER 6

"*Volitan's guillotine*," Bella calls out, spinning a finger and creating a crackling blue circle of light. She flicks it forward, sending the ring around the huge man's neck where it tightens. "Who's the weak wench now?"

"Ack." The man wraps both hands around the ring and strains to widen it. "Okay." He wheezes. "You're a magic user. We can deal."

Bella snaps her fingers and the ring puffs into mist. "Our destination will be the West Labyrinth. Your compensation will be five gold coins and a five percent share of any treasure found. Don't even ask for artifact privileges."

I like her negotiating tactics. Start low and take artifact privileges off the table from the get-go. It can be risky, though, Some NPCs' lust for artifacts runs so deep they will refuse to join without them.

"Hmmmm." The man wraps a hand around the top of his mace's shaft and pounds the head into the floor. "Twenty gold coins and a ten percent share."

"No way," Bella says. "We will go ten gold and a twenty percent share."

The man grips his goatee, tugging on it. "The name's Salo, and your terms are accepted."

Bella cracks a smile. "Meet us at the gate."

In my vision feed, an icon with Salo's face appears above Bella's accompanied by a transparent square.

ADD: **Salo Fatback, Fighter.** *(-10 Gold/-20% Share/No Artifact Privileges)*

Fighter: A man-at-arms trained for battle. May use any armor and weapon.

Primary abilities: Strength.

AGE: 24 LEVEL: 4 ABILITIES: 60 ALIGNMENT: Neutral

WEAPONS: Mace: Melee Weapon Attack: Bludgeoning damage.

Shield Bash: Melee Weapon Attack: Bludgeoning damage.

SUBTRACT: 10 gold coins to Salo Fatback. New gold coin balance: 8

"Hey," I gripe. "I just got ripped for ten gold coins."

"As party captain," Bella reminds me, "the funds drain from you. Don't worry though. That gold is well spent. I've hired questers before. Ten gold is a steal for a fighter of Salo's stature, and that mace of his should provide good front of the line offense. What kind of stats does he have?"

"He is at level four, and at sixty for abilities."

"Low abilities for a big man. But better than anything I had on my initial run. Consider him your beef."

I dig in my bag and run my fingers through the contents. "That hire leaves me with just eight gold coins."

Bella glances at my bag and weapons belt. "You're going to need all of them to complete our party and purchase yourself a better weapon." She points to my knife. "Although I've heard tough slabs of filet mignon in the north are quite susceptible to your current ginsu-esque saber."

I cover my knife's sheath with a hand. "Not funny." But she's right. I need a better weapon badly. "How much gold do you have, and what about Hans? We need to pool our resources to hire the best party. By the time we're done, I'll be down to pennies."

"Hans and I spent all our gold on healing from that last run. I have nothing, and I'm sure Hans doesn't have anything either. Whatever pennies you have will just have to do."

"The quality of even an eight coin sword bothers me." I am not going to fight with some knobbed stick. I have to find a way to acquire more gold. "Speaking of weapons, that magic strangle circle you put on Salo was nice. But do you think it was wise to waste a spell on such a situation? Most magic users I play with save their limited spell power for life and death encounters."

"It was nothing more than a parlor trick I learned from a book." Bella holds a fingernail to her lips and blows on it. "It may have looked deadly, but after a brief strangle that spell times out. A few more seconds and the circle would have disappeared on its own, and I would have lost our negotiating leverage. Non-deadly magic cost nothing off my spell power, it does always make one of my fingernails burn."

It looked pretty deadly to me. "And what about Hans?" I ask. "What can he do?"

Bella pulls me toward a large gambling table surrounded by a dozen ale-guzzling NPCs, and four men-at-arms in black red buck tunics. "I hope that fool still has some spell power left. He's always showing off to the locals."

We squeeze our way in at the table between a man and dwarf. Gambling wasn't my ideal way to earn coin, but what other options did we have? The man on my left has thick gray hair and a Fu Manchu-style mustache. He hunches over the table with eyes fixated on the dice, not even noticing us. The dwarf on my other side grumbles and moves as far away from us as the step stool he's standing on will allow. He is short and stocky with a shaggy, untamed reddish-black beard. Both men smell like a week-old mix of garbage and spirits.

I glance at the dwarf and feel a bit choked up. I am about to play dice with Gloin inside of my favorite game. This is epic.

Two dice tumble down the table between short stacks of silver pennies and stop at our end. One die shows five, the other four.

A man-at-arms thrusts a curved stick behind the dice. "Nine, Nina. You should have seena." He drags the dice back and points at us. "Feed the rack or move back."

Bella elbows me and taps on the grooved railing that surrounds the table. "Put a few pennies in the coin rack. This table is where we add questers to our party on the cheap."

I put four pennies in the rack. Then whisper to Bella, "I don't know how to play craps."

The stickman gives a nod and continues to stack recovered coins. "Place your bets."

Bella turns to the gray-haired man. "How's the action?"

The man picks up the only two pennies in his rack, places them on the playing surface and grunts. "You can freeze a side of beef on this dastardly-ass thing. I'll change my mind about it if this guy rolls a ten. Come on five, five."

Great. Gambling on a cold table when our lives depended on my coin pouch. I turn to ask Bella if she's *sure* this is the best way to win some coin, but she leans my way first and whispers, "All we have to do is wait here for one of these guys to go broke, then make a lowball offer. Unless you have another idea on how to build our party."

Understanding clicks. I grin and fold my pennies, one over the other. It wasn't about winning. It was about watching everyone else lose. I could certainly do that. Bella had brains, I'd give her that.

A bald man with indecipherable tattoos and metal stud armor tosses several gold coins onto the table. "Give me twenty-two inside and five each on the hardway, mule teeth, and Nina." He snatches the dice up in one hand, shakes them in his fist, and whizzes them down the layout.

One die careens off a stack of coins and stops, showing a five. The other bounces off the back wall, spins and halts to expose a two.

"Seven-out!" The dealer scoops in all the pennies and gold. "Five two, you're all through."

"Whore." The bald man throws his arms up and leaves the table.

The gray-haired man slams two fists on the rail. "Up pops the devil." He rakes his head with choppy fingernails. "That was the last of my... Awwwww damn." He tugs on my tunic. "Building a party, aye?"

I raise a skeptical eyebrow. "You heard us?"

"I'm gray, but not deaf yet. My name is Biff, and I will run with you for twelve pennies and the rights to the Goblet of Plenitude." He pulls a tankard from under the table, raises it up high, and lets the last few drops of brew drip into his mouth. "But I will need a pint of ale as a retainer right now, and another three pints at every town we enter on our run."

I look the man over. He is wearing a thick patchwork leather vest riddled with cracks and lines. "Well, we can use another fighter. Where's your weapon?"

"First of all, I am no fighter. I am a ninja, and projectiles are my specialty." He opens his vest to reveal a strap across his chest with a sling, several small war hammers, and a pouch. "I have tricks up my sleeve to kill more treacherous monsters then you will ever know."

"You're a ninja?" In DCQ, ninjas are an elite class of character reserved for those level five and up. This guy looks more like a low-level Highwayman.

He clasps his hands together in front of his chest, bows, and then snaps back into an attacking position. "I am Ninja. I am cold, colossal."

Ninjas have always fought well on my teams in the game. I pick my pennies up from the rack and step away from the table. Even if he is a washed-up ninja, that's better—and cheaper—than an experienced fighter. Time for my first official party member offer. "Our destination will be the West Labyrinth. Your compensation will be three pennies and one pint at every town. But no goblet. All artifacts stay with me."

The man looks down into his empty cup. "I will require a pint right now as a retainer. No pint, no deal."

I place four pennies in his hand. "For your payment, and for your ale."

He clutches the coins and manages a black-toothed smile. "Your terms are accepted."

I grin. That was easy—I didn't even have to offer a percentage of the treasure. Biff's icon appears between Salo and Bella's along with a transparent square.

ADD: **Biff Thunderpunch, Ninja.** *(-4 Pennies/-1 Pint Per Town/No Artifact Privileges)*

Ninja: A fantastic fighting machine. May use any armor and weapon. Primary abilities: Agility, Wisdom.

AGE: 47   LEVEL: 4   ABILITIES: 85 ALIGNMENT: Neutral
WEAPONS: Sling: Ranged Weapon Attack: Bludgeoning damage.
Mini War Hammer: Ranged Weapon Attack: Bludgeoning damage.

SUBTRACT: 4 silver pennies to Biff Thunderpunch. New silver penny balance: 13

"Meet us at the gate," Bella tells him flatly.

"I will," Biff says. "Right after I wet my whistle." He hobbles straightaway to the bar.

"That's actually not a bad idea." Bella says with a cringe, after Biff is out of earshot. "I could use a drink after a hire like that. Look at him Riff, he's got a peg leg."

I watch our newest party member pull up to the bar across the room, his left leg a wooden stump from the knee down. "A ninja with a peg leg. Who would have thought?"

"And he's a lush on top of it. You do know Biff is the type of NPC that abandons his party in a battle, right?"

"How do you know? In my experience ninjas are always trustworthy and brave." I put my arm around Bella and pull her toward the bar. "What I know is that we just added a level four ninja to our party, on the cheap. Dirt cheap. All we need to do now is hire a thief."

Bella and I approach the bar just as two curvy-fit females with long black hair get up and leave. They both wear sparsely placed plate mail armor and have dual cross-mounted katana swords strapped to their backs.

I take a seat and look back at the girls. "Why don't we hire the twins? They look like excellent fighters to me." Sexy too.

Bella sits, holds two fingers up and waves to the man behind the bar. "They aren't fighters. They're real ninjas. That kind of skill will run you over a hundred gold coins, each. Too rich for our blood."

VIEW THE STAG AND HEN TAVERNS BAR MENU: **Yes/No?**

I gotta see this.

THE STAG AND HEN TAVERN BAR MENU: *Ten Silver Pennies (SP)*			
= One Gold Coin (GC)			
Ale	1SP	*Rye Bread*	1SP/2 Slice
Large Beer	1SP	*Fruit*	1SP
Bark Tea	1SP	*Crisples*	1SP/Half Dozen
Hydromel	1SP	*Salted Pike*	1SP
Wine	2SP	*Gruel with Honey*	1SP/Bowl
Honey Mead	2SP	*Cheese*	1SP/Wedge
Oxymel	3SP	*Soup*	1SP
Melomel XO	5SP	*Stew*	2SP
Rumor Table Glance	1SP	*Roast Fowl*	3SP
Rumor Table Scroll	5SP	*Roast Joint*	4SP

My standard gaming session includes an energy drink and a bag of Takis Fuego. Don't see that here. "No energy drinks on the menu, huh? What did you order for us?"

"Hydromel," Bella smacks her lips. "It's kind of a fermented honey water. I'd say low on alcohol content, but high on refreshment. I've grown to like the taste."

"Hello, Bella." The barkeeper is a heavy round man. His thick beard has crumbs of food stuck in it, and his shirt is stained from sweat and spillage. He drops two wood cups on the bar splashing golden liquid over the rim. "Who's paying for this?"

Bella lifts her cup slightly and dips her head my way. "Captain Goblinmasher here knows how to wine and dine his new party members."

"Captain, you say?" The man squares up in front of me. "Would ya like to see today's rumor table? I can give you a glance for a penny, or you can keep the scroll for five."

I thrust my hand down in my bag. "This one's on me." I can't get the pennies out of my bag fast enough. "Rumor tables can be really informative."

Bella pushes my hand down. "If you must, just go for the glance. This guy's tables are ninety percent false."

"Nonsense." The barkeeper stiffens and holds both arms out wide. "I guarantee, uhh, eighty-five percent truth on today's scroll. It's well worth five pennies, young Captain."

This man must be pulling my leg. It's rare a rumor table is ever over forty percent true. "How much for the drinks and a glance?"

He growls and glares daggers at Bella. "Three pennies."

I hand him three pennies, and he drops a cigar-sized scroll on the bar. "You have till I come back to look at it."

SUBTRACT: 3 silver pennies to Derf Goodslog. New silver penny balance: 10

I unroll the scroll and lay it out on the bar between Bella and myself. He never said I couldn't share. "You start at the bottom, I'll start at the top."

THE STAG AND HEN RUMOR TABLE:

1- Cells in the East Dungeon contain individuals that will reward rescue.

2- Hawkwinds cadence has changed.

3- Several artifacts can be found hidden in a West Labyrinth chamber.

4- Nobody has ever survived an overnight stay in Ranida.

5- Beware of Setan Kober in the West Labyrinth.

6- An undead presence in Keighley has animated new atrocities.

7- The spicer's Red Maca root increases abilities by ten.

8- A huge hollow oak in Bradford produces fairy creatures.

9- The end is near.

10- The Liergarnin King has a gem as big as an acorn in his quarters.

11- Beware of a portcullis trap in a dead-end corridor.

12- A cell door in the West Labyrinth leads to another realm.

CHAPTER 7

I run my finger down the list. "Well, I don't quite know what to make of this. Rumor number nine worries me."

"No luck from my end either," Bella says, turning her focus to watching the barkeep fill our tankards.

A hand wraps around my shoulder. "Today's table is all fable. Except for the one about Setan Kober. That's a mean, ugly monster that is not to be disturbed. Mess with him and you're gonna have a bad time."

A tall skinny man steps between my barstool and Bella's. He has a long coat of leather plate armor, and a three-cornered beaver-fur hat cocked low over one eye. "My crony Biff informed me you all are in need of a thief to satisfy the gate requirement. I think we can help each other out. My name is Gregarious Slim, and I am a master thief."

Bella leans back from the bar. "I've seen you around here, Gregarious. You don't run with anybody."

He covers his mouth with a fist and chuckles. "First of all, my friends call me Slim. And second, I gotta say you got me all wrong. I run with parties, but only strong ones that pay top coin. And parties like that don't get formed around here no more."

This guy wants top coin? "No need to waste our time. We can't pay that kind of coinage."

Slim waves his hand. "No payment needed, Captain. Sometimes you have to get out of town to really put it down. I have a business associate in Cittadella that requires my help, and I need to join a party to get there. The catch is I won't be fighting, doing thievery, or providing any insight to you all. We will be doing each other the favor of satisfying the gate requirement to get out of Chittor. That's it."

"That doesn't work for us," I say. "We have business in the West Labyrinth and have some adventuring to do along the way. We need a thief that will fight by our side, open locks, disarm traps, and tell us what they know about the areas ahead." On a whim, I add nonchalantly, "We'll be giving him sixty percent of the treasure."

Slim tilts his hat up. "The game is to be sold, not told. You will have to dig deep into your bag to receive that kind of thievery, captain, especially if you plan on going into that nasty West Labyrinth. You gotta grease my palm like a prince for this questin'." Looks like a sixty percent share in the treasure isn't enough to grease his pinky finger. "And since you all aren't into that kind of work, I don't expect it. What we have here is a simple deal to get out of town."

"No way," Bella squints at Slim in disdain. "We'll find another thief."

"You can try to find another." Slim eases back from the bar. "But thieves don't work for pennies. Only gold, and a lot of it."

"Don't be so quick with that no, Bella." I have never added a thief for less than fifteen gold coins, and I am down to just eight. "This guy may be our only option." Maybe we could find another thief on the way.

"Mmmm," Bella grunts. "Your compensation will be zero coins, zero percent share of any treasure found, and no artifact privileges. Do you understand that?"

"No artifact privileges?" Slim tilts his head slightly. "Damn, you all are stingy. But okay, terms accepted."

Slim's icon appears beneath Bella's in my vision.

ADD: **Gregarious Slim, Thief.** *(-Services Clause/No Artifact Privileges)*

Thief: Trained in the arts of stealing and sneaking. May use only light to mid-weight weaponry and armor. Primary abilities: Agility.

AGE: 25   LEVEL: 3   ABILITIES: 40 ALIGNMENT: Neutral

Quarterstaff: Melee Weapon Attack: Bludgeoning damage.

Slim points to my Grimoire. "Besides, I've always wanted to run with a Compass-Keeper."

How do these NPCs know about Grimoires? "Umm." I look at Bella from the corner of my eye. She shrugs.

I take a hold of my Grimoire's sheath with one hand and shake it. "What do you know about these, Slim?"

He raises an eyebrow. "A real worldly wizard came in here with one a few days before Bella and Hans arrived."

"A wizard?" Bella sits up. "My father is an old school Dungeons & Dragons player, gamer, and programmer. He once told me having a wizard in your party is the best thing you can do, and I never forgot that. What did this wizard look like? Where did he go?"

"He had that eccentric wizard look about him. Older gentleman, fancy robe, slumped cone hat, obviously a Compass-Keeper like yourselves. He came to the bar, had a drink with me, and purchased a rumor table. What amazed everyone was what he did when he left Chittor. He walked out the gate by himself. No party with him at all. I've never seen anything like it. This man was truly a powerful wizard to do that."

Bella plunks her drink on the bar and stands in front of Slim. "What was his name? Did he say where he was going?"

"You know what?" Slim steps back from Bella. "I've said too much. I gotta sew up a few loose ends before we leave town. I'll see you at the gate."

Bella sits and drops her head to her hands.

I pick up my cup and drink down the hydromel. It's smooth, with the peculiar taste of burnt caramel in sweet wine. "It's not that bad of a hire, Bella. At least we got some useful information out of him. If we find this wizard guy he was talking about, I'm sure we can talk him into helping us."

Bella lifts her head and rubs a hand down her face. "We're wasting precious time. We need to recruit one more quester and get on our way."

Bam! A hooded figure in a fur lined cloak thrusts the point of a sword into the floor behind us. It has a simple blackened hilt and tempered blade. "Twink-a-doodle-doo, I brought this for you, Riff. As a cleric, it's of no use to me." Hans pulls back his hood.

"For me?" I jump up and wrap a hand around the sword's hilt. "Thanks, Hans." Maybe he's not such a bad guy after all. I have swung a few novelty swords and replica lightsabers in my time, but never a real sword. "Where did you get it?"

He looks from side to side. "Do you want to be asking questions, or do you want to be having a decent weapon?"

I may not fully trust Hans yet—or even like him—but that doesn't stop me from pulling the sword from the floor. It soars up, of its own accord, and pulls me around in a circle. Without even thinking, I slash, parry, and thrust like I've

68

been doing it for years. My muscles know exactly what to do and how to react. "How did I do that?" I release my grip and the blade clangs to the floor.

Bella picks up the sword and holds it upright. "You're a fighter with an abilities number of fifty, that's how. I had the same sensation when I first cast magic." She peers at Hans. "So, will you be questing with us?"

"Well, Bella." Hans looks at me with a crooked smile. "After reviewing my character sheet, and the server countdown, I only have one thing to say: your terms are accepted."

An icon of Hans's face appears beneath Bella's, and two transparent squares with it.

ADD: **Hans Talhoffer, Cleric.**

Cleric: Can cast magic spells and dispel the undead. May not wear armor or use edged weapons longer than a normal dagger. Primary abilities: Wisdom.

AGE: 23   LEVEL: 3   ABILITIES: 35 ALIGNMENT: Error

Spellcasting: 4 / 2 / 1

WEAPONS: Shillelagh: Melee Weapon Attack: Bludgeoning damage.

Dagger: Melee or Ranged Weapon Attack: Piercing damage.

I focus in on the alignment field. "Hans, why is your alignment an error?"

"You know this game is glitchy," he says. "It should say 'good'."

"I call B.S." Bella looks at Hans with an unrelenting stare. "That same error message appeared when he joined me for our first run. It should say *evil* and *butt ugly*."

"Shows how much you know, Bella." Hans fastens the clasp of his cloak. Clerics can't be aligned evil. I'm as good as the day is long."

"Good and terrible." Bella lowers the sword.

"I just got experience points," I say excitedly. "Two hounded and fifty of them." I'm already on my way to level three.

Bella dips the sword my direction. "I hope this blade isn't cursed."

"Cursed?" I take the handle and slide the blade down into a newly formed sheath.

"The quality is tagged as defective." I adjust my belt and stand tall. "But it can't be that bad. It felt way to good when I swung it around." I look over the tavern with a new confidence. "Jareth Goblinmasher finally has a real weapon."

CHAPTER 8

Bella takes a few heavy steps away from the bar and turns back to me. "I know you're happy about your new toy, but please quit your daydreaming. Don't forget, we're on a countdown to death. Let's go talk strategy."

The three of us navigate to the back of the tavern. We duck into a small dark booth with tall mahogany partitions and a single candle burning in the middle of the table.

Bella slams a fist down. "This is what I know. We have less than a day and a half to kill the goblin and ride the portal behind him back home. We need to arrive at the chamber with at least four party members alive, and one of us needs to be at level five or higher. With those requirements in place we use Hawkwinds cadence to take down the force shield, awaken the goblin, and get the 'password, flee, or fight message'. That's where your expertise comes into play, Mr. Level Ten," she turns to me. "How do we proceed from that point?"

That's the million-dollar Blizivision Studios cash prize question. This was my moment to shine. "Well, before we even get there, we'll need a pair of Bombardment Boots to kick down the door. I've been able to find them in Cittadella." I push the candle away and rest both elbows on the table. "Once in, I will need to land multiple blows to the goblin's weak spot. The good news is I know where that weak spot is. The bad news is I don't have the weapon needed to exploit it. I don't even know what weapon is needed."

Bella clasps her hands. "A completed Keris of Knaud might kill the goblin. Supernatural power and extraordinary ability, remember? We just need to find the other two parts."

"What is a Keris of Knaud?" Hans asks. "Some kind of legendary sword?"

"Not a sword, a dagger." I pull the handle from my bag and lay it on the table. "Bella, I know you say this will be special when complete, but there's no way I'm taking on the goblin with such a small blade. I've engaged the beast with some of the best weapons DCQ has to offer. The Vania Spear Whip, The Wakkablitz Blade, and even The Saber de Chaos. They all snapped like twigs upon impact. What evidence do you have that a completed Keris will do the deed?"

Bella looks around and lowers her voice. "A rumor table I paid up for before my first run had the information. Once the Keris is completed, I'm confident it will do the job."

Hans chuckles and falls back in his seat. "She believes a rumor table. Oh, that's rich."

If the dagger was on the rumor table—even if the information was false—that was evidence enough for me to place a bit more hope in it. I pull the map from my back pocket, unfold it, and lay it flat in front of us. "Putting our life at risk on rumor table fodder is a bit of a long shot, but I *do* have this." I tap a finger on the map and slide it toward Bella. "This will guide us to the other two dagger parts. I got it from the developer in my level nine package."

"A map from the developer?" Bella holds it down at both ends and peers at it, eyes wide. "If these marks show exactly where the sampir and taguban are located, we can complete the Keris and kill the goblin. We'd be golden!" She lifts her gaze to mine and her next words come out breathless, disbelieving. "We can really do this."

Hans snatches the map, holds it up and stares at it. "These marks are located far off the main road. They almost look out-of-bounds. Who knows if we'll even be able to access these areas? Not to mention there's probably some big monster boss guarding them."

I pinch the map, pulling it away from Hans, then fold it and return it to my pocket. "There's another problem. A black poison smoke fills the chamber every time I get a critical hit on the goblin. Even if I kill it, the smoke will send us all to the graveyard."

I pick up the Keris handle and look it over. "My theory is that the chamber password stops the smoke. I thought the password was going to be engraved on this pommel."

"We can figure out the smoke part along the way," Bella says. "For now, we need to get on our grind."

Hans raises his hand. "I got a question. Bella and I are at level three and you are at level two. How is one of us going to reach level five in just a day and a half? In order to level up that quickly, we'll have to rack up an unprecedented amount of experience points. We don't have the time or firepower to pull that off."

I groan. "Good point, Hans." I need to stop analyzing this game as though I have my fully-healed Jareth Goblinmasher character at my fingertips. Jareth is now *me*. And his statistics reflect that unfortunate combination.

My abilities number is good, but I'm not going to kill too many difficult monsters with my current arsenal—a kitchen knife and a defective sword. "Do experience points work any differently here in the live game?" I ask.

"We can pull this off," Bella insists. "I have a plan. Just like in the game, all surviving members of combat receive experience points. The amount we get depends on the difficulty of the combat. All we need to do is grind on one or two high level monsters that dole out heavy experience, like an earth giant, or maybe a few of the undead. I know several spots where creatures like that consistently spawn."

"Ha." Hans puts a hand on his chest and crashes back in his seat. "Now she wants to take on giants and the undead. Great. We're all burnt Streuselkuchen for sure."

"You're a cleric." Bella points her finger in Hans's face. "You have the ability to dispel the undead. Skeletons, zombies, and hags shouldn't be a problem for you."

Hans leans forward. "Shows how much you know. Experience points are not awarded for monsters you dispel. And I have yet to effectively dispel a freaking hag. The percentage chance that a dispel will work is dismal in general." His voice rises with every disheartening piece of information, as though he relishes crushing our hopes. "Riff, your little quester girl is going to get us killed before we even reach the West Labyrinth."

A few heads turn our way. "Quiet down," I say. "The bottom line is we are going to have to speed grind like our lives depend on it. Because they do."

Hans clasps his fingers, looks up at the ceiling, and then at me. "We're going to have to do what? There is no such thing as a speed grind. It's not a thing. A grind is a freaking grind. I'll see you in the courtyard." He stands up and walks toward the tavern's exit.

Bella looks at me with a slight smile. "Speed grind? That's an oxymoron, you know."

I hold out both hands and shrug. "So, let's make it a thing?"

Outside the tavern, we step into the courtyard. The sun has passed its peak and is heading toward the opposite horizon. The training grounds are active with trainers and trainees. One young man has a large crowd watching him. He thrust and parries a wooden sword into several hanging dummies, grunting every time.

A girl with brown hair and skull tattoos has her arms wrapped around Hans. She gazes into his eyes as they hold each other close.

Bella nudges me with an elbow. "NPC love." Her eyes narrow at the couple. "Pathetic."

Hans takes the girl's hand and waves to a nearby group of five hooded men. He puffs out his chest as they gather around him. "I'm going back into the valley for a quest."

The brunette breaks away from his grip. "No!" She gasps, pointing at Bella and shaking her finger. "I won't let you go with her, again. She almost got you killed last time." The girl wraps her arms around Hans's waist. "Don't do it. Stay with me."

Hans nudges her away and raises his palms. "I'm a cleric, so I must quest. These people need my help desperately."

The girl drops to her knees, clutching one of his legs. "Please, I love you."

Hans runs his fingers through the girl's hair and looks at me. "I need a moment to handle this. I will catch up with you in the marketplace."

The brunette buries her head into Hans's groin. "Don't go with that incompetent wench."

Wow. Hans really has some fans up in here.

Bella shakes her head. "You're going to need some provisions, Riff. I know a good spot."

We walk through an area with several small booths. Noisy groups of people wander between them talking, gesturing, and negotiating.

A young man in a knee-length tunic walks by us with a tray of wooden bowls containing various dry greens. "Spicers special," he calls out. "Herbs to cure many a myriad condition."

I look over his tray as he passes, wondering if any of that stuff works.

The strong smell of fish wafts from a stall with glistening meat in wet hay-filled crates. I stop to take a look and get pulled away by Bella. "Trust me, you don't want any of that nasty Gooberfish."

When feeding my virtual character Jareth, I always got what was cheapest. But now that my taste buds are actually going to encounter these provisions, I wish I had just a bit more coin.

We walk past a few more booths and stop in front of a small one with a patchwork fabric roof and wood counter. Torches, ropes, shields, and several swords line shelves or hang from ropes stretching across the back width of the canopy. Loaded sacks are piled up on the ground, and a large barrel in one corner overflows with red apples.

A smiling dwarf waddles up the steps of a small stage behind the counter. "I have all the equipment you need for adventuring." He looks down at my sword and scrunches his face. "I wouldn't fight a vorpal bunny with that steel. You look like a high-level fighter. Let me fix you up with a Were Slayer. Only nine thousand gold coins for you."

---

*VIEW CATLOB'S TRADING POST MENU: **Yes/No?***

These menus are so cool. I focus on the yes.

CATLOB'S TRADING POST MENU: Ten Silver Pennies (SP) = One Gold Coin (GC)

Tinder Box (Flint/Steel)	5SP	Sack of Wheat (2)	1SP
Torch (6)	1SP	Apple (5)	1SP
Flask of Oil	2SP	Single Day Ration	1SP
Lantern	1GC	Wine (One Quart)	3SP
Paper Dragon	1SP	Water Skin	1SP
Small Sack	1SP	Rope (50' Length)	1SP
Large Sack	3SP	Mirror (Hand Sized)	5SP
Small Backpack	5SP	Thieves Tools	3GC
Large Backpack	8SP	Holy Symbol	3GC
Heavylessness Bag	5GC	Huo-Yau (Sack)	300GC
Small Shield	10GC	Helmet	20GC
Large Shield	30GC	Gauntlets	25GC
Robe	3GC	Leather Armor	20GC
Chain Mail	40GC	Plate mail	60GC
Sling w/25 Stones	2GC	Spear	3GC
Club	1GC	Hammer	5GC
Hand Axe	4GC	Quiver (15 Arrows)	5GC
Dagger	5GC	Staff	2GC
Poleaxe	10GC	Mace	5GC

Short Bow	*25GC*	*Light Flail*	*10GC*
Short Sword	*10GC*	*Heavy Flail (Two-handed)*	*20GC*
Long Sword	*15GC*	*Pootang Whip (LVL6)*	*Error*
Were Slayer	*9000GC*	*Blade Viridian (LVL8)*	*1500GC*

I'm familiar with most of these items. Wait, does that say Blade Viridian? So, they do exist. I gotta get my hands on it.

I will the menu away and scan the merchandise for the blade. An ornate two-handed saber rests in a single tier stand on the shop's top shelf. Unlike my plain sword, this one has mirror polish with a blue-green tinge, and an expressive swirl pattern engraved on the hilt and blade. "How much for that one?"

"Aah." The dwarf raises his eyebrows. "You have a keen eye. Cost for the Blade Viridian is fifteen hundred gold. Note that you must be at level eight or higher to equip with it."

If only I had the bankroll from my character back home.

"Actually," I sigh, "I am just here for some basics today."

"Pick up rations for the whole party, just in case." Bella says. "I can produce fire with my magic, so no need for a Tinder Box."

"Okay. Give me the small lantern," I direct the merchant, "a flask of oil, a water skin, eleven days' rations, and a backpack." I point to a small pack hanging from a rope between several paper dragons. "The one right there will work. What's with those origami dragons?"

The dwarf pulls down the small pack with a hooked pole. "A wizard makes them for me out of enchanted parchment. Just one penny for the toy, how many would you like?"

"Add a purple one to my order."

"The color of kings. Yes, sir." He hooks one of the dragons and maneuvers it over to my hand. "It's yours."

I take the paper toy and look to the training grounds. The little kick-butt quester girl that was so disappointed by Hans's disappearing dragon is running around a circle of kids sitting in the dirt. She is armed with a small sword, and her pigtails bounce up and down as she spins, stabs, and thrusts the weapon between them with crisp precision. "Hey, hey, little girl!" I wave a hand. "We got something for you over here."

The little girl stops, sheathes her sword, and points to her chest.

"Yeah." Bella waves her over. "Come here. You're gonna like this."

The girl glances around, as though to check for some sort of trick. But then her curiosity gets the best of her and she runs up to us, arriving out of breath. "Hey, I'm Harleen."

I set the paper dragon in her hand. "Don't mind that evil cleric from the tavern. This is for you."

Bella points to the dragon and says, "*Educ ad vitma.*" Purple glitter puffs out of her finger and cascades over the toy.

The dragon flaps its wings and flies up to the little girl's shoulder.

"I love it." She smiles from ear to ear. "Thank you." She runs back to the training grounds, eliciting an explosion of squeals as her friends surround her.

"Why did you do that?" Hans steps around the booth's corner. "She's just a stupid NPC kid, hardly a quester that could ever help us. That coinage would be better spent on something that could aid us on our run."

"The quester who ignores the NPCs never fully plays the game." Bella says, folding her arms. I like her spunk. And her appreciation of the DCQ world.

The merchant dwarf pulls the drawstrings of my now-loaded pack closed and drops it on the counter. "Your order is ready. Three gold is the cost."

I flick three gold coins to him and toss the pack on my back. "Are you sure you're not aligned evil, Hans? I mean, weren't you just hugged up on an NPC in the courtyard? I'd like to know what she could help us with."

I let the statement hang just long enough for him to open his mouth with what I assume would be some annoying retort, then I cut him off. "Let's go."

One by one, the transparent boxes flash in my vision.

SUBTRACT: *3 gold coins to Catlob Whaley. New gold coin balance: 5*

ADD POSSESSION: **Small Backpack** *(-5 Pennies)*
Holds up to four hundred coins.
ADD POSSESSION: **Flask of Oil** *(-2 Pennies)*
Provides light for four hours.
ADD POSSESSION: **Lantern** *(-1 Gold)*
Cast light thirty feet in all directions.
ADD POSSESSION: **(11) Single Days Rations** *(-11 Pennies)*
Unpreserved food for one day.
ADD POSSESSION: **Water Skin** *(-1 Penny)*
Holds enough water for one day.

As we walk across Center Square, I see a man sitting on the ground talking to the goats. "You think that guy can really communicate with animals?" I hadn't seen that in the game before.

"Nope." Bella chuckles. "He's just crazy as a shambler. He also happens to be a member of our party that you hired. Do we have to stop and get him?"

Is that Biff, our Ninja? Oh man, it is. "Hey, Biff." I hold out a hand and pull him up, trying not to gag at the waft of goat stench. I'm not sure if it's coming from the animals or his clothing. "Are you ready to quest with the best?"

He stumbles and nearly pulls me down with him before he plants his peg leg firmly on the ground. He picks up a small pack and secures it to his back. "I am all packed and can't wait to reach the next town."

Hans shakes his head. "Please tell me you didn't hire Hong Kong Phooey. I don't mean to rain, piss, break your crayons, or pop your balloons, but this man sucks."

Biff pounds his chest, hocks, and spits a loogie to the ground, an inch shy of Hans's boot. "Clerics say a lot, but only fight a little. We'll see who sucks when it's time to do battle." He moves in close to my ear and whispers. "Drunken kung fu is all about cold-blooded attacks and colossal evasions. Rest assured, you made an excellent choice in hiring me."

Salo walks up to us and glares at the goats from the corner of his eye. "Aaa… Aaaa… *Aaachoooo!*"

"Salud," I say. "Welcome to the party, Salo. Does the goats smell bother you as much as it bothers me?"

He scrunches his nose and sniffs. "They are nasty, dirty animals. What is salud? Aaa… Aaaa… Aaachoooo!"

"That means 'bless you,' my good quester." Other than dirty words, salud is the extent of my Spanish.

"It means bless you in what language? I am not familiar." Salo pinches his nose and squints at the animals.

"In the language of—the Compass-Keepers." That sounds way more mysterious than just saying Spanish.

Hans looks Salo up and down. "What else are you allergic to?"

Salo wipes his arm across his nose. "Fake-fool clerics like you."

81

I give Salo a nudge forward. "Let's get in this valley already."

The five of us cross the remainder of the courtyard to the stronghold gate. A large crowd of henchmen, hirelings, and men-at-arms loiters there. Slim emerges from the crowd, takes a stance behind us, and nods my direction. "I'm ready to accompany the team, Captain."

Castilian steps out from a guard shack and looks us over. "Welcome to the edge of town. Who leads this party?"

Bella gives me a push. "That's you."

I step up to Castilian and assume a regal pose. "I think you know that's me."

He holds out a hand. "Let me see your paperwork."

I pull out my Grimoire, open it, and touch the red welcome screen dot. A new screen pops up with a green dot in the middle.

FINGERPRINT VERIFIED

JARETH GOBLINMASHER: CAPTAIN

LEVEL: 2 - ABILITIES: 50 - CLASS: FIGHTER - TOOLS: MAP+3

PARTY OF SIX WITH THIEF CONFIRMED

TOUCH HERE TO VIEW YOUR CHARACTER SHEET

●

I put the Grimoire in Castilian's hand.

He studies the screen. "Some would say it's not wise to start a run to Cittadella so long after midday. Not me, though. I applaud your bravery. Anyway, enjoy your time in Ranida." He turns, looks up to the left tower and cups his mouth. "We got an accredited questing team here. Open, says me." He puts his arm around a nearby man-at-arms, slides something in his hand,

and speaks low. "Thirty gold coins on they don't. Hurry. This is a winning bet for sure." He looks at me and nods. "Best of luck."

Did Castilian just place a bet against us?

Grating clanks ring out as the gate rises upward and stops with a bang. Castilian waves us through with the continuous circling of his hand. "Go now. Enjoy."

Bella tightens the shoulder straps that connect her pauldrons and walks alongside me. "Chittor is a safe haven compared to what we are walking into," she warns me. "As soon as we step beyond this gate, we're fair game for all monsters."

I take a step under the gate and get a shock.

NEW TASK: **Pass Ranida's Gate.**

Pass under Ranida's Gate into the Central Valley.

CHAPTER 9

A dirt road winds in front of us, meandering into the valley below. On either side of it, a dense forest of lush green trees climbs up sharp mountains that disappear into white clouds. Already, the air smells clearer. But it carries the threat of unseen enemies.

I lead the way, away from Chittor and toward the real adventure. A single blinking prompt appears in the upper corner of my vision as I walk.

> *PARTY STATUS:*

I focus in on the prompt and a transparent sheet appears in my vision.

> *REORDER THE PARTY:* **Yes/No?**
>
> *Set the marching order of your party. Remember, only the first three members of a party can attack monsters with weapons while in a dungeon. Note: Only NPCs are bound to follow marching order instructions. (* = NPC)*
>
> | | | | |
> |---|---|---|---|
> | *Jareth Orcslauter, Fighter.* | *HP: 30/30* | *AC: 3/20* | *LVL: 2* |
> | **Salo Fatback, Fighter.* | *HP: 21/50* | *AC: 6/20* | *LVL: 4* |
> | **Biff Thunderpunch, Ninja.* | *HP: 7/65* | *AC: 7/10* | *LVL: 4* |
> | *Madmartigan Galladoorn, Mage.* | *HP: 25/40* | *AC: 3/10* | *LVL: 3* |

Hans Talhoffer, Cleric.	*HP: 21/40*	*AC: 2/5*	*LVL: 3*
*Gregarious Slim, Thief.	*HP: 27/40*	*AC: 5/10*	*LVL: 3*

Whoa! Biff only has seven hit points? He is already close to death. I focus on the 'No' and the sheet disappears. "Bella, Hans, let me talk to you for a minute." I take a few steps away from the NPCs and wave the two gamers into a huddle. "Let's talk about our marching order. Salo has twenty-one hit points, and I have thirty. The problem is Biff only has seven. But he has a max of fifty. Who has a spell that can bring his hit points up?"

"He'll be fine with what he has," Hans says.

"You think?" I ask. Hans had already shown he didn't like the ninja. Did he even care about Biff's survival? "A couple blows from a level one monster will check him into the boxed condo. Remember, he is a ninja. Our only party member with elite class status."

"Your ninja won't live no matter what we do." Hans looks down at Biff. "I'll bet coins on it. He's old and has a handicap. Nobody wants a party member with a handicap."

"I'll take that bet," Bella interjects. "A ninja's dexterity and intelligence make them hard to hit. I bet his armor class is a Sherman tank-like ten."

"Sherman tanks don't have peg legs." Hans walks in a circle with a mocking limp. "On top of that he's always sauced. That makes him more like a butt-naked zero."

"Biff has the highest armor class in the whole party," I point out, glancing at Hans, who doesn't even have a weapon. Why is he talking so much smack when he can't defend himself against physical attacks? "Let's talk about magic. What do you two have in your arsenal? If Biff gets killed, one of you is going to have to advance to the front line."

"I'm at 4/3/2," Bella says. "That means I can cast four first-tier, three second-tier, and two third-tier mage spells. The best healing spell I have right now will only restore one to eight hit points of health. That number will increase once I hit level four. I am also pretty handy with my dagger and flail when I need to be." She pulls a short wooden haft with a studded metal ball attached by a chain from her belt. "If you need me on the front line, I am there."

Hans pulls open his cloak. A thick knobbed stick hangs on his belt almost to the ground. "Us clerics are not much with hand-to-hand combat, but we are the strongest magic users in the game. I am at 4/2/1 with cleric spells. Another kill or two should award me the next level, and a few spells with semi-nuke type potency. I am content to stay on the back row to heal or cast spells on our enemies, but if Biff and Bella eat grass I can step up with my shillelagh. It packs a wallop, and I'm not afraid to use it against any threat."

His words sounded great and all, but I hadn't forgotten Bella's story about him ditching her in her hour of need. "Well let's get on with the foraying then," I say. "Just be ready to heal Biff, if he needs it." I walk to a nearby tree, break off a branch, and take a deep breath of the crisp air. I still can't believe I'm in the Valley of Fear.

Bella cocks her arm back and hurls a baseball-sized rock into the shrubbery.

"Baaaaaaawr." Bushes smash and trees sway as an unknown entity scurries deeper into the forest.

"Don't dally, Riff." She continues ahead. "Our plan doesn't include lost time and hit points to wandering monster attacks."

Biff hobbles up next to Slim and we resume our march. "I agree wholeheartedly that we should not pussy-foot," our one-legged ninja says.

"There is a small village on the other side of the gate with a lovely little pub. We really must get there quickly."

"Preach." Slim points a long cane with an ebony shaft forward. Its top features the carved ivory bust of a gape-mouthed Asian man with a ponytail. "The sooner we pass Ranida's Gate, the better. This area has an ugly reputation at night."

"Don't put it so damn lightly." Salo turns around from his position in front of the party. "We're dead in this part of the valley after dark. The scum that comes out of this forest at night will rip us to bloody shreds. Ranida's Gate closes at sundown, we need to be on the other side of it before then."

What is wrong with these NPCs? I have been through Ranida many times in the game, even camped out here overnight. Sure, there were wandering monsters, but they were always easy to kill—level up fodder, really. But maybe the real game is different.

"What exactly happens here after dark?" I ask.

"It's a different terror every night." Salo removes the mace from his belt and rests the shaft over his shoulder. "The wall has been erected to keep those terrors away from the populated areas to the north."

"It won't be a problem," Bella says. "We'll be on the other side of the wall long before nightfall."

I take up a position alongside Salo and scan my map. *I can't wait to see what A-Sampir has in store.* "We have one order of business about halfway to the gate, but it shouldn't take long. Let's pick up the pace, Salo. I'd like to keep this party on schedule."

After twenty minutes of trudging the dusty road and scanning the forest lines for monsters, the greenery gives way to a set of identical man sized statues, one on either side of the road. They are square blocks of white stone topped with oversized humanoids with webbed feet, three-digit hands, and no heads.

Bella looks up at one of the figures and shivers. "Those things are so creepy."

I touch the statue's foot and look up the road. "According to the map, the fourth set of these is where we need to make our turn. I wonder who knocked their heads off."

"Sirens," Biff says. "Lovely young ladies, and quite accommodating, if you know what I mean. Contrary to what Salo says, not everything that comes out of Ranida after dark is so bad. I was once a member of a party in this land that got attacked by two-dozen bandits and an earth giant. The encounter took us so long to snuff out that we missed the gate curfew. My party hunkered down and prepared for the worst when we saw them."

Biff looks up into the sky with a smile. "Dozens of gorgeous sirens came down from these hills. Blondes, brunettes, and redheads in all shapes and sizes. They sang to us all night, and made fire-roasted treats consisting of marshmallow, chocolate, and honey cracker. Just before sunrise, the girls lopped off all the statue heads along this road. I asked one of the beauties why. Why desecrate the statues? She gave me a kiss on the cheek and said sirens only like real men."

"You are a true player, Biff," Slim says. "A true one-of-a-kind player."

"Let's keep going, guys." Bella resumes the march, but it doesn't redirect the conversation.

"Bah," Salo frowns. "Those weren't sirens. They were succubus. Killers, all the same."

"I think I know the difference." Biff rubs his hands together. "They were killers though. Just not the way you're thinking."

An hour later, the sun has dipped below the tops of the trees, and we reach the fourth set of statues. I walk around the one located on the right side of the road. "Somewhere back here a path will take us to the map point." I prod through the bush with my sword and find a faint dirt trail heading back into the forest. "This has got to be it. I'll take the lead."

"We don't have time for this." Slim jogs after me. "Sunset's not far off."

"Neither is the map point." All the same, I quicken my pace.

We duck under branches and step over fallen tree trunks into the dense wilderness. The path widens and turns muddy as we approach a two-story stone compound set against the mountain cliffs. The walls are pitted and crumbling with piles of fallen rubble at the base. A modest gatehouse in front has a crashed portcullis in a pool of sludge.

"What a dump." I kick a rusty iron bar at my feet into the sludge. Several small tree frogs jump from the slop into the forest.

Hans walks to the sludge, raises a boot and smashes it down onto a frog mid-hop. "Slimy little green roaches." He twists his boot on a bar to clean the entrails off. "Let's go in."

We step under the gatehouse into a large open courtyard littered with rotting wood tables and chairs in pools of water and mud. A hallway with an open pair of wood double doors leads into the compound in front of us. We weave through the debris and take a stance at the hall entrance.

Slim glances into the opening and steps back. "In my experience, places like this are death traps. Since I am not being compensated for this run, I'll wait safely right here for you all."

That's right. He has a no services clause.

"More loot for us." I shrug and move to the threshold, looking in. The corridor is long and straight, with cracks and gaps in the rough stone brickwork. Water drips down the walls, dampening the floor. The air is cold with a salty tang. Dingy stained-glass skylights high above dimly light the way to a closed set of wooden double doors far at the other end.

I step into the hall, my foot slipping out from under me, and fall to a knee. "Watch the floor. Looks like there is some grime build-up." I stand carefully and try to regain my composure. What a bad start to my dungeon crawling career. I draw my sword. "Let's do dungeon number one. What we came for is just behind those doors down there."

Salo takes a position to my left and points the jagged metal hunk on his mace forward.

Biff spins a war hammer in each hand and stands to my right. "Colossal."

We walk slowly to the center of the hallway and stop at an ornate carved door set in the right wall. A painted gold crown decorates its black cast iron doorknob.

Salo eyes the knob. "What say you, Jareth?"

"Treasure." Biff points to the knob. "There is sure to be something of value behind a door with a crown knob like this."

At home, I would never pass this up. But we have serious time constraints now. "You'll have to come back for it on your own time, boys. This door is not on the map. Our treasure lies behind the double doors ahead." As if hearing my comment, the double doors open with a clank.

We all freeze, and I brace for my first real encounter.

Two green humanoids step into the hall, speaking to each other with squeaky clicks. They have shiny slime-covered skin, and paunchy bodies topped with toad heads. Each has a dagger at its hip and holds a three-pronged trident spear. One puts his hand on the other's shoulder and doubles over with laughter.

90

Salo pulls the shield from his back and positions it in front of him. "Liergarnin guards."

I know this monster from the game, but I simply call them Toad-Fish Men. They are level one foes, but vicious none the less.

The upright Liergarnin notices us and yanks his partner upright by a leather shoulder strap. He points at us, and opens his toad mouth to croak out, "Kurpla."

They both tilt their tridents forward and charge at us full speed. "Kurplaaaa!"

LIERGARNIN

LEVEL: 1 *(200XP)*   **HIT POINTS:** 11

ARMOR CLASS: 10 *(Natural armor)*   **FREQUENCY:** Rare

NO. APPEARING: 2-24   **DAMAGE:** By weapon or 3 - 7

SPECIAL ATTACKS: Bite, Leap

SPECIAL DEFENSES: Amphibious, Slippery, Speak with Frogs and Toads

INTELLIGENCE: Low   **ALIGNMENT:** Neutral   **SIZE:** M

TYPICAL WEAPONING: Dagger, Three-pronged trident spear, Weighted throwing net, Harpoon

DESCRIPTION: Liergarnin have paunchy humanoid bodies with a toad's head and huge fishlike eyes. Skin is shinny green, gray, or spotted yellow with sheen from slime covering. Liergarnin only wear leather harnesses with shoulder straps for their weapons and personal effects.

CHAPTER 10

Salo raises his shield. "It's going to be frog legs for dinner." He sprints forward. "Aaaaaah!"

I raise my sword and run to catch up with him. Energy pulsates through my hand into my body. Feels like that abilities number is kicking in. I'm ready.

Both of the guards launch their spears at us in unison. Salo blocks one projectile with his shield, and then slams the business end of his mace onto the oncoming monster's head.

I duck under the soaring trident intended for me and slide feet first into the toad-fish man's legs, upending it into a face plant slam.

Biff crashes his peg down on the fallen toad's back. "Kill it, Jareth."

I raise my sword and pause. Am I about to kill something for real?

The toad stretches out its neck and bites my ankle. "Arghh!" I roar as pain shoots up my leg. "It bit me."

The toad looks up at me with bulging fish eyes. "Kurpla!"

Biff pounds his peg down on the creature's head. "Kill it already."

I slice down across the back of the toad's neck, then raise my sword up and quick slice down again. With the second slice its head lops off to the side, attached only by a few thin strings of oily meat.

The smell of dead fish rises from the sprawled monster. I pinch my nose, gag, and move away from the carnage. Did I really just do that? Killing had been a lot easier with a computer between me and my enemy, and it had never gotten my heart racing like this. Then, I get a flash in front of my face.

DUNGEON CRAWL QUEST PRIVATE BETA 1 WARNING

You were hit for damage! There are currently no safeguards against real pain, and real death in this private beta version of DCQ. If you die while immersed in the game, you will die in real life.

If your character drops below 200 HP it is strongly suggested that you exit the game at one of the following locations:

ERROR...

Quality control write up and bug report due upon reentry. This message will not repeat.

"I got the death warning," I stammer. And my pain confirms it. "This is bad."

"Are the exit locations still in error?" Bella asks.

"Yes." I kneel and rub my ankle. "That's bad, too."

"Hesitation is bad." Bella steps around the dead Liergarnin. "Next time, don't wait to bring down your sword. Is your leg okay?"

I look over the wound. "That thing tried to bite my foot off." The laceration is only skin-deep, but stings badly. I won't hesitate again. It is me or them. "I'm good," I say, hoping its true.

Liergarnin (2) has been killed! For killing the monsters each survivor earned 80 experience points.

"I leveled up to three." This requires verification. I pull my Grimoire from its sheath, touch the red dot and look over my stats. "I took four hit points of damage, but I made level three. Look, my abilities number went up too." I flex my right bicep and feel it pulse. "I can kind of tell my strength has increased." It feels good.

Hans smacks me on the back. "Bella and I leveled up after our first kills too. All three of us are at level three now. If you want to impress me, reach level four."

Biff flips the nearest corpse over and runs his hand along its harness. He pulls out a small leather bag, rips it open, and holds out three silver pennies. "The spoils of a clash."

Salo drops two pennies in Biff's hand. "I found these on mine. Liergarnin never have anything good. Their tridents and daggers are rusty, dull, and of no value."

"All gains go to the captain." Biff holds his hand my way. "The booty is divvied up after the run."

I look over the five coins. "Not much loot on these guys."

Biff kicks his peg against the wall, scraping off fishy guts. "A timid captain's coffer is often deflated of riches."

I drop the coins in my bag. "I guess I'll have to make my hustles bold to fill this bag with plenty of gold."

96

Salo creeps down the hallway in front of us. He examines the floor and sidewalls with each step. The rest of us catch up to him at the end of the hall. He nods and points to an imbedded iron lever and keyhole lock. "Is this door more to your liking?"

Is he throwing shade because I didn't go for the treasure room door? "According to my map, yes, this door *is* to my liking." I reach for the lever.

Salo slaps my hand down. "A good captain would provide his party with a thief to determine if this door was booby trapped or not."

"I'll take care of this." Bella circles the handle with an open hand and says, *"Exarmo periclum."* A red spark snaps from the keyhole. "Aha. Good call Salo, that poison needle would have sent Jareth all the way back to the temple at Chittor."

I glue my curious hand to my side. "Good looking out, Salo. I owe you an ale for that."

"And me too." Biff says. "I saved you from the Liergarnin with my peg."

Bella smashes the needle with the hilt of her mace, then waves me forward. I grab hold of the handle. "I'll pay off double at the next town, Biff." I twist and pull but get no movement. "It's still locked."

Salo nudges me aside. "Prepare for a fight."

I draw my sword and look over the blade. *This thing sliced toad-fish neck nicely for being defective. I kind of like it.*

"Uhraah!" Salo blasts the heel of his boot to the side of the lock with a booming kick. The door cracks in the center and bursts open.

We step into a rectangle room with a glowing yellowish-green ceiling. A heavy iron door is at the back wall, along with a rack of three harpoons and several weighted throwing nets piled in a corner. The smell of an unsanitary fish market on a hot summer day wafts over us.

Three little toad-people quickly shift to the back of what looks like a small oval hot tub filled with bubbling greenish muck. They start yapping quiet but snappy croaks.

I return my sword to its sheath. These guys don't look too threatening. "We mean no harm," I say. "I am here for an item."

The door in the back of the room swings open. A giant Liergarnin, twice as big as the ones we beat in the hall, takes a firm stance in the jamb. He is muscle-bound, wearing a complete set of plate mail armor, and has a belt lined with daggers and a gem-encrusted gold crown riding low on his head.

Frothing at the mouth, he croaks with a deep bass several times and waves to the others. One by one the little toad-people hop from the pool and scamper through the door behind him, dripping sludge as they go. The giant takes a step my way and stares with shiny black fish eyes.

"Croak."

I am okay fighting toad-fish men, but this well-armed giant is another story. Maybe I can use some diplomacy. "I have no grudge with you, toad-king. I have come for the Keris of Knaud's blade."

"He has it," Bella says in a low tone. "It's on his belt."

Hans stretches his fingers. "I have a spell that will weaken him quite a bit. Just say the word, and I'll blast him with it."

"Why did you call him toad-king?" Salo grumbles under his breath. "We stand before the illustrious king of the Liergarnin, not a toad-king. I'm pretty sure you insulted him."

The Liergarnin king covers a wavy blade on his belt and shakes his head. "*Croak.*" He snatches a harpoon from the rack and hurls it at me in one smooth motion.

I step to the side just in time for it to whiz by my head. It crashes into a wall behind us and smashes into pieces.

Salo raises his shield.

"*Acedia.*" A bolt rips from Hans fingers into the creature's chest.

"*CROAK.*" The toad stumbles back into the doorway, snatches another harpoon, and thrusts it at Salo, who dives to the right and deflects it off his shield into the pool of muck.

Biff tumbles across the floor, hops behind the door, and punches it shut, sandwiching the toad between the door and the wall jamb.

Bella and Hans rush in, pressing against the door to keep the toad pinned.

"Hurry, Riff." Hans wedges his foot in a crack of the floor and pushes hard. "My spell won't keep it weak much longer."

Trapped, the toad-king struggles to reach its weapons belt and howls. "*Crooooaak!*"

I dart forward and pull the wavy Keris of Knaud blade from its belt. On the other side, I get a peek of the three small toad people desperately trying to pull their king to safety.

Hans whips a small dagger from a sheath on his calf and holds it to the toad's throat. "Did you get what you came for, Riff? Can I kill this slimy *wichser* yet?"

Biff grunts. "We can't keep him trapped like this much longer. He's regaining strength."

Salo joins the party in pushing the door. "Orders, captain?" he grunts.

I take a step back, but I can still see one of the small toad people grasping at its king's leg. It looks through the crack at me with pleading eyes and a quivering lip.

"Let him go," I command.

Biff, Bella, and Salo let go of the door as I kick the toad king in his chest. He flings back into the room and the door slams shut.

Chains, slams, and the clicks of closing locks vibrate through the room as the Liergarnin secure the door from the other side.

Hans throws his fists in the air. "Why did you let it go? I could have leveled up twice for killing a Liergarnin king. *And* I could have had its head and that crown."

"We got what we came for," I say. "Besides, I think the king was the little toadlets' daddy."

"Toadlets?" Hans challenges me, putting his face an inch from mine. "They are monsters. And we need to kill them to level up. I used my only level three spell, and for what?" He spins and grips his fists harder. "This is exactly why I need to be captain of this run."

He has a point, but I can't admit it in front of the party. Not after leading them in our first successful encounter. I look at Bella and shrug. "That man has to be aligned evil."

And I have got to get used to killing these monsters.

I hold the wavy blade up with two hands. It is a foot long and razor sharp on both sides. Its tang is lodged in a cracked bone handle wrapped in soiled strips of cloth. But there are no numbers on it that I can see.

"It's a work of art," Bella says.

"Except for this cloddish handle." I pound the hilt on a nearby wall. "I need to get it off."

"Let me see that." Biff grips the Keris by the bottom of the handle and holds it upright. "This is the proper technique for removal." He taps the top of his wrist with a fist. *Clank.* "This is a colossal looking blade." He bows and presents it to me, free of its former handle. "Blessings."

I pull the sooang from my bag and slide the sampir into it. The steel flashes red-hot then cools. It forms one flawless piece.

"Sheath it." Bella points to my belt. "It's got to have some damage ability now."

I slide the dagger into the perfectly fitted sheath on my belt and a box appears in my vision.

TASK COMPLETE: **Complete the Keris of Knaud II.**

For completing the task you earned 400 experience points!

ADD POSSESSION: **Keris of Knaud -1 (Sooang/Sampir)**

Damage: 2-5. Range: N/A. Frequency: Error. Quality: Incomplete.

Melee Weapon Attack: Piercing damage.

Soulbound to 'Jareth Goblinmasher' - Item cannot be traded or sold.

NEW TASK: **Complete the Keris of Knaud III**

Acquire the taguban to unlock the Keris of Knaud's true power.

"Task two of the Complete the Keris of Knaud saga has been accomplished," I announce. "I got four hundred XP for it. And the Keris now has some damage ability, but it is still at a minus one and of incomplete quality."

Bella wipes both hands across her face. "So, we still need the sheath to make it right."

"That's our new task—Complete the Keris of Knaud III."

Salo snatches the final harpoon from the rack and snaps it in two. "Rubbish. The Liergarnin are all about rubbish." He pulls a net from the pile and hurls it onto the floor. "This is also rubbish."

"Wait." Hans pokes his shillelagh into the net pile. "There's something—"

Salo plunges his hands into the nets and throws them off, one after another. Within seconds, he's uncovered a large iron chest sealed with heavy bands and multiple dome locks.

Biff inspects all the sides carefully. "It's a Hamid-Jazari chest. If the locks are operated in the wrong order, it will not open. They are also known to have poison stunners."

I wrap my fingers around the chest's top corner. It's a real treasure chest. I love finding these in the game, and now I've found one for real.

The muffled sound of a horn blows outside, and somewhere beyond our room heavy doors slam and chains crash.

"Not good." Biff's body stiffens. "The king is sounding the alarm."

Salo points to the largest lock on the chest. "There are great treasures in here. We gotta get it open. Where is that damn thief when we need him?"

Biff leans over the chest, and I see him slide the long, pointed fingernail of his right pinky into the lock and jiggle it. "Even a great thief would need some time to pop a chest this well fortified." He moves and puts his ear to the wall. "We will be having a lot of unfriendly company very soon. We either need a powerful spell or some huo-yao to pop this chest open."

Bella shrugs. "I can disarm small bobby traps, but not open locks like this. I've got nothing for it."

"What is huo-yao?" I ask.

Biff pulls a small sack from his belt and shakes it. "It's a blasting powder. I have some, but not enough to blow open a chest this robust. It would take quite a while to rig, and the help of a fire-throwing magic user to ignite it."

I put my hand on Biff's arm. "Maybe you shouldn't be shaking that stuff." I look in the sack of black powder and jerk my head back. "Smells skunky." Hmm, with a little engineering, I bet I could turn this powder into some kind of easy-dynamite, chest-busting explosive. Hans isn't the only one who has taken chemistry classes.

Salo moves to the exit door and opens it. "No sense in wasting our time trying to do things we are ill equipped for. We need to be on the other side of the wall by sundown." He continues down the hall.

"And I need a drink." Biff rests his hand on my shoulder. "We have to leave this chest behind. Onward."

The first chest I encounter, and it goes unopened. This is an embarrassment to my DCQ prowess.

Outside the compound, we step into dwindling daylight. Slim, the useless thief, is talking to two girls in the courtyard. One is skinny as a pole with dull black hair and a beak of a nose. The other is beautiful and voluptuous, with wide hips, a narrow waist, and ample breasts. They both wave goodbye to Slim and take a path into the forest as we approach.

I hold my arms out wide. "You missed out on some fine looting in there."

Slim turnes from the girls. "No use looting when I don't get a share of the treasure."

"There was a huge chest we would have loved for you to examine."

"What a coincidence." He points in the direction the girls went. "There was a huge chest out here I was indeed enjoying examining. Besides,"—he gestures to my head—"I don't see the Liergarnin king's crown on you up there.

Anything else in there is worthless. I don't know if you heard the sound of that horn, but we need to be on our way. One of my girls is very familiar with the horn signals. Apparently, the king has decreed that he wants your party dead, and since I'm part of your party, we need to get out of here before we're knee-deep in killer minions."

Back at the main road, we take a right turn at the headless statues and continue on to the gate.

Who were those girls Slim was talking to? I think there is more to our non-fighting thief than we know. I drop back in the marching order and walk alongside him. "So, who were your friends back at the compound? You neglected to introduce us. That one was super pretty."

"Just re-connecting with a few of the locals. It's funny you should ask. Juliette, was eye-balling you for sure. She said she thinks you're fine as Melomel XO wine."

"She said that for real? Wait. Which one was Juliette?"

"I'm not telling. I don't play matchmaker. Besides, don't you see the way Bella looks at you? You need to be holding hands and kickin' cups with her."

"You think Bella likes me?" I glance over at her. She is fine and a gamer girl. Mack just might approve of this one. Besides, she and I can continue this back in the real world once we've saved DCQ. None of the NPCs can follow me home.

I can always find out more about Slim later. Right now, I need to investigate his Bella theory. I work my way to Bella's side. But what to say? "So, what spells do you plan on using against the goblin?"

She looks down at her fingertips. "I have two level-three spells that could distract him. Leveling up is the key. If I can hit level four before we get there my options get better. At level five, I can really do some damage."

"You really know your way around DCQ. I don't run into too many players like—well—like you. I mean, you are officially the finest girl I have ever met that plays the game."

"You must not get around much." She flushes a bit, despite the cooling air. "I have a few really good-looking girlfriends who play in my dorm. I kind of consider it research. My major is Game Production Management."

"Okay." This is way too good. We are into the same business. "My major is game development. But Management is good too. How'd you get into that?"

"My dad pushed me in the management direction as a trade-off for tuition. It's worked out, though. I already have an internship set for this summer. I'm super excited about it."

"I would take that trade for tuition any day," I say. "Keeping up with the financial end of college has been tough. The best schools in the video game design field are no joke on cost. I'm going to make it, though. Hey, maybe we'll meet on the professional level at E3 someday." It felt oddly freeing to talk about life beyond the game. A crisp reminder of what we were fighting for.

"I'm definitely looking forward to that." She smiles and kicks a rock from the path into the bushes. "You know, I have a few friends that are diabolical when it comes to school finance."

"If we survive this, I'm gonna need their info," I say.

"If we survive." Bella fidgets with her Grimoire. "I got in an argument with my dad over my internship selection before I got sucked into the game. It was heated. I hate to think that was the last conversation we will ever have."

"I feel you on that." The way things happened between Mileena and I doesn't sit well with me, and I didn't even have a chance to say goodbye to Mack. "I left a few loose ends back home too." I give Bella's shoulder a playful shove and smile. "But we're going to live-for-real-live. This is Madmartigan and Jareth we're talking about. We're like the king and queen of DCQ."

Bella and I talk college life, magic powers, and game design until the wall comes into view. Mack would *definitely* approve of her. But what if she already has a boyfriend? Bella and I sure have a lot more in common then Mileena and I ever did.

The wall cuts through the mountains on both sides of the valley to a gate in the middle of the road. Amazing. I imagine this is as close as I will ever come to seeing the Great Wall of China in person. I love this game. The optics are incredible.

The road curves to a tree-lined straightaway leading to the wall's gateway. Two watchtowers flank a closed iron spike door.

Salo looks up at the trees as the sun dips. "We're cutting this close."

"Why does the gate look closed?" Biff asks.

"Because it is," Slim says flatly.

"But the sun's not fully set yet!" I break into a jog. The others follow, clanking and croaking and hobbling behind me until we finally arrive in front of the watchtower.

A man at arms looks down from the top of the wall and waves. "No entry until the morning."

Salo grabs the gate with both hands and rattles the bars. "But the sun has not set yet. We demand entry."

The man shrugs. "The monsters of Ranida have been encroaching on the valley earlier and earlier as of late. No entry for you, despite your demand."

"We have gold." Bella glances at me then back up at the man.

The guard turns away. I catch a few mutters as though he's speaking with someone out of view. Then looks back down. "I can send the gate master for three hundred gold coins." He lowers a rope down the wall with a sack attached to the end.

"Would you accept five?" she asks.

The man holds up five fingers and leans over the wall. "Five hundred?"

"No." I cringe as Bella clarifies. "Five gold coins."

The sack and rope instantly ascend back up the wall. The guard stands up straight. "I should place an arrow in your forehead for asking." He disappears behind the wall.

I put my hand on Bella's shoulder. "Looks like we are going to stay the night here."

Biff looks up. "They are being unreasonable."

I turn to the forest and look up into the hills. "Hey, Biff, any chance we get sirens tonight?"

"It's a full moon, so not likely." He walks back along the tree line, stops, and looks up at one. "This one looks excellent. Salo, lift me up a few branches. I will do the rest."

Salo and Slim lift Biff up to a lower branch, where he grabs hold, swings, climbs, and disappears into the tree.

Bella and I look up. Leaves and small twigs snap and fall in our faces.

"Look at him go." I guess he really is a ninja. "Are you going up there to scout a way over the wall?" I call after him.

Slim clasps his hands into a step and holds them down. "You're next, Bella. Up you go."

"What's up there?" she asks.

Salo positions himself alongside of Slim. "Several trees along this road have wooden platforms to ride out the night. Each can hold two of us at best."

Bella takes the offered hand-step and gets launched up to where she can grab a branch and climb. I watch her navigate a few limbs before I lose sight of her in the leaves. "Are you okay up there?" I call.

"I made it to the platform," she says. "It's not so bad. You can see everything from up here."

"I'll take care of her, Jareth." Biff calls down. "You all try to find sturdy platforms. And be quick about it."

I really should have thought this through so that I'd end up on a platform with Bella for the night. If nothing else, to plan strategy for tomorrow. It seemed a waste to go to sleep so early, but what else could we do?

Slim walks a few trees deep into the forest and turns to us. "One of my thoroughbreds has a luxury platform a little ways back. I'm going to spend the night with her. I will see you all at the gate in the morning. If you survive the night."

Salo looks up into several trees then stops. "Nice, very nice. I claim this one."

He sure seems excited. There has to be a solid platform up there. "I'm with you," I say.

Salo points up to a neighboring tree. "Hans, that one looks to have a semi-steady platform. You better take it. I'm going up." Salo scales the tree.

"You good with that one, Hans?" I ask.

He grabs hold of a low branch and glances my way. "I bet five gold coins I'll be on my platform before you." He jumps to the next branch but drops down when it snaps off in his hand. "Oof."

"You're on." I jump to the lowest branch, dig my boot onto a limb, and double time scamper up doing my best to follow the route Salo was so quick to negotiate. Branch after branch I ascend to a circular platform around the tree trunk. I look over to Hans's tree and try to catch my breath. "I beat him Salo. He's way down there."

Salo squats on his heels with his mace pointed downward. "We will take turns. One sleeps while the other guards. If anything tries to get up here during the night, kill it. You sleep first." His sentences are terse. Clipped.

With so many amazing things going on I haven't even thought of rest. "Getting some sleep is probably a good idea." I lay on my back and stare up at the moon. I can tell Salo isn't happy with me. I'm not sure I want to hear the answer, but I ask anyway. "So, how do you think I am doing as captain?"

"Worst I've seen," he says briskly. "When you passed up on the ornate door, let the Liergarnin King go free, and had no means to open that chest, you cost me gold and experience. I could have made the next level and had a trove of sweet, precious gold. Now, we're stuck in Ranida after sun down with no riches. So far this run is a bust."

Gold is not exactly the primary objective on this run. But if our NPCs knew that, they wouldn't have agreed to join us. "Is there anything you think about other than gold and leveling?"

"Yes," he answers quickly. "The Pole of Pounding. The experience points I would be granted for equipping with it would bring me up to the elite class of Lord. I want that pole more than anything. But, of course, capable captains make artifacts exempt, and the incapable are not good enough to get anywhere near one anyway."

Ah, the elite classes. You can switch from your basic class to lord, wizard, bishop, or ninja, once you become more powerful. The special requirements for abilities, alignment, and allowed possessions turn me off of making the switch. But for NPCs it's probably the greatest thing that can happen to them.

I know what can cheer this man up. "A rumor table back in Chittor boasted that several artifacts could be found in the goblin's chamber, and that's where we're headed. If we come across that pole you crave, it's yours. I got you."

"Your party members will kill you for giving up such a valuable item." The corner of his mouth turns up, hinting at a smile. "But I accept your generous offer, Captain Goblinmasher."

TERMS AMENDMENT: Salo Fatback, Fighter. (-10 Gold/ -20% Share/ + **The Pole of Pounding Artifact Privileges)**

"It's official then, my man. I hope we find it." I look into the trees and close my eyes. What scourge is going to come down from these hills tonight?

CHAPTER 11

"Ribbit, ribbit." I open my eyes to find a bloated, yellow and black tree frog sitting on my groin. Its mouth opens to reveal spiked teeth dripping with mucus.

"Don't move," Salo whispers. "One bite will paralyze you, not to mention end your love life." He gently positions the handle end of his mace against the frog. "Lift your pelvis. Coax it to leap."

A bubble of sticky slobber builds up around the border of the frog's mouth. "Nice froggy, froggy," I whimper.

Just as I move my hips, the frog opens its mouth and bears down. "Rrrri–"

Whack! Salo launches the frog off my groin like a golf ball from the tee.

I sit up and watch the green streak fade into the darkness. "Way to tee off Kermit, Salo.

"Shhh." He holds a finger at his lips. "It has friends at the base of the tree, millions of them."

I dip my head down and listen. The sound of wildlife fills the air with hoots, buzzes, and ribbits. But mostly ribbits. "I guess the king sent his minions."

Branches thrash in a neighboring tree. "Help!"

I peer into the darkness, but only make out leaves and a faint flicker of light. "Hans, is that you? What's going on?"

"Frogs keep trying to hop on my platform," he says, out of breath. "They're trying to bite. Frogs aren't supposed to have teeth, are they?"

Salo peers in the direction of Hans's voice. "Listen up. You will have to keep fighting them off until daybreak. Do not get bit."

"What? Daybreak? I can't." Branches snap and leaves rustle. "Take that, you nasty little sheisse. Ugh, the guts are putrid."

Salo lies down. "Your turn to take watch," he says to me. "Hold your stance, punch out to defend, and strike like a Medusa Demon."

"Got it." I draw my dagger. "Why aren't they swarming us like they are Hans?"

Salo closes his eyes and crosses his hands over chest. "Your friend has the scent of toad guts on his shoe from the one he stomped at the king's compound. It's drawing them in." Is that a smile I hear in his voice?

I have to warn Hans before he gets bit and dies. "Hans!" I yell. "Toss your boots away from the platform. They can smell the toad guts on them."

"Arghh." Branches snap downward. "I did it. But they are still coming. Not as many. But they are still... Ugh."

Crap. Well, he did kill one on his platform.

"Don't sleep, Hans," Biff calls out from the distant darkness. "That's definitely a smile in his voice. "When the master is away, the frogs hop in and bite."

"Yeah, Hans," Bella calls out. "Stay strong."

I sit with my back to the tree trunk, with my dagger out and ready. This is going to be a long night. For the first hour, I'm on high alert. Only two more frogs make their way up, but I nudge them off the platform, making sure not to kill them and send their scent into the air. After a while, I don't see them again. I don't hear them.

I close my eyes, straining my ears for any *ribbit* or sound of attack. In fact, I think I hear better when my eyes are closed. My tired, tired eyes…

"Wake up."

I raise my eyelids just in time to see Salo's head descend below the platform. "You make a poor watchman."

I grab my dagger from my lap and stand, putting one arm around the tree trunk. Brightly colored sunrays blast orange and yellow through the trees. I can make out Hans's empty platform in the tree across the way. Did he survive the night, or succumb to the wrath of the tree frogs?

I position myself to climb down and my stomach rumbles. *What I wouldn't do for some Roscoe's right now. I'm hungry as a hostage.* A sharp pain in my abdomen causes me to double over. *What was that?*

YOU HAVE BEEN DEDUCTED A SINGLE DAY'S RATION: -(1)
Single Day's Ration
Eat once a day to avoid a loss of hit points.

It seems I forgot to eat.

Hunger pains cost you 2 damage. Status: 24/40

And it cost me hit points. I put a hand on my stomach and stand as the pain eases away. I guess by 'deducted' the game means I ate. Well, I'm not hungry now. Unsatisfied, but not hungry.

113

I climb down the tree and plant both feet firmly on the ground, hoping everyone else made it through the night.

A couple dozen questers talk amongst themselves at the foot of the gate. They all have loaded packs and various weapons. Bella, Biff, Salo, and three other men kneel over a body stretched out on the ground.

Oh no! Hans?

I run up to my party members, kneel next to Bella, and look over the body. A man with a mangled face and multiple yellow blisters on his arms shivers uncontrollably on the ground. It's not Hans. I blow out a breath. "Who is this? And where are Hans and Slim?"

One of the men in the circle runs a hand through his hair. "Yesterday was the worst. First, an encounter with an infuriated knot of Liergarnin cost us three men. Then, when we finally made it to the gate, it was closed. The three of us were lucky enough to make it onto tree platforms. Osnat here picked a tree with no platform and took the brunt of the frog's fury."

"Unlike this sad sack, I survived." Hans elbows his way into the circle and kneels next to me. He hacks like a barking seal. "This guy was a welcome diversion for me, though. I was close to getting overrun."

"Hans." I pat him on the back to help with the cough. His hair is an absolute mop, lips are cracked, and eyes are bloodshot red. "You're alive."

"But you look half dead." Bella interlocks her fingers and pushes her hands out until her knuckles crack. "Scratch that—he looks whole dead."

"Fighting those frogs off kept me up most of the night." Hans looks at the bottom of his left boot. "I got my footwear back though. Vindictive little arschlochs."

Bella spins a finger in a circle and rests her hand on the man's chest. "*Parva sanitatem.*" The man stops shaking and moans. "I did what I can, but unless someone here is willing to use a level eight spell, he's going to die."

Two of the men lift the injured man by his arms. "Thank you for the help," one says. They drag their friend toward a shaded area in the forest.

Slim passes by them, flanked by two slender females. He has a steaming mug in one hand and his cane in the other. Both ladies are wearing short, form fitting robes. The girl on the left has long curly blond hair and holds a large serving tray with several round loaves of bread. The other has pale skin, leaf-shaped ears, and holds her head down with a hand on Slim's shoulder.

"Good morning, Captain. I brought breakfast for the whole party." Slim hands his cane to the pale girl and raises his cup. "For health."

"Slim, you're alive." I guess I'm not such a bad captain after all. My whole party made it through the night.

"Slept like a baby thanks to the family here." He sips from the top of his mug and tilts his head to the girl with the tray. "Ahhh. You make a mean cup of java, Melusine."

Biff plucks a loaf from the tray and bows in the girl's direction. "Some ale would go nicely with this."

I pick a loaf and take a bite. The bread is soft and warm. "Bella, you gotta try this."

Bella takes one, breaks off a hunk, and gives a cautious bite. "Mmm. I was just about to ask you for a ration, but this is actually very good."

Not to mention free.

"She mashin' for a ration, Riff." Slim nods his head. "The secret is nutmeg and cinnamon. Makes these things a true delight."

Bella, Salo, and I all partake in the bread. Hans comes over slowly with one hand massaging his temple.

Slim steps back. "Woah, Hans." He shields his eyes. "You're looking like Baba Yaga this morning. I could carry a bushel of kumquats in those bags under your eyes."

Hans glares at Slim. "The gate is about to open. Let's be there when it does."

A man and boy walk cautiously toward Hans. The man raises a shaky hand like a child asking permission to speak. "Excuse me, sir. Are you Hans Talhoffer, the cleric from Chittor?"

Hans stands up straight. "You've heard of me."

The boy steps forward. "Can you show us the dragon?"

Hans raises his left hand and chants, "*Partum a malum magia dracone.*" He snaps his finger and white smoke puffs up from the ground. The little purple dragon tiptoes out of the smoke, spins in a circle, and disappears. "That's all I can reveal today. I have a major run in the works on the other side of the wall."

"I loved it." The boy jumps up and down. "You are truly great, Mr. Talhoffer."

The man walks backward with a giant smile. "Thank you. Your sorcery is second to none."

Wow. Hans has fans. If only that dragon could fight for us instead of just looking cute. I don't get what these people see in Hans.

Slim kisses each of his lady friends on the cheek. "Bye, babies."

I watch the girls go back into the forest. "What's the deal with all these forest girls you know?"

"I go way back with Melusine and Manchette. It's good to have acquaintances throughout the valley. Be known on the outer-planes, recognized on the inner-planes, and accepted in the local kingdom, young captain."

The gate cranks up, and the crowd streams through ahead of us. We step under the portcullis into a wide, open clearing. A large building on the left side of the road has several guards in front of it. To the right, a small two-story building has questers going in and out.

"Anything here worth exploring?" I ask.

Slim gives me a slight push toward the two-story building. "Yes. If you want to catch a severe case of haggish herpes, that brothel has the worst concubines the valley has to offer."

A heavy woman with a large crooked nose leans out of a top story window. "Bifford T. Thunderpunch!" She waves our direction. "You best come and see me."

Biff ducks his head and hobbles away fast. "We should keep going. This is not a good place to be brought into temptation."

TASK COMPLETE: **Pass Ranida's Gate.**

For completing the task you earned 400 experience points!

NEW TASK: **Touch the pillar at Cittadella.**

Touch the pillar located at the four-way crossroads in the center of Cittadella.

"Our new task is the pillar at Cittadella." I pull out my map and flip it open. "It's about an hour's walk." Cittadella is the center city of The Kingdom of Fear. I can't wait to see it in person. "Once in the city, we will need to find a cobbler with a blowout sale on Bombardment Boots."

As we continue along the road, I slide out the Keris to admire the blade. The morning sun shines off its sharp edge. *That sheath better turn this weapon into a cat-eyed goblin slayer.*

"Nice dagger." Slim says.

I return the blade to its sheath. "It will be even nicer when I complete it. I've been promised artifact-level killing powers."

"My weapon has some decent killing power." Slim wraps his hand around the carved ivory bust that tops his cane. "This end is great for bludgeoning." He thrusts the shaft forward and then pulls it back to reveal a four-inch spike protruding from the bottom. "And this end for piercing." He twists the bust retracting the spike. "It can also cast a powerful spell versus the undead that I haven't used because it drains a level."

"Okay." It's like something from out of Assassin's Creed, but with magic ability. "Where can I get one?"

"I acquired this from a Chinese polymath monk." He returns the cane to his side and resumes his shoulder-dipping limp strut. "I can do some uncommon damage with it."

I'd like to see Slim in action with this cane, preferably in my party. What were the chances of me changing his mind about fighting with us? "So, Slim, strong parties and top coin are your requirements, if I remember correctly. Why are you so picky about who you quest with? If you're as good with that weapon and thief skills as you say, I think you'd be a popular hire across the board."

"Prosperity over popularity." Slim raises his cane high and steps forward like a proud drum major. "I have a personal policy when it comes to joining questing parties. Only do so if your team captain is a wealthy wizard. You live longer that way."

Bella looks down at her palms and spreads her fingers. "Quests must come few and far between for you, then. I haven't seen a wizard since I've been here."

"They don't come around like they used to," Slim says. "At one point I ran with a wizard captain named Spliff. After my last run with him, he told me that the Kingdom of Fear no longer had anything to offer that wouldn't kill him, and that he would not quest again until the new world is unlocked."

Wow, that pretty much sums up how DCQ lost its popularity in a nutshell. Without an expansion, people got tired of the same old thing. "Our endgame is to unlock that new world," I say.

"Is that right?" Slim raises an eyebrow. "Then you must think you got what it takes to beat Setan Kober, the cold-hearted greater hobgoblin warlord that keeps the new world from us?"

So, my arch-enemy has a name.

"Did you here that, Riff?" Bella says, echoing my thoughts. "The cat-eyed goblin is named Setan."

A MONSTER HAS BEEN IDENTIFIED: The monster 'Cat-eyed Goblin' has been revealed as 'The Greater Hobgoblin Warlord Setan Kober' by Gregarious Slim.

This monster is now known to you and your party.

"Most people don't like to say it," Slim says. "I quested with the great captain Spliff on a few runs at Setan. Some of them even made it all the way to the monster allocation chamber." He looks down and grimaces. "Combat there left a lot of men dead. You know, we never so much as made that freak bleed. It's a nasty place to go."

"A completed Keris is the key." I show him the dagger again. "I'm two-thirds of the way there. When I complete this, we're going to kill Setan. Before sunrise tomorrow, in fact." My pulse double-timed as I realized I'd not likely sleep again unless I was dead or back in the real world.

Today was game day.

"Oh, really?" Slim smirks and looks at me from the corner of his eyes. "Just remember, my contract with you ends in Cittadella, Captain."

Well, I tried.

The road we're on continues to a circular wall, spotted with towers and ringed by a moat. Tall structures and smoking chimneys of the enclosed city rise from inside.

Slim straightens his collar. "I love this city. It is the meeting place for all the humanoids of the valley. Human, dwarves, halflings, gnomes, elves—"

"—and all types of half-breeds." Hans cuts in.

Slim continues as though Hans is nothing more than a fly that buzzed across his path. "Half-elves, half-orcs, brownies, succubi, and I'm pretty sure I've met at least a few half-demons in the dead of night. There is a whole lot of coin to be made off the fools in here."

"Any elf rangers ever sighted in Cittadella?" Bella smoothes her outfit and leans Slim's direction.

"Not that I have noticed," Slim says.

"Good." Hans smirks. "If I run into Legolas, I'm slapping him."

"Ha." I cover my mouth.

Bella takes firm steps forward. "You two are some haters."

We continue over the moat bridge, between two towers, and down a building-lined road to a circular clearing in the inner city. There, the road splits in four different directions, roughly corresponding to the points of the compass. We continue to the center of the roundabout where a waist-high stone pillar stands, crowded with rotten fruit and small trinkets. A rusty cast-iron pole with direction arrows rises from the pillar's center.

West - The Labyrinth at Keighley.
North - The Haworth Caves.
East - The Dungeon of Denholme.
South - The Stronghold at Chittor.

"The pillar of Duomo." Salo rubs the stone's top corner. "This is where all the great quests start. A rub of the stone will bring us good luck in any direction."

Slim and Biff each rub opposite corners of the pillar. Slim wasn't even coming with us. Where was he heading?

Hans pushes between Bella and me. "Stupid NPCs. Only gaining hit points will bring us what we need." He snatches a small clay figure off the pillar and crushes it to dust in his fist. "You're all idiots."

Bella rubs the pillar and glares at Hans. "When karma strikes, you better stay far away from me."

I step next to Bella and give the pillar a rub. "Me too."

TASK COMPLETE: **Touch the pillar at Cittadella.**
For completing the task you earned 500 experience points!

NEW TASK: **Enter the West, North, East, or South-East dungeon.**
Explore Cittadella to gather information and gain possessions for your dungeon run.

"Task complete." I circle around and look down each of the city's four streets. "Bombardment Boots time." My usual place at the North end of the city won't even let you in the door without a hundred gold coins in your possession. "Who knows the best place to purchase cheap footwear?"

CHAPTER 12

"No footwear for me." Biff says, staring at a single-story house at the corner of the intersection. It has several open windows with propped top-hinge shutters. A scruffy man sits in a window sill, his legs dangling out. He sways back and forth with a large mug in his hand. "Oooh." Biff exhales slowly. "That looks blissful. I believe it is time for some liquid compensation. The Pub of the Left has a colossal mead I enjoy."

"It's way too early for alcohol," Bella says. "Can't you wait 'til afternoon?"

"Might not live that long." Biff faces me and holds out a palm. "Come on now."

I do owe Biff one pint per town, so I dig in my sack. "Do you know a spot for Bombardment Boots?" I pull out a penny a drop it in Biffs eager palm.

> *SUBTRACT: 1 silver penny to Biff Thunderpunch. New silver penny balance: 14*

He clamps it in his fist. "Nope, my expertise stops at drinking establishments." He hobbles off to the pub.

Salo follows. "I will be at the pub as well."

"Alcoholic NPCs." Hans scoffs. "I should have handled the hiring duties."

"I know a place for boots," Slim says quietly. "Come on, Captain."

We follow Slim down a narrow, twisting alley lined with houses crammed in the small space.

"Hey, look." Bella stops and rests a hand flat on a large glass picture window. "Potions. All different kinds."

I look up at the shop's marquee: *SOREN'S POTIONS & SCROLLS – Rare, Medium, Well Done.*

This could be good. A few emergency healing potions can be a questing captain's best friend. I step up beside Bella and look inside. Four rows of glass bottles have various colored liquids in them. They are all different shapes and sizes, ranging from simple two-inch vials to flamboyant multi-bubbled decanters. Some are topped with swirling glass corks while others have solid gold stoppers.

"They are beautiful." Bella points across the lower row. "All those are healing potions. The cheapest one, a potion of curing, is five hundred gold coins."

"Look on the top shelf," I say. "What I wouldn't give for that oil of overpowerism. Too bad it costs eight thousand gold. Damn."

"There are better deals for this kind of thing elsewhere," Slim says. "Soren charges extra for the fancy bottles and prime location. Come on."

We move on, and he soon stops at a door with an oversized boot overhang, tapping on its square window. Inside various styles of footwear are displayed on several different sized wood chests. "This is The Mad Cobbler's shop. He also repairs string instruments, is a jeweler, and dabbles in apothecary." He turns the doorknob. "I hope he's in."

The four of us walk in, accompanied by the ring of a coil spring doorbell. The smell of leather and incense fill the air. Shelves along the shop's interior are lined with shoes, boots, strips of leather, and buckles. The low-hanging ceiling has exposed wooden beams carved with fancy needle and hammer decorations.

"Giles!" Slim calls. He looks at himself in full-length tri-fold dressing mirror and straightens his collar. "I have a captain in need of Bombardment Boots. Are you in?"

"Good morning." A short man with a thick tool-lined leather apron saunters around a stacked pyramid of old footwear. "I do have that style available. But it will cost lots of gold, Mr. Slim, even for your associates."

"Huh." Hans looks at me, reaches in his coat, and wraps a hand around his shillelagh. "Did he say lots of gold?" He leans over to my ear. "There are other ways of acquiring high-priced merchandise."

"Let's see how this plays out first." I distance myself from him.

Slim picks up a stringed instrument with a deep round back and plops down on a plush chair. "Give us a look at the product then. We'll be the judge if it's worth a high price."

Giles pulls a pair of scuffed black boots from a lower shelf and rests them on a wood box. "This is what I got. Price is two hundred gold. Firm."

They're way more stunning in person than in pixelated miniature form on my computer screen. Thick leather, hefty buckles, the promise of destruction. I could almost feel them on my feet already, empowering me.

Bella shrugs and picks a thin book from an upper shelf. "Two hundred is a steep price," she murmurs, flipping through the pages.

Two hundred gold is actually a great deal for Bombardment Boots. I have paid over a thousand in the game before. Too bad I am one-hundred ninety-five gold coins short.

Giles doesn't respond to Bella's comment. He doesn't look desperate to sell, so we likely won't talk him down much, if at all. So, I step in.

"Two hundred, you say?" I dig in my pockets to bide time and feel something small and round. It's a ring. The ring Mileena gave back to me by depositing it in the toilet. Have I had it all along? It must have been in my pocket when Mack and I went to The DCQ Den. Damn, that seems like eons ago. Slowly, I pull out the promise ring and hold it up, maintaining an air of confidence. "I should be able to outfit my whole party for the trade of this."

"I'm not big on trades," Giles says, but I can tell the ring has caught his eye. I rotate the ring slightly, allowing the sun to catch its edge through the window.

"But, let me see." He takes the ring, places it under his nose, and sniffs hard. "Where have you been storing this, a lavatorium? It smells abysmal." He pinches his nose and holds the ring to an eye. "The gold seems to be of semi-decent quality. Let me run this by my appraiser." He snaps his fingers.

An oversized golden grasshopper jumps from a rafter, to the pile of shoes, to a shelf, and then onto Giles's palm. "Hello, Sir Thomas."

Hans's eyes widen, and he shoves past me to get a closer look. He bends down slightly and looks over the grasshopper. "It's mechanical."

"Partially." Giles holds the ring near Sir Thomas' antennae. "Several of them live up in the rafters of my shop. Some are trained killers, ready to aid me in the event of a robbery." He lets that statement settle for a moment. Hans takes a step back from the grasshopper and peers upward in alarm.

Meanwhile, Giles listens closely to the gold insect's clicks and chirps. "I understand, thank you, Sir Thomas." Giles scowls at me. "What drossy merchandise are you trying to push off on me? You can't trade this. It is soul-bonded to another."

> *AN ITEM HAS BEEN IDENTIFIED: Your item 'Ring' has been revealed as 'Gold Promise Ring' (Soulbound to Mileena Tobias) by Giles Latumapic.*
>
> *Promised items cannot be bought, sold, or traded by anyone but the person they are soulbound to. The person to whom the item is promised may release it to the holder, if asked, by answering with a verbal yes, or no. If released, the item can be sold, or traded by its holder.*

So much for that. We were so close. I swallow hard. It's a promise ring, and I didn't keep my promise concerning it. It is cool that the game incorporates real world stuff like that. And it sucks big time. "But she returned it to me," I whine at Giles, hoping for a loop hole.

"Apparently, not in a way that would release the soulbind," he says, handing it back to me. He's disappointed. If the ring had been mine, he would have bought it. For a lot.

"Who is it promised to?" Bella asks.

I don't want to get into that. "Doesn't matter—" A vibration comes from my hip, and I stiffen. "Wait a sec." I open my Grimmoire and see a new message.

PLACE THE RING ON THE RED DOT TO PORT MILEENA TOBIAS INTO DCQ.
ONCE THE CHARACTER IS IN THE GAME, SHE CAN BE ASKED TO OFFICIALLY RELEASE THE PROMISED ITEM, AT WHICH POINT IT CAN BE SOLD OR TRADED.

●

What the—? The last person I want to see is Mileena. She broke up with me because of the game I've been sucked into for real. She hates DCQ. And me. I can't even imagine how much that hate would increase if I summoned her into it now. And what does porting her in really mean? Would it be some kind of hologram or virtual Mileena that I could ask to release the ring, and then she'd poof back to reality? No, it says, "Once the character is in the game." That sounds much more permanent. I can't do this. And yet, I have to. I can't use the ring to get the boots until I break its connection to Mileena. And I need those boots to save myself, Bella, and Hans, not to mention the game. Mileena will be mad, but she'll get over it. I won't get over being dead-for-real-dead. But if I pull Mileena in and I fail, would she die too? And once she gives over the ring, *IF* she gives over the ring, what then? Would she be trapped in DCQ? Would she be bound to our quest, or be able to stay somewhere safe and out-of-the-way until we save the world? Or it ends. Mileena doesn't have an avatar *or* a Grimoir, so how would she even function in the game?

This is the hardest choice I've ever had to make in DCQ. There are real things at stake here. Real people.

I glance at Bella. She's looking at me, eyes full of hope and curiosity. I'm starting to care about her. A lot. Bringing in Mileena may save us all, but what will Bella think of my ex? What will she think of me after Mileena starts bad-mouthing me?

"So, what is it?" Bella finally asks, nodding at my Grimoire. "Can we sell the ring or not?"

I have no choice, really. I'm the captain of this party, and I have to do what is best for all of us, even if it screws my chances with Bella.

I turn to Giles. "I can get the ring released," I say. "Or at least I can try."

"Really?" Giles smiles, the gold insect hopping onto his shoulder. "I'd like to see that."

"Make it quick." Hans says.

I hold the Grimoire flat in my palm and place the ring on the dot. *I can't believe what I am about to do.*

Would you like to port Mileena Tobias into the world of Dungeon Crawl Quest?
Yes/No?

I focus on the 'Yes'.

My Grimoire vibrates.

I pick up the ring and see a new message.

WARNING!

THE INCOMING PARTY MEMBER DOES NOT HAVE A GRIMOIRE,
OR A DCQ CHARACTER SHEET.

THIS TEMPORARY CHARACTER WILL BE PORTED OUT OF THE
GAME IN:

00:05:00

00:04:59

00:04:58

I let out a huge pent-up breath. So, I'm not dooming Mileena to the fate of DCQ.

But, I also only have five minutes to explain where she is, why she's here, and what I need her to do for me.

Mileena materializes in front of me and stumbles into a stack of crates. She is wearing a skimpy black and purplish-red leather outfit with an exposed midriff.

I help her to her feet. "Mileena, it's me, Riff." This is about to get really awkward.

"What happened? Where am I?" She turns, looking around the shop, and catches her reflection in the dressing mirror. "What am I wearing?" She runs a hand along the side of her hair and tightens her ponytail. "I mean, I look good in it." She pushes her breasts up with both hands. "Really good."

She's not wrong. She looks great, but I force myself to focus on her character sheet.

ADD: **Mileena Tobias, Assassin.** *(Error)*

Assassin: Trained in the arts of stealing and sneaking. Can use any armor and weapon. Primary abilities: Agility, Evasion, Sneak attack, Cunning

AGE: 22   LEVEL: 0   ABILITIES: 0   ALIGNMENT: Neutral

00:04:13 minutes until port out.

Hmm, no level or abilities number, but an assassin though? That's an elite class of thief. How did that happen? She doesn't even like these games.

Mileena wraps a hand around my arm. "You've bulked up, Riff." She lets go and spins around. "This looks like something from Harry Potter. What is this place?"

Mileena is really here, in DCQ. This is crazy. "Um," I stammer. "Do you remember that game I like to play so much? Well, you're inside of it."

"I'm inside of what?" She asks. "Really, what is this all about, Riff?"

Wow. She's handling this transition way better than I did.

Slim stands with a smile and adjusts his hat. "Introduce me to your friend, Captain."

"Yeah, Riff," Bella says, raising an eyebrow. "Introduce us."

I hold up a palm to Bella and Slim. "I only have five minutes to handle this, guys. There's really no time for introductions."

Bella pushes my hand away and extends hers toward Mileena. "Sorry he's so rude. I'm Bella. Welcome into the game."

"Riff, rude? Tell me something I don't know." Mileena shakes Bella's hand. "Nice to meet you." She looks at me. "Riff, please explain where I am and why. This isn't funny."

I hold up the ring. "It's about this." I look my ex-girlfriend in the eye. I needed to do this right. "And the fact that I need to apologize to you for messing up our breakfast date. Not just that one, but many of our dates. The way I treated you was way wrong. I wasn't a good boyfriend, and I'm sorry for that. It's not an excuse or even a valid reason, but I just get too caught up in,"—I hold my arms out—"this game stuff."

Bella looks at me with a furrowed brow and turns away, peeking at her Grimoire.

"It's all good, Riff." Mileena looks over the glistening gold grasshopper on the shoemaker's shoulder and smiles. "I really wasn't feelin' you like that anyways." She looks around the room. "If your game is always as enchanting as this, then, I really can't blame you for being so deep into it. This whole place is amazing." She looks herself over and runs fingers down the sides of her body. "And look at what it did for me. Not that I didn't look good before, but this body is bangin'."

"You look great." I say low.

"I don't mean to interrupt you two, but"—Bella taps her bare wrist several times—"it was a five minute countdown, right?"

I take Mileena's hand. "Will you release this ring to me? It's a matter of life and dead-for-real-die death."

"Eww, did you fish that thing out of your nasty toilet?" Mileena pushes my hand away. "I don't want that back. Not ever."

Was that a yes? A no? How detailed did the verbal confirmation need to be? "So, you release it to me? Officially?"

"Yes." She pats down her thighs. "Hey, where's my phone?" A blue streak whisks around her feet and climbs upward. She raises a leg to step out of it, but her foot gets pulled back down as though tethered with a bungee cord. "What is happening?" she asks, sounding a little scared. "Am I going back home? Are you going to be all right? Do I get to keep these—" The swirl covers her head and she disappears in a snap.

> *AN ITEMS STATUS HAS CHANGED: Your item 'Gold Promise Ring' (Soulbound to Mileena Tobias) has been released by Mileena Tobias and is no longer soul-bonded.*
>
> *The item can now be bought, sold, or traded by its holder.*

"You Compass-Keepers are something else." Slim falls back down in his chair. "Really something else."

"I liked your friend, Riff." Bella walks across the shop picking at nickknacks. "She was cute."

"Drama." Hans says. "Can you give the ring to the man already?"

I hand the ring to Giles. "Let's make this deal."

Giles once again holds the ring near the grasshopper's antennae and listens closely to its noises. "Good. The bond is gone. I accept the trade." Sir Thomas hops down to Slim's shoulder and creates a melodic chirp by rubbing its hind leg.

"Hey there, old friend," Slim looks at the grasshopper fondly. "You want to make some music?"

Giles drops the ring in a small upper vest pocket and pats it down twice. "Be wise with your usage of these boots." He snaps a rag and spins it around a tin of black compound. "They only have one charge left in them."

"One charge?" This guy is trying to rip me off. I hold my left hand out and place the other on my sword. "I'm going to need that ring back. I need boots with at least five charges. One kick may not be enough for the door I got to bust down."

"Easy, Captain." Slim plucks a beautiful melody on the lute. "The only way you're going to acquire a pair of boots loaded that high, if you can find another pair at all, is with a teetering stack of genuine gold coins."

I guess I will just have to make the one charge count. "If you throw in that guitar," I say, "we have a deal."

"You want that old lute?" Giles buffs the leather on the Bombardment Boots and looks at Slim. "We have a deal. The instrument is yours. You know Mr. Slim can mesmerize with those licks. I've seen him perform many times."

I take the boots and stuff them in my pack. "You do play well, Slim. I got some skills on the guitar too, you know."

ADD POSSESSION: **Bombardment Boots + (1)** *Charge. Bombardment. Damage: 0-1. Range: N/A. Frequency: Rare. Quality: Poor.*

Melee Weapon Attack: Bludgeoning damage.

Bombardment: Strike with a verbal "Bomb" to cast one or more of its 'Bombardment' charges. Use to kick down the sturdiest of door.

Slim stands and holds the lute my way. "You've just acquired a charming instrument, Captain. You know I'd rather play than thieve, but no one wants to provide the correct pay to a musician. The troubadour's guild just isn't what it used to be."

I take the lute and look over the front. "Nice. I like it."

ADD POSSESSION: **Lute + (7) Charge.** *Charm person.*

Damage: 1-2. Range: N/A. Frequency: Uncommon. Quality: Average.

Melee Weapon Attack: Bludgeoning damage.

Charm: Play instrument with a verbal "Charm" to cast one or more of its 'Charm Person' charges. Makes a humanoid you can see a trusted friend for five minutes.

Soulbound to 'Jareth Goblinmasher' - Item cannot be traded or sold.

A plucked string musical instrument.

"Real nice." This lute not only plays music, it also has spell power. I strum through all six strings with an upstroke. "And it's in tune." Wait, where am I going to carry this thing?

Slim shakes Giles hand. "I'm going to need a new pair of boots soon myself. The leather on mine is getting a bit stiff."

I look at Slim's boots. The leather is made up of small triangular scales. "Are those gators?"

"Gators? I would never wear any ugly-ass gators." Slim rests a foot on a square chest and twists his ankle. "Look at the symmetry in the pattern. These are dragon scale."

"Real dragon scales?" I look close at the shoes. "Those are really nice. You got a cool sense of style, Slim. But what I really need to know is where can I get a hat like yours?"

Slim tilts his brim even lower over one eye. "I already gave you my connection for boots. The Mad Milliner's hatworks is a completely different thing. Maybe when your pockets are fatter, I'll introduce you."

Hans kicks the chest out from under Slim's boot causing him to stumble. "Enough about hats and gators already. It's time to go."

I set the lute against the wall where Slim found it. "Giles, if you don't mind, I need to leave this here until I can afford a suitable carrying case. It's soulbound to me, so take good care of her."

Giles rolls a hand in a circular spiral and bows. "It was a true pleasure trading with you."

We leave the store and make our way to the roundabout. Several civilians line the road watching a party of eight questers make their way to the East gate.

Slim eyeballs two underdressed ladies in black leather across the road. They both gaze in a shop window and point at various articles of clothing. "See that," he mumbles. "Those two just sitting on their butts watchin' the questers go by, when they need to be tappin' their toes on them roads to get this gold." He tugs his tunic down, brushes off the shoulders, takes a deep breath, and exhales. "This is where I leave you, Captain. I wish you all great success in your quest to open the expansion." He steps onto the road and looks back. "Beef up on your defenses against the undead before you go West. There are some real weird walking corpses out there. Oh, and, Bella." He points at me. "Watch out for this guy. I think he has eyes for you."

Bella smiles. "Bye, Slim."

"Good riddance." Hans sneers.

"Travel safe, Slim, and good luck with helping your business associate." I watch him strut across the street, sneak up behind the two girls, and surprise them from behind. *I really need a hat like that.*

NEW TASK: **Assemble a party at Cittadella.**

Assemble a party of six adventurers in order to enter the valley.

I clear the message with a shake of my head. "We need to hire a new thief in order to leave Cittadella." And all I've got is chump change to pay someone. "Let's meet up with the rest of our party before they get overly intoxicated."

Bella, Hans, and I go back to The Pub on the Left. We step through a rickety wooden door into a small establishment barely lit by flickering candles and the low light from the open windows. The walls are lined with various nooks and crannies perfect for shady dealings. There are a few tables in the center, and a bar that stretches across the back.

A stubby, pointy eared man with a brown cloak and pointed cone hat stumbles into me as he crosses the floor. He has two frothy mugs of beer in each hand. "Merry New Birthday to you all," he says in a slurred British accent. "I have been named Sir Abbot—*hiccup*—Wychwood, and I am the only Boggarf in Cittadella. I am at your service on all promising quests to the—"

He pauses and slurps from one mug, then lowers it and chugs from another. "To the East Dungeon. Yes, the East Dungeon is where a Boggart-Dwarf does his best work. Destructive, skilled at household chores, and handy I am for sure—*hiccup*—in a tuss." He covers his mouth with a mug and emits a bubbling belch. "Be at the bar, I will—*hiccup*. To talk any and all business dealings with you." He continues into a dark booth and passes out across its bench.

Well, this is a pleasingly gloomy place. Perfect for a booze-up. No wonder Biff likes it.

A young man in pristine leather armor approaches from the bar. "I am Castel Franco, The Master of Cittadella. And you, questing captain Jareth Goblinmasher, are a thief short of an official party. May I suggest The Snatch near the East gate. All hirelings there are members of the Thieves Guild and will serve you well. You're on your own hiring in places like this." He heads to the door. "See you at the gate."

"Hey, Jareth." Biff stands and waves to us from the bar. "It's three pints for a penny in this truly colossal establishment. Come join me."

"Wait, Jareth." Salo approaches from a snug corner with a petite person wearing a dark robe with a shield strapped to his back. "I have befriended a thief for hire."

The figure pulls back its hood. "I am William Thomas Flukermayne the third," he says in a squeaky voice. "But you can call me WTF Mayne. I am a thief extraordinaire, specializing in impossible chests and unlockable locks. I have a short sword to fight and am the holder of this." He pulls a dark wood dowel from his belt. "A fully charged staff of immortuos. With this I can strike down any undead entity my party encounters."

Okay, let's get straight down to business with this one. "We would like to hire you as our thief, but for little compensation."

"Tis a nay." William lowers the dowel into its sheath. "You are the luckiest captain in Cittadella today. If my acquaintance, Salo here, did not introduce us, I would slit your throat for uttering the words 'little compensation' to a master thief like WTF Mayne."

"I said little compensation, not no compensation." *Looks like I am going to have to step up my hiring tactics with this guy.* "It just so happens we are on our way to The Snatch to start our hiring process. Are you a member of the Thieves Guild?"

Williams face scrunches. "The Whore's Snatch is the worst place to find a thief and they are not fond of you Compass-Keeper types. Salo tells me you are running on a budget of sorts. This I understand. Make me a fair offer I can't refuse."

"We will give you a fair deal," Bella says. "Three gold, a ten percent share, and no artifacts."

William squints with an open mouth. "Thieves, on average, demand more than fighters, and I know how much you are compensating Salo. Thirty gold, twenty cut, and I always get artifact privileges."

"No." Bella shakes her head. "Five gold, a twenty-five percent share, and no artifact. That's the most we'll go."

William sneers. "I need more up front. Word is you all have had horrible luck with the looting."

He's trying to drive a hard bargain, but the fact he's considering our offer at all tells me he wants a quest. Maybe even needs one. So, I hold my ground. "Take it or leave it, William." Anyone hanging out in a bar like this can't be worth that much gold. "We are on our way to The Snatch." I turn toward the bar.

"Wait." William steps in front of me. "Add artifact privileges and your terms will be accepted."

"Hmmm." I can't believe he's going for this deal. "Okay. You got your artifact privileges."

"Terms accepted, then." William looks at Salo and shakes his head. "Barely accepted."

An icon of William's face appears beneath Salo's with three transparent squares.

ADD: **William Thomas Flukermayne III, Thief.** *(-5 Gold/-25% Share/+Artifact Privileges)*

Thief: Trained in the arts of stealing and sneaking. May only use light to mid-weight weaponry and armor. Primary abilities: Agility.

"Meet us at the North Gate," I say.

"Welcome to the party, WTF." Biff stumbles with a cup in hand and latches onto Salo's shoulder. "See you at the West Gate after I quench."

"North Gate, Biff." I say. "How many have you had?"

Bella looks at me with slanted eyebrows. "We will meet the three of you at the North Gate within the hour. The sooner the better."

Biff upturns the cup and takes in the last drop. "Quench complete. North Gate it will be. Sooner and better."

Salo puts his arm around Biff. "The three of us will meet you all there." He leads Biff to the door with William following.

"Misfit NPCs." Hans shakes his head. "You have assembled a motley crew."

Bella looks down and rubs the scar on her leg. "At least we have upgraded to a thief that will fight with us."

"A quick drink for luck." I step to the bar and slam down a penny.

"Three hydromels please." I put a hand each on Hans's and Bellas' shoulders. "Let's drink to finding the Taguban. Map point number two awaits us."

CHAPTER 13

Bella, Hans, and I walk down the center of the road toward the North Gate, as groups of men, women, and children point at us from various storefronts along the way.

Hans slides the side of his boot in the dirt and kicks rubble up at the closest onlookers. "What are you looking at?" Then to me he grumbles, "These wandering NPCs make me sick. I should clobber a few just for kicks."

"We are a questing team, Hans," I say. "We're like heroes to these people. You should be flattered." How did he even get into DCQ? He seemed to hate so much about it.

"They're just sizing us up to make bets." He pulls out his shillelagh, flipping and catching it in one hand. "I really want to clobber a few."

Ahead, an arch crosses between two gate towers with barely visible words etched into the crumbling stone. "North Gate – Here There Be Caves," it says.

Biff, Salo, and William fall in line behind us from a side street.

"You're right on time, guys." I grin, the excitement building again. "The North Gate Arch will lead us to the most quested area of the game."

"I rarely quest The North Caves," Hans says. "Real pros stick to the East Dungeon."

Castel breaks away from a circle of men-at-arms and greets us with a smile. "Gentlemen, one beautiful lady, and you, William." He holds out a hand. "Paperwork, please."

I open my Grimoire, touch the red dot, and put it in his hand.

He looks at the screen. "Party of six with a thief confirmed." He focuses in closer and his smile widens. "Oh-ho, and a map plus three." He looks at me, then at William, then back at me. "Accredited you are."

We walk under the arch and over the moat bridge. The road meanders slightly to the right and then ahead between a gently flowing river on the left, and lush forestry on the right.

"It's breathtaking." Bella beams at the view in front of us. "Haworth's river valley at high noon is truly a sight to see."

Hans continues forward. "Don't take it all in for too long. High noon means we only have twelve hours until the server shuts down."

> *PARTY STATUS:*

This message again? I focus in on the prompt and get the transparent sheet.

> *REORDER THE PARTY:* **Yes/No?**
>
> *Set the dungeon marching order of your party. Remember, only the first three members of a party can attack monsters with weapons. Note: Only NPCs are bound to follow marching order instructions. (* = NPC)*
>
> | | | | |
> |---|---|---|---|
> | *Jareth Orcslauter, Fighter.* | *HP: 24/40* | *AC: 3* | *LVL: 3* |
> | **Salo Fatback, Fighter.* | *HP: 21/50* | *AC: 6* | *LVL: 4* |
> | **William T. Flukermayne III, Thief.* | *HP: 16/40* | *AC: 5* | *LVL: 3* |
> | **Biff Thunderpunch, Ninja.* | *HP: 7/65* | *AC: 7* | *LVL: 4* |

Madmartigan Galladoorn, Mage.	*HP: 25/40*	*AC: 3*	*LVL: 3*
Hans Talhoffer, Cleric.	*HP: 21/40*	*AC: 2*	*LVL: 3*

I focus on the 'No' and the sheet disappears. Questing through Ranida with an underpowered party is one thing. Entering Haworth with one could be a death sentence. Questing parties are only as good as their front three are. And if that's true we're in nothing but deep trouble. My armor class is a paltry three, and William has only sixteen hit points. That's better than Biff's meager seven, but I really need all my guys to be at full strength before we get into the goblin's labyrinth.

As we walk, I keep a close eye on the tree line. Last thing we need is to get surprised by wandering monsters of any level. After about twenty-minutes, we come to an area where the river twists through a jumbled patch of jagged rocks.

Biff grabs his groin. "Wait." He makes a sharp turn into the forest. "Needing to relieve myself."

Bella takes a few steps to the river's edge, crouches, and dips in her water skin.

Hans follows behind her and does the same. "Do NPCs really need to relieve themselves? It just seems stupid. This world is ridiculous sometimes."

Salo points ahead and up to the snowcapped North Mountains. "I have logged many a quest in those hills."

I stand next to Salo and gaze at the sight. "It's surreal to see these mountains in real life—I mean in person." I pull out my map and survey the road ahead. "We are making good progress. I'd say we are about an hour away from our destination."

William steps next to me and leans in. "Your map looks to show a true representation of the mountains." He points to an upper area on the map. "See this spot right here. I once popped open a chest filled with—" He pinches his nose and coughs. "Ugh. Biff. Are you dropping a hellacious turd out there or what? You stink. Wait. That's not the smell of poo. That's—"

A clammy hand wraps around my throat and a sharp object pushes into my back.

"Anyone moves, and the captain here is going to collapse into a heap of dead," snarls a guttural voice.

Salo and William spin around and receive javelin tips to their chests. Two humanoids with crusty, wart-like skin lesions on their faces push their javelins forward slightly. They wear hide armor. I can't tell what animal—or human—the hide was taken from.

"Movement makes me unstable," grumbles the attacker in front of Salo. "Be still, or I stab."

I can't believe we've been surprised by—I don't know what. Their faces don't have the piggish characteristics of orcs, and there are no tusks. Otherwise, they look just like the orcs I've seen in DCQ–brownish green coloration, bristly black hair, stooped posture and all. Maybe this is some type of half-orc. Whatever they are, their odor is repulsive.

Two more of the monsters have stepped up behind Bella and Hans. One rests the blade of his scimitar alongside Hans's neck. He looks similar to the others, but has a shiny, spiked helmet. "Move and you'll *be-heading* down river in two pieces."

An overweight slobbier version rumbles behind Bella and cocks back a bulky tapered hunk of wood with large iron spikes in its end. "Keep your hands in the water, or I'll knock off your dome."

144

The helmeted beast presses the blade of his scimitar into Hans' neck, nearly breaking the skin. "We got two Compass-Keepers down here, chief. Should we kill them now?"

"No," says the voice behind me, its musty breath wafting over my ear. "Setan needs slaves, and Compass-Keepers are worth triple." He tightens his grip around my neck. "Hear me clear, captain. If you guide me to some treasure, I might forget I captured you."

If we didn't have to retrieve the third piece of the Keris of Knaud, I'd let them take us straight to Setan. That would probably save us a lot of time and battles. But, we weren't prepared to defeat the goblin yet.

The fat brute standing over Bella runs a slobbery tongue across its upper lip. "I like this girl. I'm hungry."

The tribe leader twists his blade into my back. "Too many deaths to haggish gonorrhea have depleted the warlords' harem. Your girl will be a prized addition. Now, captain, spit it out before my tribe member Sazerac satisfies his bloodlust on your tender little girl. Where's the treasure?"

I gotta buy some time. "I have this." I raise my hand with the map in it and twist my wrist. "This shows the way to a great horde of treasure. Only I know how to read it, though."

A chattering sound comes from behind, and then a brown rat with patchwork fur and scabs jumps across my shoulder to the ground in front of me, spins around, looks up, and hisses through seething incisors.

"What do you think Splintleton?" The tribe leader snorts. "Is his map legitimate?"

I arch my back to ease the sting of the sword. "Let my party go, and I–"

The rat screeches and bolts into the forest.

Thwack! The monster behind me falls to the ground with a thud. The boulder that smashed into his cranium rolls down to the river. I draw my sword, stick it into his back, and watch several more stones hurtle through the air. Biff is rapid fire slinging rocks. And he's my new hero.

The two monsters next to me get popped in their heads simultaneously by flying projectiles. One falls down, knocked out cold. The other takes several steps back, shakes his head, and wobbles from side to side.

Salo whips out his mace, jumps on the unconscious beast, and bashes its head in.

William draws his sword and bangs weapons with the dazed beast several times before managing a straight thrust through its heart. The monster slides off the sword, dead.

DING! A rock hits the helmeted one, sending the helmet bobbing downstream and the beast tumbling down the river bank into the water. Hans raises his shillelagh and slams it down on the creature several times. He then lowers a boot on the thing's neck, pinning its head underwater until it goes limp.

The fat monster side-steps a flying stone and takes a whooshing swing at Bella's head. She ducks but gets clipped in the shoulder and slips backward into the river with a splash.

I rush her attacker with my sword raised. "Hey!"

The brute turns and runs towards the forest.

Oh, there is no way this fool is going to outrun me.

A reddish-blue ball of haze whooshes past me and explodes across its back. The slob falls to the ground and rolls several times to a stop. I run up to the sizzling monster and hack my sword across its neck.

> *Weird Humanoid (5) has been killed! For killing the monsters each survivor earned 200 experience points.*

Weird Humanoid? So, we were fighting an unidentified monster. I thought I'd fought everything DCQ had to offer. It's been forever since I've encountered anything new.

> *You were hit for 2 damage. Status: 22/40*

Hans wipes his hands together and blows white smoke from his palms. "I'm really good at this magic thing. Did you see the way I lit that dummkopf up?"

"Bella's hurt." I run past Hans and wave. "Come on."

Salo helps Bella out of the water and sits her on a large flat rock.

She covers her eyes with both hands and doubles over. "Aaaah." Blood and river water drip from her shoulder. "It's dislocated," she moans. "And it hurts like the devil. I'm down seventeen hit points from that one blow."

Biff holsters his sling and picks up the chief's sword. It has a solid black handle and a blade with a semi-circle cut out in its lower section. "Good thing for us my sling aim is as good as ever. I don't know how the fat one managed to duck me." He hands me the sword and sits next to Bella. "Sorry I couldn't get him before he got you."

Hans wraps his hands around Bella's shoulder. "Let me come to the rescue, once again. *Medicor summus seco.*"

"You mean, 'Let me come to the rescue like I should have on our last ques—*aggh!*" Bella cries as her shoulder flashes white hot, then returns to normal.

I rub my neck and sit next to Bella. "Did that work? How is it?"

She drops her hands and rolls her shoulder backward, then forward. "Wow, it feels a lot better. Thank you for doing that, Hans. This time."

He looks over his palms. "That spell should bring back ten to fifteen of your hit points. But I am running through way too much of my spell power on minor objectives, Riff. I hope I have something left in the tank for the big boy at the end. I am down to just four level one spells. You all need to help me level up."

"That's the plan, Hans. We all need to level up. This battle helped." But we were running out of time. I stand and swing the chief's sword from side to side. "Nice balance. I don't know about this strange notch in the blade though."

William drops five small worn leather sacks on the rock. "What you have there is an executioner's sword. The wielder can use the circle to decapitate an opponent with ease. It is surely a lot better than your current weapon." He rips open the sacks and spreads the contents on the rock. "Seven gold coins and eight pennies from the foulest Evon clan. I hate them."

"You know what those freaks were?" I ask.

William looks at me slack jawed. "Do you Compass-Keepers know anything? Evons are Setan's personal guard. Word is they come from the expansion world. I hate them and their little rat companions."

"That rat was a companion of theirs?" I ask." I think the chief called it Splintleton."

"And you let it get away." Williams says aggravated. "The little snitch is sure to lead reinforcements our direction."

> *A MONSTER HAS BEEN IDENTIFIED: The monster 'Weird Humanoid' has been revealed as an 'Evon' by William Thomas Flukermayne III.*

This monster is now known to you and your party.

EVON

LEVEL: *1 (240XP)*   **HIT POINTS:** *10*

ARMOR CLASS: *12 (Hide armor)*   **FREQUENCY:** *Rare*

NO. APPEARING: *2-30*   **DAMAGE:** *By weapon type*

SPECIAL ATTACKS: *Aggressive*

SPECIAL DEFENSES: *Speak with rodents*

INTELLIGENCE: *Average*   **ALIGNMENT:** *Evil*   **SIZE:** *M*

TYPICAL WEAPONING: *Club, Dagger, Javelin, Scimitar, Shield*

DESCRIPTION: *Evon are foul smelling humanoids with crusty, wart-like lesions on their face, brownish green colored skin, bristly black hair, and a stooped posture. They keep rats as pets and can communicate simple concepts with them and some other rodents.*

Evons? I had never heard of them before. If they have anything to do with Setan that's good, though. It means we are getting closer to our objective.

Salo drops a dagger, a scimitar, two javelins, and a small round shield on the ground in front of the rock. Then, he flings the fat Evon's club into the middle of the river. "These weapons are workable. They had nothing else of value."

Time for some upgrades. I toss my sword and feasting knife into the pile and sheath the executioner's blade and dagger.

NEW PRIMARY WEAPON: **Executioner's Sword**

Damage: 3-10. Range: N/A. Frequency: Uncommon. Quality: Average

Melee Weapon Attack: Slashing damage.

> *ADD POSSESSION:* **Dagger**
>
> *Damage: 1-3. Range: 40 ft. Frequency: Common. Quality: Average*
>
> *Melee or Ranged Weapon Attack: Piercing damage.*

Now, this is more like it. Up to ten hit points of damage for a primary weapon is much more to my liking. Nothing special about the dagger, but it's better than the feasting knife. I grab the shield, strap it to my arm, and take a hard step forward. I move it up, down, and thrust it forward. "This will work." I strap it to my back.

> *ADD POSSESSION:* **Small Shield**
>
> *Damage: 1-2. Range: N/A. Frequency: Common. Quality: Average.*
>
> *Shield Bash: Melee Weapon Attack: Bludgeoning damage.*

> *YOUR ARMOR CLASS HAS BEEN INCREASED! Armor Class increased to 4/20.*

A boost in armor class! That's what I'm talking about. Only one more point, but all good.

Bella looks at the pile. "None of this stuff will do anything for me."

"No surprise there." Hans kicks one of the javelins and turns his head. "These scrub monsters never have anything a magic user can equip with. We need to encounter some higher-level monsters."

Salo secures the javelins and sword to his pack and points to the pile. "WTF, you grab the rest."

I scoop up the coins, drop them into my bag and pull the drawstrings tight. "Well, this fighter is happy. First a weapons upgrade, and now things are looking up on the monetary side."

Bella lifts a hand toward me from her seat on the rock. "That monster said he wanted to take us to Setan, and that Compass-Keepers are worth extra gold. How does Setan know about Compass-Keepers?"

I take Bella's hand and help her stand. "Could it be that Compass-Keeper wizard from Chittor that Slim spoke of? Maybe the wizard fought Setan at some point. Maybe Setan is scared of him."

"Or he got killed by Setan," Hans theorizes.

Bella strides down the road. "Wizards don't die so easy. We're wasting time. Let's go."

After walking for another ten minutes, the valley begins to widen. We follow along the right tree-line for fifteen more minutes and finally stop where a narrow dirt path cuts to the right between lush trees.

I look up and to either side of the opening. "This has got to be it."

We follow the path for about five minutes, until a low single-story compound with a dark square tunnel entryway reveals itself amidst the overgrown trees. I take a look at my map. "Map point number two is located in the center of that building."

"I know this death trap." The corners of Biff's mouth dive into a deep frown. "This is the Bonnacon's Lair."

CHAPTER 14

11:40:15 HOURS UNTIL DCQ SERVER SHUT DOWN.

"The what's lair?" I haven't heard of Bonnacon before. "What do we need to know, Biff?"

A wrinkle-faced man with a long gray beard hobbles out of the building's tunnel. He spreads his white cloak, sits on a stump in front of the entryway, and lowers his head.

Biff looks at the wrinkle-faced man and waves. "Hello."

The man stands and motions for us to come forward.

Biff turns to me and lowers his voice. "Bonnacons have the shaggy mane of a horse, but in all other respects resemble a powerfully built, yet stubby bison. Their hides are as tough as plate mail armor, plus three, and they have colossal curved horns. The big draw is they all have barrel collars around their necks with different treasures inside. You will need to find the Bonnacon with the item you seek in the barrel around its neck. The challenge here is that they don't give up the barrel easily. As far as dangers go, the Bonnacons's inward-curving horns are no good for butting or goring. They have developed a secondary means of defense…"

BONNACON

LEVEL: *3 (3000XP)*   **HIT POINTS:** *40*

ARMOR CLASS: *14 (Natural armor)* **FREQUENCY:** *Very Rare*

NO. APPEARING: *1*   **DAMAGE:** *1-12*

SPECIAL ATTACKS: *Charge, Excrements*

SPECIAL DEFENSES:

INTELLIGENCE: *Simi*   **ALIGNMENT:** *Neutral*   **SIZE:** L

TYPICAL WEAPONING:

DESCRIPTION: *Bonnacons are giant bull-like creatures with the shaggy reddish mane of a horse. They have horns that curl in toward each other and have a hide so hard it repels spears.*

The wrinkle-faced man squints and looks us over. "Who seeks what here?"

Go time. "I am Jareth Goblinmasher. I seek the sheath belonging to the Keris of Knaud."

The man bends over, holds his chest, and cackles. "You are brave to seek that item."

I step forward and wait for him to recover from his laugh. Why is this so funny? Is he ever going to come up for air? I wait a few more moments and can't take it anymore. "The sheath belonging to the Keris of Knaud. That is what I am here for. Can you help me?"

The man steps backward and sits back down on his stump. "I will release the Bonnacon called Paeonia into the labyrinth. He indeed has what you seek."

154

Labyrinth? Neither Biff nor the map said anything about a labyrinth. Was it inside the building? Beneath it?

The old man pulls a small wooden hourglass with black sand from under his cloak. "When the powder runs out, this entrance will seal, and a clarifying flush will commence." He gestures to the building entrance.

Looks like I'd be going underground.

"If you fail in acquiring the item today," the man continued, "it will not return for another twenty moons. You can take two party members in with you." He flips the hourglass.

Biff steps into the entryway and points inside. "It's all in the smell. Bonnacons have a unique fragrance. It will help guide you to the animal. Follow your nose."

William raises his hand. "I can help you find him."

"Aaa-Aaa-Aaa-Choo." Salo drops to a knee. "Aagh." He clears tears from his eyes, sniffs, and rubs his nose. "So irritating. I won't be any good at tracking such an animal."

I turn to the wrinkle-faced man and shake a finger at the hourglass. "What do you mean the entrance will seal?"

Bella lights a torch and steps into the corridor. "Like sands through the hourglass, slackers. Come on. We'll be back before the sand runs out, if we act fast."

"Let's go then." I lead Bella and William down the hall to a four-way intersection. Each of the three paths lead into complete darkness.

Bella sniffs hard down each corridor. "All four smell like a dank old dungeon." Her torch illuminates the few feet of ground ahead of us.

I peer down the forward hall. "We're not at the map point yet. Let's continue straight down." I wave the team on and break into a jog. Bella keeps pace with me holding the torch, so we can keep our footing.

We continue until the corridor turns right, then left, then right again to a two-way split. I mutter the turns to myself so that we don't get lost on our way back.

Bella sniffs to the right, then to the left, gags and coughs. "Something smells like dog crap to the left."

I sample the air and pinch my nose. "Oh, that's awful. Left has got to be the way."

"WTF, Mayne." William nods with a scrunched nose. "Left is absolutely the one."

We follow the foul air, passing several fresher smelling outlets. At the end of the hall, we turn right, then left down to another four-way intersection.

Bella takes a step down each of our three options then steps back. "They all smell equally of sour ass."

"Let me take a whiff." I take a step down the left hall and my boot slides across a wet clay-like substance. A putrid ammonia-like smell rises from it, hitting my nose with a noxious penetrating burn. "What is this stuff?"

Bella holds the torch down and turns her head. "Oh, my damn."

My boot is covered in brownish green goo. "I think I stepped in a pile of Bonnacon dookey." I kick and drag my boot against the wall and floor. Chunks of the gunk scrape off in a smear. I pinch my nose and bend down to get a closer look. "Hey guys, it looks like Bonnacons eat corn. Look."

But the Bonnacon gets the last laugh. The sole of my boot starts turning red-hot. It pops, bubbles, and puffs white smoke. "Um, ouch, it's burning now." I stomp my foot down several times and flip my boot off down the hall.

Thankfully, I'm wearing the normal boots I entered the game with, not the Bombardment Boots, which are in my pack for safe-keeping. "I guess Bonnacon's have acid doo-doo."

William fans his nose. "I can't believe you stepped in it."

"Wow, Riff," Bella says. "The smell is really coming out." She steps around me and continues down the hall. "At least we know we're on the right path."

I follow behind Bella and William to the end of the hall, leaving my contaminated boot behind and walking with one socked foot. Soon, the corridor makes a sharp right into a basketball court-sized cave lined with lit wall torches. We freeze at the entrance.

A giant bull, with reddish fur shading to black, stares at us down from the middle of the chamber. It blows black smoke from snotty nostrils and lowers its head our direction.

"Hello, Paeonia," I mumble. This thing is twice as big as any bison I have ever seen. I pull out my dagger. "You two attack him on the right. I will slide by on the left and try to slice off the barrel. Take slow steps forward and go hard on the count of three. One. Two."

CLANK! A thick wooden panel drops down behind us, blocking the entrance we just came through.

William sprints back to the panel and runs a finger along it edge. "WTF, Mayne. We're trapped in here with this monster."

Paeonia grunts, grinds its hooves into the gravel, and shakes its mane.

A rock wall slides open at the other end of the room, revealing a dark hallway.

"Aha, there's our exit," I say, adjusting my sock foot on the gravel. "Once I secure the barrel, we all run for that hallway. Okay, here we go, on the count of three. One."

157

The animal turns around in a wobbly motion, lowers its front legs and lifts its short black tail in our direction.

William peers over his shield and nods. "It is submitting to our superior strength. Go get the barrel, Riff."

The Bonnacon grunts and sways its rear from side to side.

Bella grips the haft of her flail and drops to a knee. "Are you sure that's a position of submission?"

"*Gaaaroooo.*" The animal machine gun fires steaming brown baseball sized dung balls at us.

Bella and William dart to the right and run toward the beast. "You missed me," Bella jukes, then sprints to the right. "Fire this way."

William raises his shield just in time for it to get splattered with several acid feces balls. They ignite and explode in a fiery dung spray upon impact. He runs behind Bella. "Over here you whiffy beast."

"Go, Riff," Bella says. "We'll take the fire."

With Paeonia distracted, I sprint to the animal's left side. It's more of a stumble as my boot grips and my sock slips in the gravel, sending rock spikes into my sole. I compensate for the weakness and launch myself toward the Bonnacon with my booted foot. I slash down on the barrel's leather collar. It comes away, drops to the ground, and breaks into pieces revealing a slick, grained, timber sheath.

That's it. I reach down and clutch the item just as Paeonia's rear hooves collide with my chest. I soar backward and tumble end over end to the rear of the room.

Bella and William slide into position at each of my shoulders and lift me up by the arms.

"You got the sheath." Bella says. "Nice."

I stuff the sheath in my belt, shake my head, and pat down my chest. "I think I took some damage," I gasp. "It's hard to breath."

Paeonia whips around in circles, lowers its front legs, and once again tilts its rear our direction.

"WTF, Mayne." William holds his shield forward. "That sheath is no good to us if we don't get out of here alive. The animal is blocking our only way out with its stinking arse."

A cloud of black smoke bellows out of the animal's anus creating a fast approaching wall of fog.

William raises his shield up just below his eyes. "What's this now?"

I'm the fighter here. I have to take this monster down, broken ribs or not. I run into the fog with a raised sword.

"Stop, Riff!" screams Bella.

I spill to my knees as the smoke burns my lungs and eyes.

William runs in and drags me backward behind the approaching smoke line. "Bad move. I could have told you that smoke was deadly."

"I think I got something for this," Bella says, twirling a finger and thrusting it ahead. "*Patet in dregs aer.*"

A bolt of electricity cracks out of her finger and strikes the black cloud. The smoke flashes a blinding white, then collapses in on itself leaving the room clear of everything but Paeonia and his rear end.

"It worked." Bella says, sounding satisfied.

"*Gaaaroooo.*" The Bonnacon looks back, shakes its mane, and again sprays a barrage of hot dookie balls.

"WTF, Mayne, I'm done." William snatches the Keris' sheath from my belt, runs to the wooden panel, and begins to lift it up from the bottom edge.

"Hey." I take a step after him but stop to dodge flying dung. "William stole the sheath," I tell Bella, just as she gets tagged in the leg with a cantaloupe-sized line drive and spins down to the ground. She lifts her head. "He's trying to slide under the door!" she yells. "Stop him."

William strains but only manages to lift the door a few inches.

The Bonnacon bolts past me full speed and rams its bludgeoning head into William's back.

"Aaahhhh." William instantly gets flattened against the wall panel like a strawberry-covered pancake.

A PARTY MEMBER HAS BEEN KILLED!
NAME: William Thomas Flukermayne III… DEAD

The beast shakes its head and staggers backward in a zigzag pattern.

"William got smashed." One look at his body and my stomach lurches.

"Gaa-ar-ooo." Paeonia dips its head and grunts.

No time to mourn backstabbing party members. I have to kill this beast before it regains its senses and flattens me too. I run as fast as I can, ignoring the pain in my ribs and the bruises forming on my socked foot. I jump and drop the executioner's notch of my sword down on the beast's neck, cutting a few inches deep. That won't do. I raise the sword once more and drop it down with all the force I can muster. It cuts a fourth of the way through and blood gushes everywhere. The beast flops to the ground, then shakily raises its hind legs.

"No you don't." Bella steps up, swings the spiked ball of her flail around in a circle and smashes it down on the top of Paeonia's head. The animal flattens out with a thud. "Gaaahh." She leverages a boot on the beast's head, yanks the spiked ball out, spins around, swings, and crashes the ball down again in the same spot.

Woah, Bella isn't playing.

"And that would be a kill shot," I say. "We got him, girl. His stank ass is dead now." Just like our thief.

I pry the Keris sheath from William's bloody hand, trying to ignore the splatter of guts on the wall. "RIP, Mayne."

The wood panel that closed on our entrance earlier slowly cranks upward.

The Bonnacon Paeonia has been killed! For killing the monster each survivor earned 1500 experience points.

YOU MADE THE NEXT LEVEL! Max hit points increased to 45. Strength +2, Intelligence +1, Wisdom +1, and Luck +1 increased! Total Abilities now 60.

You were hit for 5 damage. Status: 17/45

"I just made level four." I focus on the message for confirmation. "Paeonia was packing hella hit points. Did you level, too?"

Bella yanks William's staff and sword away from his body and slides them into her belt. "No, but I must be close now." She straps William's shield to her back, pulls a small sack from his pocket and sits on the ground with a raised knee. "I took some damage. It burns." A three-inch scrape runs across her calf.

I run water from my drinking skin over the wound, then tie a torn strip of my tunic around it as a bandage. "How many hit points did this set you back?"

"I'm good." She stands with a slight wince. I offer her a hand for support, but she shoves it away. "We have less than five minutes until the sands run out."

Several sharp snaps and a booming crash ring out from the opening across the room.

"Something's coming." I take Bella's hand and we hurry to leave the way we came. I look back one last time to see a flood of steaming chunky brown sludge flowing into the room from the rock entrance across the way. "Just what we were hoping for—a wave of weird hot lava." That must be the clarifying flush.

Bella covers her nose. "That's not hot lava." She snatches a torch from the wall and tugs on my tunic. "The flow is not slowing. Let's move. And watch your step." She jogs down the corridor.

I follow Bella's lead. She takes each turn with precision remembering our route out with ease. We hit the final turn and see light at the end of the tunnel. Salo, Biff, Hans, and the old man are yelling and waving for us to hurry.

Just as we exit the tunnel, a stone wall drops down behind us.

I turn to Bella and try to catch my breath. "We made it."

The old man holds up the hourglass and watches the last few grains of sand run out. He then presses an ear up to the stone wall. "Let's see." He jerks his head away. "From the sound of the splash, you might have had a few seconds to spare."

I slow my breathing and hold my chest to ease the tightness. "That smoke and hoof kick got my chest all messed up."

Bella stairs at me with wide eyes. "How many hit points did you get set you back? Do you need a heal?"

I take a few deep breaths and rub my eyes. "I only got hit for five. I'm sure I will be all right."

Hans points to my feet. "You forgot a shoe. And where's our other party member? I hope you didn't leave him in that giant flushing toilet."

163

"William was a flat-out disappointment in the battle with Paeonia." I hold out the sheath. "We did manage to bring back the prize, though."

Salo lowers his head. "So, WTF didn't make it?"

"Doesn't surprise me," Biff says. "The Bonnacons have remarkable flatulent defenses. They can launch their excrement for distances up to two or three furlongs, some say."

Bella stands in front of me and looks over the sheath. "Don't be too sad, Salo. Your friend snatched the sheath and tried to run out on us."

I pull out the Keris. "Let's see some magic here." I insert it into the sheath. A shock winds through my body, and I'm knocked off my feet to the ground. "Whoa!"

TASK COMPLETE: **Complete the Keris of Knaud III**

For completing the task, you earned 500 experience points!

NEW PRIMARY WEAPON: **The Keris of Knaud + (5) Charge.**
Distinguished Hack.

Damage: 10-50. Range: N/A. Frequency: Err. Quality: Grand-Master

Melee Weapon Attack: Piercing damage

Distinguished Hack: Strike with a verbal "Hack" to cast one or more of its 'Distinguished Hack' charges.

Soulbound to 'Jareth Goblinmasher' - Item cannot be traded or sold.

Equip with this blade to administer damage to the most robust of monsters.

"Hey, this thing packs a wallop." I stand and pull the Keris out of its sheath. The blade is now covered in shimmering gold leaf. "And has an excellent new look. Stats say the damage range of this thing is ten to fifty, and there is a bonus. It is packing a magic ability called Distinguished Hack." I should have known there was going to be magic involved with this weapon. I hold the dagger up and look it over from tip to butt. A green glow at the bottom of the blade catches my eye. I look closer and see four glowing green numbers–1264. Lotto numbers, finally.

Bella gives me a satisfied high-five. "The gold leaf is what I needed to see. It's completed. We're going to kill Setan."

I whip the blade from left to right. "This is all right." A pulse runs down my arm. "I feel I can do some quick damage with this weapon. It's like it was custom made for me."

Bella kneels and drops William's sack to the ground. "Let's see what our backstabbing ex-thief has for the cause." She sifts through the contents. "Hmm, some thief's tools, and this." She holds an open palm my way. "Five gold coins."

"So, we get a refund on that bad hire." I scoop the coins from Bella's hand and drop them in my bag. "I'm going to invest in a few healing potions when we get back to the city." I realize, for a moment, that I'm talking as if we'll be in the game forever. I'm talking as though I've forgotten about returning to real life. But we have less than half a day to find Setan and defeat him.

ADD: 5 gold coins to Jareth Goblinmasher. New gold coin balance: 12

Biff looks in the sack. "These tools are of decent quality. Should fetch seven or eight gold coins at the Cittadella."

Bella hands Salo our dead party member's sword and shield. "These should be worth something too." She spins William's staff around like a baton and sheaths it on her belt. "I will keep the staff of immortuos for myself." She gazes at her status sheet. "Only six charges in this thing. But still, it works for me."

"Ouch." I pull a thorn out of my dirty-socked foot. "I can't be questing with only one shoe."

"You might as well break in the Bombardment Boots," Bella says.

"Don't do that." Biff pulls a pristine brown leather shoe from his pack. "I would hate for you to accidentally set off the charge. You can have this. It is the other from my pair. It does not fit my peg, so I don't need it."

I stuff my foot in the shoe and take a few steps. The fit is tight, and its heel is lower than my other. I walk in a circle up and down like a carousel. "Awkward, but it will do. Thanks, Biff."

Bella looks at my new footwear and shakes her head. "Mismatch. That's not a good look."

I run in place and dip from side to side. "Not a good look? I'm 'bout to bring this style back."

Bella passes by me and looks over her shoulder. "You're not bringing nothing back if we don't keep it moving. Eleven hours, twenty minutes until shut down."

CHAPTER 15

After an hour's walk, we pass under the arch back into Cittadella, and a group of a dozen young boys and girls run our way.

Hans holds both hands up. "The great cleric of Chittor returns from his quest."

The kids run past him, hardly glancing his way. Instead, they surround me. A little brunette girl sporting a double top knot slips through the group, stopping in front of me. She digs in her pocket and pulls out a wrinkled piece of parchment and a sharpened piece of charcoal. "Are you Captain Jareth Goblinmasher?"

Hans shoves his way through the crowd of kids and snatches the parchment from her fingers. The piece of charcoal tumbles to the ground. "What's this?" he asks.

Biff grabs the paper from Hans and runs his finger down it. "This is a list of betting opportunities." He hands the paper back to the girl, who retrieves her charcoal and shoots Hans a glare.

Biff clears his throat. "Ahem... Captain Jareth Goblinmasher is returning five of six, less his thief, who lost his life in a fierce battle with a Bonnacon."

The children cheer, then scatter, disappearing into local businesses and down dark alleyways.

Biff beams in approval. "We came in high on the over-under, Riff. You will now be considered an up-and-coming captain in wagering circles."

NEW TASK: **Assemble a party at Cittadella.**

Assemble a party of six adventurers in order to enter the valley.

"An up-and-coming captain with an incomplete party," I point out. "We need a new thief." Not to mention the fact that my fame means nothing unless we save DCQ by midnight. I nod toward a nearby building with its double doors propped wide open. "That looks like a good place to start."

"The Routier's Rest, excellent call." Biff hobbles toward it. "They have a colossal selection of beverages, as well as questers for hire."

"Salo," I call. "You're familiar with arms. I need you to sell our surplus and meet us back here. We will need as much gold as possible to hire another thief and keep this quest going."

Hans frowns at me. "I will go along with Salo to supervise." Then, in an undertone he adds, "Trust an NPC with our loot? Real smart."

"Salo is neutrally aligned." I shrug.

"Unlike your evil ass, Hansel," Bella says. "Just get us as much coin as you can."

"That is not my name," Hans mumbles. "Du drecksau."

As Bella, Biff, and I step into the pub, we are inundated with the smell of sweet, exotic tobaccos. I do my best to wave away the smoke and guide the party to a table.

We sit, and Biff looks around the room. "Do you see a serving wench? I'm quite thirsty. The pint-per-town payment option is truly colossal, and I'm due for an installment."

Bella pulls a metallic black scrunchie from her hair. Long brown and red ombre curls fall over her shoulders. "This place is crazy with hookahs." She whisks her finger in a circle. "*Discutio vapos.*" The smoke around our table vaporizes into fresh air. "I can't stand smokers. That spell should keep the smoke at bay long enough for us to figure out how we're going to acquire a new thief."

I inhale the fresh air through my nose. "It smells like roses and lavender. Nice." Then a thought hits me. "Bella, could you use that same spell in the goblin chamber against Setan? I mean, you used it against the Bonnacon."

"The spell I used on the Bonnacon is a level three that can also extinguish flame or steal breath, depending on the situation," she explains. "I have one left. The small rose and lavender spell, however, is non-lethal. I can use it a few times a day."

"Then save that level three spell for Setan, no matter what." If Bella's spell doesn't stop the smoke, maybe it will steal Setan's breath. Either way, we need a backup plan. I glance over at the bar. A group of carousers take their drinks to a nearby table, leaving the bar open for the moment. "I'm going to speak with the barkeep about our thief situation."

"Ask about our drink situation, as well." Biff massages his throat. "Colossal thirst needs to be quenched."

I take a seat at a bar and look over the shelf of bottles. The bar tender hurries back and forth, concocting several drinks at once. He stops in front of me and dabs his brow with a hanky. "Drink for you?"

---

*VIEW THE ROUTIERS REST BAR MENU: **Yes/No?***

I focus on the *no*. "I need two hydromel, one ale, and information on thieves for hire."

"Three drinks coming up." He holds the hanky to a temple, looks up, and squints. "But gold is what jars my memory when it comes to quality questers for hire." He tilts his head. "I will be back with your drinks."

Someone pulls out the barstool next to me and a small glass of dark brown liquor slams down on the bar. "How was your run up North?"

I turn to see Slim standing there with an eyebrow raised. "Slim!" I greet him with a firm handshake. He is wearing a brown tunic and the hat I've always admired. "We got what we needed up North but lost our conniving-ass thief to a Bonnacon goring."

"A goring?" He takes a seat, wraps a hand around the glass, and stares into its contents. "That's a terrible way to meet your maker."

"Tell me about it." I pat my chest and blow out a breath. "The Bonnacon tried to do me in, too. I'm only now recovering." Slim seems different somehow. Less sure of himself. "Were you able to help your business associate?" I ask.

"I'm afraid not." His brow crinkles in a frown. "But I was able to find some information on their whereabouts." He glanced to the right side of the bar. "Do you know those two girls over there?"

I look over and see two well-toned girls in scant leather armor. One, with light brown hair, smiles our direction and sips seductively at her drink. The other runs a finger down her long blond hair in a twirl and winks.

"No, but if they are thieves for hire, I'm down to investigate." I stand, but Slim grabs my shoulder and pushes me back down.

"Don't be so quick about it. Let them come to you." He takes a swig of his drink. "So, what's your plan after you acquire a thief? Are you still heading West?"

"We hope to level up off the undead in Keighley, enter the West Labyrinth, and then kill Setan before midnight tonight."

Slim's eyebrows pop up so high they almost disappear beneath his hat brim. "Ambitious, to say the least. Here come your prospects, just like I said they would."

I turn in my seat.

The brown-haired girl stops a few steps in front of me, smiles, and looks at her friend out of the corner of her eye. She is sexy, with smooth skin and long eyelashes.

The blonde slides up to Slim and runs her hand gently down his arm. "What's your choosing fee?" She flicks her tongue out to reveal a beautiful silver ring pierced through the tip. Slowly she runs that tongue across her moist red lips.

Wow. This girl may have some special skills. Is she even human?

Slim strokes his chin. "First, let me see what we're working with." He glances at me from the corner of his eye and whispers, "This world has way too many freaks. And I like it." He stands up and looks the girl over.

She runs her hands down both sides of her hourglass figure and asks coyly, "Do I pass?"

"You, there," the barkeep grunts from behind me. "Three silver for the drinks."

"One moment." It takes every ounce of my willpower to turn away from the girl in front of me, even for a second. I turn and look at the drinks on the bar. I completely forgot about this round for Bella, Biff, and me.

Slim raises a finger at the barkeep. "Hold up on those, Ted. I need four shots of ambrosia, hors d'age."

"Yes, sir." Ted lines up four shot glasses, fills them with dark brown liquor, and heads down the bar. "Who else needs a drink?"

Slim's eyes narrow and he cocks a crooked smile. "Eenny Meeny Miny Moe." He picks up a glass and motions for us to do the same. "May these shots reveal the ho." He drinks half the shot and returns the glass to the bar.

I drink the whole thing in one quick swallow. The liquid has a warm burn as it flows down my throat. "Okay," I cough out. "Sorrows officially drowned."

Both girls throw back their shots and hold their liquor. Impressive. The girl with brown hair sits next to me with a hand resting on her chest. "That was a strong, strong drink. Good though."

"So, are you a thief by trade?" I ask, and then can't resist adding, "Because you're stealing my breath away."

She giggles. "I don't quest. But if I did, I think I would like to be a fighter. I have skills in several areas."

"A pretty fighter with skills in several areas would be a deadly combination. Maybe we can make that happen. I'm Riff. What do they call you?"

"My name is Meridiana." She looks around, then pulls in close to my ear. "Watch out for my friend. She is always up to—"

"Application denied." Slim flicks his fingers at the blonde, dismissing her. "Bye."

The blonde scrunches her face, grabs Meridiana's hand, and stomps away.

"It was nice meeting you, Riff," Meridiana calls over her shoulder. "And thank you for the drink!"

"Slim, what the hell?" I hiss. "I was getting somewhere with mine."

"Well, mine was an undercover hag," he says. "Those two are man killers. You don't want to mess with them."

"You call that a hag?" She looked good to me. They both looked good. "Did you see the tongue roll? I was about to get her to join my party."

"Be cautious of everyone and everything, young captain," Slim says. "Not every monster in the kingdom has toad heads or skin lesions. When I say undercover hag, I mean those girls were succubi. Their hag owners send them into town to get questers drunk until they pass out. Once you're unconscious, they turn you over to their hag owner, and that's where it gets ugly. The hag will either press on your chest to suffocate you, molest you to propagate their nasty-ass species, or slip their skin and enter your body to drive you crazy with nightmares. No, you don't want one of them messing up your careful plans."

I take one last look at the retreating Meridiana. Suddenly her brown locks and curvy form don't seem all that enticing. Thank goodness Slim broke up our conversation before I started making real recruitment moves on her.

"Succubi that run solo can be turned out from their hag owner," Slim says. "But never when they run in pairs. You got to separate them. The whole thing takes time."

"Good looking out." I toss some silver on the bar. "And speaking of time, I'm dealing with dead-for-real-die if I don't get my party moving. Do you know of any good thieves for hire?"

SUBTRACT: 3 silver pennies to Ted Nummies. New silver penny balance: 18

"Perhaps," Slim says cryptically. "But first, I need you to meet somebody." He makes a quick triple-click sound with his tongue, and a small animal appears from under his hat. It has a consistent mix of orange and black fur, short-legs, large walnut shaped eyes, and prominent curled whiskers. It moves to his shoulder and licks a paw.

"Is that a sniffer?" A few lucky gamers in DCQ have been able to unlock sidekicks known as sniffers. Disterbingly, I have yet to figure out the formula to unlock one myself. The consensus in most forums is that they are an extremely random subscription gift, but I don't believe that. Most of the sniffers I've seen are weasel like animals that can sense traps, evil, and magic. This one looks different from the any I've seen. It's more muscular and has an unusual spade-tipped tail.

Slim scratches the animal lovingly under its chin. "This is Skookum. I found her in a trash heap with her half-sister when they were kits. Sniffer breeders don't keep mongrels. I'm guessing she is a cross between a sniffer and some kind of pseudo-dwarf dragon."

Slim extends his arm, and Skookum scurries down it, hops onto my lap, circles, and looks up with big brown glossy eyes. "She got all the best abilities of a sniffer, plus she can breathe fire and whoop up on enemies with her dragon tail. Skook has saved my life numerous times and has aided me in acquiring coin constantly."

I stroke the animal's silky fur. "She's awesome!"

Skook licks my hand, hops up to Slim's arm, and scampers back to his shoulder. "Look Riff, I came to you for a reason." Slim toys with one of the empty shot glasses. Uh-oh. Did he need gold or something? He must be mighty desperate if he was coming to *me* for help. "The information I uncovered about my friend is that I need something from one of Setan's cells to help them. Therefore, I would like to join your party as a full member on your run to the West Labyrinth."

Had I misheard? *Slim* wanted to use his skills to aid us? "Slim, you know I can't afford you."

Slim waves his hand. "No payment necessary, Captain. All I'm after is a direct quest into the monster allocation chamber and Setan's lair. Oh, and artifact privileges."

My man. "You got it."

Slim grabs my hand and shakes it hard. "Terms are accepted then."

ADD: **Gregarious Slim, Thief.** *(Direct quest to Setan's lair/Artifact Privileges)*

Thief: Trained in the arts of stealing and sneaking. May only use light to mid-weight weaponry and armor. Primary abilities: Agility.

AGE:25   LEVEL: 3   ABILITIES: 40 ALIGNMENT: Neutral

WEAPONS: Quarterstaff: Melee Weapon Attack: Bludgeoning damage.

A smaller icon of Skookum materializes beneath Slim's.

ADD: **Skookum Tortie, Sniffer.**

Belette: Trained to sense traps, evil, and magic. Primary abilities: Wisdom

AGE: 3   LEVEL: 2   ABILITIES: 25 ALIGNMENT: Neutral

WEAPONS: Detect: Can detect traps, evil, and magic within 30 feet.

Bite: Melee Weapon Attack. Piercing damage.

Fire Breath: Can exhale fire in a seven-foot cone.

Tail Strike: Melee Weapon Attack. Bludgeoning damage.

TASK COMPLETE: **Assemble a party at Cittadella.**

For completing the task, you earned 50 experience points! Complete additional tasks and kill monsters to earn more.

"One more order of business." Slim stacks two gold coins and three silver pennies on the counter. "Ted, this is for my drinks, your tip, and a glance at the latest rumor table."

Hmm, Slim seems to like rumor tables as much as I do. I drop four pennies next to his two. "Make it a rumor table scroll, and not the fugazi-fable version either."

SUBTRACT: *4 silver pennies to Ted Nummies. New silver penny balance: 14*

Ted scoots the coins into his palm and drops a cigar-sized scroll on the bar. "Only the very, very, very best and most current table for anyone who quests with Slim."

I unroll the scroll and lay it out on the bar.

THE ROUTIER'S REST RUMOR TABLE:

1- A Lich now stalks Keighley.

2- The mountains above the West Labyrinth are hag-ridden.

3- A countdown to obliteration has begun.

4- Keris's are ineffective versus the blood of greater goblins.

5- Remove the Zuni Fetish doll's gold chain for luck +10.

6- A cell in the West Labyrinth contains a dead entity with riches to pilfer.

7- The value of huo-yao is on the rise.

8- Dusting off a model galleon in the North Caves will bring luck.

9- Beware of wandering Evons.

10- The West Labyrinth's corridors have shifted.

11- The Liergarnin King has vowed to kill all humans.

12- A notched stick of wishes can be found in a forest troll's hoard.

I drop a fingertip on rumor number one. *A Lich*. "What are the odds this one is true?" Fighting undead monsters is one thing. Fighting an undead wizard is another. "We're not equipped to take on a Lich."

"Hopefully that rumor is false," Slim glances down the scroll. "Or just Whipstitch."

"What do you mean, Whipstitch?" I ask.

Biff pushes his way between Slim and me and snatches his ale from the bar. "Colossal thirst." He chugs the whole of its contents. "Aaaaa, comforts the heart."

"Excuse me, Riff." Bella reaches over me and picks up a cup. "You were supposed to bring these to our table." She nods Slim's direction. "Hello, Gregarious."

Hans drops a sack onto the bar. "We're back. While you were all drinking like fish, Salo and I sold everything we had for eight gold coins."

"Way to go, Hans." I roll up the scroll and stuff it in my pocket. I'll ask Slim what a Whipstitch is later. No need to alarm the party with Lich talk, yet. "I didn't think you would get over six or seven." I empty the coins into my bag.

ADD: 8 gold coins to Jareth Goblinmasher. New gold coin balance: 20

"Listen up, team," I insist. "We have re-acquired the services of Slim here as our thief. He is bringing his sniffer, Skookum, and will join us as a full-fledged fighting, thieving member of our party."

Bella gives me the stink eye. "I hope you didn't over pay."

I shrug. "How could I overpay? You've seen my wallet."

She looks Slim up and down with a frown. "I look forward to seeing you fight, Greg."

Skookum peeks out from under Slim's hat and sniffs the air.

Bella's frown turns to a smile at the sight of the sniffer. She gently pets Skook under her chin. "Oh, she's beautiful."

"And deadly in a skirmish." Slim picks up his shot glass and maneuvers it under Skook's mouth where she laps up the liquid.

"We need deadly." Bella pauses to examine her player's sheet, then shakes it out of her vision. "And more time." She slowly breathes in, blows out a sharp breath, and chugs down her hydromel. "Let's talk strategy. This party has a level-up problem that needs to be addressed. We will be taking on some high level, heavy-experience-point-giving monsters on our next leg. Our best melee skills will be needed. Hans, re-acquaint yourself with your deadliest cleric skills. Your ability to dispel the undead is sure to come into play."

"My abilities have been in play," Hans says. "I've saved this resource-draining party from death several times already. Though I am low on spells, as usual, I will carry you all on my back."

I raise my cup. "So, let's get on with it. Who will drink with me to the slaughter of Setan?"

My toast is met with a chorus of cheers and the splash of liquid.

Our drinking done and our thief secured, we step outside the pub and run into a large two-wheeled handcart being pushed by an old pockmarked man. "Unique magical provisions available here." He waves us over. "My prices are cheaper than any stone-and-plaster shop and superior in quality. Ask anybody about Cheapjack's papyrus and elixir."

Cheapjack runs a hand up and down his cart's multi-tiered display as if it is a game show prize package. "Feast your eyes." All three tiers are loaded with brown rolled up scrolls and simple glass bottles filled with multicolored liquid topped.

"Okay." I look over the merchandise. "We are far from being maxed-out on abilities or hit points," I say to my crew. "We should get some liquid healing." This is the last chance we will have to purchase anything before taking on Setan, so we better spend wisely.

Hans pushes himself between me and Cheapjack. "Please tell me you are not going to buy anything from this roach coach, Riff."

Slim picks up a bottle of red liquid, shakes it, and holds it up to the sun. "Cheapjack is no gypsy hawker. You can tell by the liquid's glimmer this potion is top quality, and you can't beat the price."

VIEW CHEAPJACK'S MENU: **Yes/No?**

Yes. "Let's see what he's got," I say. We only have six hours until midnight. There's no point saving our money when we'll soon all be dead if we don't succeed. Might as well spend it now.

CHEAPJACK'S MENU: Ten Silver Pennies (SP) = One Gold Coin (GC)

Vial of Vigor	7GC	*Parchment of Pain*	10GC
Potion of Heal	14GC	*Scroll of Hurt*	20GC
Potion of Health	14GC	*Scroll of Harm*	28GC
Potion of Curing	300GC	*Scroll of Affliction*	5000GC
Water of Life	1000GC	*Roll of Death*	10,000GC
Potion of Paralysis	1000GC	*Scroll of Protection*	3000GC
Liquid Di Giorgio	1400GC	*Chronicle DiFloryshe*	12,000GC

"You call these good prices?" I only see one item that we can afford that would really help us. "Give me three Vials of Vigor," I tell Cheapjack.

"Not so fast." Slims eyebrows tense. "Cheapjack is out of pocket with these prices. A few carts closer to the gate have better deals."

"Who offers better bargains then me?" Cheapjack snaps.

"Quark Gint has been very competitive lately." Slim cocks an eyebrow. "And Porgi Poke had some two-for-ones last time I stopped by his cart. Let's go, captain."

Cheapjack sidesteps to block our way. "I have a special deal for you. Half price on the Potion of Heal. It's three to five times more potent than the Vial of Vigor. No one else in Cittadella can make you this offer. I promise you that."

Slim nods. "I like it."

"I'll go with the three Potions of Heal then," I tell Cheapjack.

ADD POSSESSION: **(3) Potion of Heal** *(-21 Gold Coins)*
Drink this potion to restore one to eight hit points of damage.

I give the man twenty gold coins and ten silver pennies.

SUBTRACT: 20 gold coins to Cheapjack Collie. New gold coin balance: 0
SUBTRACT: 10 silver pennies to Cheapjack Collie. New silver penny balance: 4

That's pretty much all the coinage we have. We are as ready as we can be for this final push. I load the merchandise in my pack and strap it to my back. "Let's get to it."

We head toward Cittadella's exit for the last time.

CHAPTER 16

06:20:58 HOURS UNTIL DCQ SERVER SHUT DOWN.

A tall hooded figure draped in a black cloak stands at Cittadella's West Arch. As we approach, he raises a hand my direction and groans out, "Paperwork."

I open my Grimoire, activate it, and put it in his hand. "Where's Castel?"

He pulls back the hood slightly and slowly raises the device to his pale face. "Party of six with a thief confirmed. Enjoy your deaths."

Hans walks under the arch. "Nobody's dying, you freak."

I step under the West arch and survey the road ahead. It is narrow with dark, twisted woods on either side.

"I don't like it." Bella wraps her hands around her arms. "The path to Setan's Labyrinth is way more wicked for real than in the game. It's like a path to hell."

"I agree." A cold wind howls around us, ruffling the trees. "We are sure to encounter the worst of what DCQ has to offer on this path."

PARTY STATUS:

Time for this again. I focus in on the prompt.

REORDER THE PARTY: **Yes/No?**

Jareth Orcslauter, Fighter.	HP: 17/45	AC: 4	LVL: 4
*Salo Fatback, Fighter.	HP: 21/50	AC: 6	LVL: 4
*Biff Thunderpunch, Ninja.	HP: 7/65	AC: 7	LVL: 4
*Gregarious Slim, Thief.	HP: 27/40	AC: 5	LVL: 3
*Skookum Tortie, Belette.	HP: 14/30	AC: 4	LVL: 2
Madmartigan Galladoorn, Mage.	HP: 18/40	AC: 3	LVL: 3
Hans Talhoffer, Cleric.	HP: 21/40	AC: 2	LVL: 3

I wave in Bella and Hans. "Okay, we need to make the West Labyrinth before sundown, and do some leveling along the way. Salo, Biff, and myself are currently at level four. One of us has to make level five in order to access the chamber. It's time for that good speed grind."

"That's still not a thing," Hans grumbles, stomping ahead. "If all goes well, I'll level up twice and save all our asses'."

"This guy." Bella shakes her head and watches Hans head down the path from the corner of her eye. "One of us has to make level five *and* survive to Setan's chamber. Don't forget the survive part. How are you holding up for the marching order? I know you've taken some damage."

"I'm going to reorder and bolster." I explain. "Hey, Biff." I wave him over. "I'm switching you to fourth in the marching order." Biff may be a Ninja, but he is only seven hit points away from death. Slim is sitting pretty at twenty-seven, best in the party.

Biff plants his peg and stands tall. "No need to drop me back. I want to fight. Ninjas are meant for the front of the marching order." He looks ahead unblinking.

I've dented his ego, and I'm bummed about that, but I must make decisions based on what is best for the party. "Slim has the sniffer. They serve double-duty if I put them in front. Besides, I need you protecting our rear." I pull a potion of heal from my pack and hand it to him. "I think I owe you another drink, my friend." I pull out another potion for myself, uncork it, and hold it up. "Here's to your good health, our party's good health, and may we all live long and prosper."

"Hear, hear." Biff lifts his vial. "To colossal peace and long life, Captain."

I clink my vial with his and put it to my lips. The liquid tastes like a mix of Jägermeister and dark chocolate. Not bad, actually.

YOUR HIT POINTS HAVE BEEN INCREASED! Hit points increased by one to 18/45.

A PARTY MEMBER'S HIT POINTS HAVE BEEN INCREASED! NAME: Biff Thunderpunch. Hit points increased by five to 12/65.

"I only gained one hit point?" Maybe Hans was right about these potions. "I'll just have to make eighteen work." I grab the final potion from my pack, bite off the cork, and spit it out. "Bella, you're next in need."

She waves off the vial. "We both have eighteen hit points now, Riff, and you're on the front line. I appreciate the gesture, but I'm fine." She wraps her hand around my arm. "I need you strong on the home stretch, so drink up." She continues down the road.

"She's right, you know," Biff says.

I drink down the contents and wipe my mouth. "I would feel better if Bella and the rest of us were closer to being maxed out."

> YOUR HIP POINTS HAVE BEEN INCREASED! *Hit points increased by four to 22/45.*

Four this time, okay. I focus on the status prompt and reorder Slim in front of Biff. "Let's do this"

"Let's." Slim raises his cane. "Watch your back. Thieves on this road will leap on any weary traveler they can take, and the undead are known to pop up right out of the ground and mug you from behind."

"Speaking of thieves and undead." I look over at Slim as we walk. "What's a Whipstitch?"

"I had hoped you'd forgotten that, Captain." Slim says. "Whipstitch is the remains of a wild and crazy little hermit magic user that embraced undeath as a means of preserving himself."

Bella looks nervously at the road ahead. "You mean a Lich?"

"No, not exactly." Slim adjusts his tunic and scans the tree tops. "Liches are great wizards that have embraced undeath. Whipstitch was an insane, low-level seer that got lucky to embrace it. I guess you can call him a minor Lich, but deadly with dark magic nonetheless."

"I am familiar with the Whipstitch Lich." Biff blurts. "He's a colossal little bugger. Rumor has it he's out and about on this very road, and physically falling apart from feeding on rodent and Kobold souls. They say that, when he was alive, he gave half of his brain to a real wizard in exchange for lichdom after death. Hardly a fair deal to become a Lich with zombie-like intelligence."

"I don't know." Hans stretches his neck and smiles. "He had the right idea. Becoming a Lich means you can live past death. Who wouldn't want that? I'm sure, with some tactical maneuvering, you can become a Lich without going crazy and becoming evil."

"All Liches are crazy," I say. "And I don't like the idea of taking on one of any type." But I bet killing one would net some major experience points.

As we head down the road, the forest encroaches upon it more and more. Rocks, mud holes, ruts, inclines, and water crossings become more frequent with every step.

I check my map as the sun dips below the treetops. We're only about twenty minutes from the West Labyrinth entrance, but with every step our chances to level up decrease. We need a fight. "Hard to believe we haven't run into any wandering monsters yet," I mutter.

Just as I say it, Skookum scampers from Slim's right shoulder to his left, rises on its hind legs, and hisses at the road ahead.

Slim stops and scowls at me. "Did you really have to say that?"

Five rusty brown humanoids in crudely fashioned hide garments scamper from the trees and form a line across the road in front of us.

The one in the middle—the tallest of the bunch—drops a rock in the pocket of a sling and swings it in a wide vertical orbit. The four monsters flanking him all pull out daggers and yip like small injured dogs.

"Kobold," Biff says. "I believe they are demanding Skookum, and a payment of gold as a toll to pass. Very enterprising for such unintelligent creatures."

KOBOLD	
LEVEL: *1/2 (50XP)*	**HIT POINTS:** *5*
ARMOR CLASS: *5 (Natural armor)*	**FREQUENCY:** *Common*
NO. APPEARING: *5 - 35*	**DAMAGE:** *By weapon*
SPECIAL ATTACKS:	
SPECIAL DEFENSES:	

INTELLIGENCE: *Low*   **ALIGNMENT:** *Evil*   **SIZE:** *S*

TYPICAL WEAPONING: *Sling, Dagger, Short Sword, Spear*

DESCRIPTION: *Kobold are small reptilian humanoids with rusty brown skin.*

"They won't be getting a damn thing from us," I say. Now this is a monster I know well from the game. What shall I dispatch them with? Not the Keris. Best to save all its charges for Setan. So...

NEW PRIMARY WEAPON: **Executioner's Sword**

I raise my sword and lift my shield. "Should be a piece of level-up-fodder cake. I'll take on the one in the middle. Let's fight."

"Agreed." Salo swings his mace around and grips the shaft. "I'll start with the reptiles on the left."

Slim uses his fingers to give Skookum a rub on the head. "We'll take the right."

A rock whizzes past my ear as I sprint forward. I dodge a weak dagger-thrust to the face by the tall Kobold, and then jab a swift stab forward puncturing the beast through its chest. I yank up, pull out, and kick the monster backward. It's carcass collapses onto the ground. One down. Four more to go.

188

Salo upends his combatant with his mace and then bashes its skull over and over again with its heavy metal head.

Biff steps up and fires three mini war hammers into another Kobold's head causing it to wobble a few steps and fall flat.

The two remaining enemies bear down on Slim. He spins his cane in a circle and then quick punches it forward, caving the first one's nose into his skull. Just as the second Kobold's blade cuts into Slim's shoulder, it gets blasted in the side by a brilliant basketball-sized ball of yellow flame. The monster spins in a circle, stumbling backward headfirst into a tree. I run up on it, plunge my sword into its scaly torso, and turn around. "Nice shot."

"Got him." Hans blow off his palms. "Slim, you owe me just like the rest of the party."

Slim looks the Kobolds up and down. "It's skinny little lizards like this thinkin' they the Last Dragon that gives questing a bad name."

Kobold (5) has been killed! For killing the monsters each survivor earned 42 experience points.

I sheath my blade and view the message in dismay. Not much XP attached to Kobold.

Bella wraps her hands around Slim's bleeding shoulder and chants, "*Vulnere remedium.*" Then she turns to the rest of us. "Is everybody else okay?"

Salo works his way from one corpse to the next. After plundering the last body, he steps my way and drops a fist full of coins in my hand. "That's fourteen silver pennies. I've stockpiled their daggers too, but they are of little to no value."

"My man," I say.

Biff examines the sling inch by inch. "The cords show signs of significant wear, but the pouch is like new." He stretches it out the full length of his arms. "It's engineered for a greater range than my current rig, I can work with—"

"*Eeeeek!*" Skookum squeals and hisses at the road ahead.

A small skeletal humanoid with black eye-sockets and glowing pupils levitates several feet above the ground in front of us. It has a diagonal stitch across its bone forehead, is wrapped in decaying red velvet garments, and holds a wooden staff topped with a green gem.

Now I understand why there weren't many monsters prior to the Kobold. All the rest were avoiding this thing.

Slim sets Skookum on the ground and wraps his palm around the ivory bust that tops his cane. Bella slowly unsheathes the staff of immortuos and says, "Hans, what's your daddy doing here?"

"It's Whipstitch." Biff loads his newly acquired sling with an ovoid led projectile and begins a swooshing vertical orbit. "The crudest of the undead."

"That's a Lich?" Hans asks. "I guess something is lost in the translation."

Salo takes up arms. "Don't underestimate it."

LICH (LESSER)

LEVEL: 5 (5100XP)   HIT POINTS: 50

ARMOR CLASS: 14   FREQUENCY: *Very Rare*

NO. APPEARING: 1   DAMAGE: 5-20

SPECIAL ATTACKS: *Touch, Magic*

SPECIAL DEFENSES:

INTELLIGENCE: *High*   ALIGNMENT: *Neutral*   SIZE: *S*

TYPICAL WEAPONING:

DESCRIPTION: *A Lesser-Lich is an undead and skeletal little person with black eye-sockets and glowing pupils. Its garments are the decaying remains of once fine robes.*

I fought stronger liches than this in the game, but I am not about to underestimate this ones power. I unsheathe the Keris and feel its pulse.

NEW PRIMARY WEAPON: **The Keris of Knaud + (5) Charge.** *Distinguished Hack.*

"Aaargh." Whipstitch points its staff forward and mutters, *"Volumina ligeti."*

Four reddish brown hellhounds sprint from behind him. They have glowing red eyes and spit a combination of black froth and red flames from between sharp teeth. Tiny skeleton warriors ride the hounds like jockeys on thoroughbreds. They have one hand under the hounds' spiked collars, and the other held high with curved sickle swords.

HELLHOUND

LEVEL: 1 (225XP)	**HIT POINTS:** 6
ARMOR CLASS: 8	**FREQUENCY:** Rare
NO. APPEARING: 2 - 8	**DAMAGE:** 4-11

SPECIAL ATTACKS:

SPECIAL DEFENSES:

INTELLIGENCE: Simi   **ALIGNMENT:** Evil   **SIZE:** M

TYPICAL WEAPONING: Bite, Breathe fire

DESCRIPTION: Hell hounds are pitch-black in color. Their eyes glow red and their bodies are muscular. They can exhale fire and have a deadly bite.

SKELETON (DEMI)

LEVEL: 1 (141XP)	**HIT POINTS:** 5
ARMOR CLASS: 6 (Armor scraps)	**FREQUENCY:** Rare
NO. APPEARING: 3 - 30	**DAMAGE:** By weapon

SPECIAL ATTACKS:

SPECIAL DEFENSES:

INTELLIGENCE: Non   **ALIGNMENT:** Neutral   **SIZE:** S

TYPICAL WEAPONING: Short sword, Dagger

DESCRIPTION: Demi-skeletons are the animated bones of dead little people, mindless automatons that obey the orders of an evil master. Garbed in the rotting remnants of a combination of clothing and armor.

"Who's got some magic for these fools?" I call out.

The Lich thrusts its staff, calling out a spell, and bolts fly from its tip, hurtling toward each of us.

"*Clipeum, Clipeum, Clipeum.*" Hans crosses his arms and then throws them wide open, creating a giant transparent rectangular shield. It absorbs the bolts with a crackle. "Somebody do something," he demands. "This shield won't last."

Bella aims her staff forward and fires six glowing blue spheres. Two of the skeleton warriors get hit and disappear into a burst of black smoke. The other two riders dodge the projectiles and continue to run at Bella full speed.

"To the rescue!" Hans drops the magic shield and flicks a finger at the riders. "*Immortuos, Immortuos.*" Bolts fling from his finger, knocking the final two riders off their mounts where they puff into black smoke. "Take out the hounds!" he yells.

Salo sprints forward and uppercuts a hound under its chin with his mace. He then spins and slams it solidly down on another dog's back, nearly folding it in two.

Biff launches his led projectile between a charging dog's eyes, causing it to yelp and die in an awkward skid.

I dive-tackle the final hound just before it reaches Bella. As we roll across the ground, I jam the Keris into its rib cage twice. When we come to a stop, I kick the animal off with the full force of both my legs.

"Aaargh." The Lich waves its staff and bolts fly from the tip. Biff gets hit in his groin, and Salo in the head. One strikes me in the chest, and we all get knocked to the ground. My skin burns, and the torturous heat sinks beneath my bones. I manage to prop myself up with one elbow to suck in a breath, just in time to see Bella and Hans dive into the trees, barely avoiding the strikes aimed at them.

Slim ducks under the blast and runs forward with his cane straight out. "*Hova glova nivlan blizman.*" A swirling gold light blazes from the eyes on the

195

bust on his cane. The light crashes into the Lich's eye-sockets, and its entire body flashes a bright white. It slumps over and floats downward.

I clutch my burning, aching chest. "You got it, Slim. You got it—"

The Lich convulses and floats back up. "*Volumina.*" Bolts crackle from its eye sockets to the green gem.

We're not going to survive another round of this thing's magic. The muscles in my arms and legs pulsate. What's this? The Keris shakes and pulls my arm up and back. I get it, ranged weapon attack, the Keris wants me to throw it as a projectile. But I can't afford to lose it if I miss.

The Lich rises higher than before and thrusts its staff above its skull. "*Voluminaaaa,*" the monster howls.

The Keris has got to be telling me something good here. I'm going for it. I run forward and launch the Keris at the Lich's forehead. "*Haaack!*" The dagger soars like a supercharged rocket with a shower of glittering dust in its wake, and jams into the Lich's skull stitching causing it to crack a quarter inch across the forehead.

"*Volumin*—aarghhh." The points of light in the Lich's empty eye sockets flash white, then turn black. It lurches backward then falls onto the ground with a final, weak. "Aarghh."

"Got it." I drop to a knee, hold my chest, and take deep breaths.

The lich rises up on its hands and looks forward with dim points of light fading in and out in its eye sockets. "*Vol...um...in–*"

"Not yet." Slim sprints toward our fallen foe. "It's trying to cast another spell."

Skookum drops down from a tree limb and swats its dragon spade tail into the Lich's head. The skull pops off its neck and rolls forward, tumbling across the ground.

Slim jumps up and bangs the bust of his cane down on the skull, pulverizing it into a cloud of black smoke. "You think I ain't?" He drops the cane and wraps both hands around his own head. "Here it comes. Aaaah! Level drain."

Bella rushes to his side. "Are you okay, Slim? What can I do?"

I pick the Keris up and wipe black dust off it onto my pants. This just might be what I have always needed to get the goblin job done. I sheath the weapon.

A WEAPONS STATUS HAS CHANGED:

Your weapon 'The Keris of Knaud + (5) Charge' has been changed to 'The Keris of Knaud + (4) Charge'

I shake the message off, causing my head to throb even worse. *I hope four charges are enough to kill Setan.*

Salo stands over Biff who is laid out on the ground. "Some help!"

Biff sits up and hacks a stream of blood. "A colossal victory."

I open my water skin and stagger over to Biff. "That Lich's bolt gave me a hell of a jolt, too." I kneel down and hold the skin his way. "Drink up."

Biff looks up at me with a pale face and bloodshot eyes. "Do you have anything stronger?" He takes the water and sprays it into his mouth. "I may need a moment." He straightens his back and winces. "Or two. A moment or two."

"Is everyone okay?" Bella slides to a stop by my side and looks around. "I think we all just kinda survived a Lich attack?"

I rub my head in an attempt to ease the ache. "Our greatest challenge still lies ahead." Time to regroup.

Hellhound (4) has been killed! For killing the monsters each survivor earned 150 experience points.

Skeleton Warrior (4) has been killed! For killing the monsters each survivor earned 47 experience points. *No XP awarded for monsters dispelled by a clerics magic.

The Whipstitch Lich has been killed! For killing the monster each survivor earned 850 experience points.

YOU MADE THE NEXT LEVEL! Max hit points increased to 48. Strength+1, Agility+1, and Luck+1 increased! Total Abilities now 63.

You were hit for 6 damage. Status: 16/48

PARTY STATUS: Multiple members' status has changed.

REORDER THE PARTY: **Yes/No?**

Set the dungeon marching order of your party. Remember, only the first three members of a party can attack monsters with weapons. Note: Only NPC's are bound to follow marching order instructions. (* = NPC)

Jareth Orcslauter, Fighter.	HP: 16/48	AC: 4	LVL: 5
*Salo Fatback, Fighter.	HP: 15/55	AC: 6	LVL: 5
*Gregarious Slim, Thief.	HP: 21/32	AC: 5	LVL: 2
*Skookum Tortie, Belette.	HP: 8/30	AC:4	LVL: 2
*Biff Thunderpunch, Ninja.	HP: 2/65	AC: 7	LVL: 5
Madmartigan Galladoorn, Mage.	HP: 19/40	AC: 3	LVL: 3

I stand and shake the menus away. "Okay team, I got good news and bad. Salo, Biff, and I all leveled up to five. We can officially enter the chamber."

"This isn't right." Bella shakes her stat sheet away. "We just beat a Lich, but I didn't level." She shakes her head and her voice comes out small. "Unbelievable."

This game can be stone cold. Bella leveling up would have been a great help against Setan, and she knows it. "Leveling is no good unless you can heal the wounds." I point to Biff. "And that brings me to the bad. He's down to two hit points."

"I'm a mage, Riff." Bella looks down at Biff. "Leveling would have recharged my current spells and given me at least one powerful new one."

Biff coughs a splatter of blood across his lap and waves Bella away. "I will be—okay."

"You need a heal." Bella kneels and clenches her jaw. "Desperately. Lay down and I will fix you up."

Biff lays on his back and hacks once again. Bella raises a finger and touches it to Biff's forehead.

But before she can speak the spell, Hans kicks her finger off with the tip of his shoe. "Let him ride it out, Bella. We have two level-five party members. We don't need three. He's expendable. The truly good news is that I leveled up to four, replenished my spell power, and learned new magic. I'm now at 4/3/1/1, including a new piece of wizardry that can freeze the goblin and give everybody time to land blows. Thanks to me, there may be hope for this party after all."

Bella's face reddens, and she returns her finger to Biff's forehead. "I'm going to give you a double dose." She chants her spell.

Two beams of white light spin around Biff and disappear into the ground. He stands up and pounds his chest. "Better. Thank you, Bella."

"Better off dead." Hans huffs. "If we fall short on spell power, I'm blaming you, Bella."

I check the status sheet. "That was a good heal. He's now at ten hit points."

Bella looks Biff over and then at her sheet. "I do need to save some spell power for the goblin. The smoke spell, in particular. I'm down to 0/3/1." She looks up in the trees. "We're losing light fast. We need to be in the Labyrinth before it is too dark to find our way."

Slim drops a baseball-sized gem into my hand. "It took some serious thieving skills to pry this from that demon's staff."

I move the gem up and down in my palm. "Your cane spell was phenomenal, Slim. We received a lot of experience points from that encounter. I am sure you'll gain back that level you lost for using that spell soon."

Salo steps up to me, twirling the four spiked Hell Hound collars on his arm. "I know people in Cittadella that will pay a few thousand gold for a gem that size."

I drop the gem in my bag. "You're all going to come out of this run with some major coin. That's for sure now."

ADD POSSESSION: **Emerald Gemstone**

"It's getting dark." Bella plants her fists on her hips. "We need to move."

We regroup and set a fast pace. It matches the quickening of my pulse as we get closer and closer to Setan. We meet no enemies on the path—as though they know we've just decimated a Lich, and we're not to be messed with. After a quarter of an hour, we stand in front of a giant cave with three evenly spaced wood doors. All three are reinforced with iron bands and studs but have shifted on their hinges and are cracked open about an inch.

Biff pulls open the door on the right and turns to me. "So, this is the West Labyrinth."

I wrap my fingers around the middle door's handle. "Biff, the door you just opened contains a monster-infested path that has a lot to offer if you're into fighting wererats. This one leads to Setan." I pull the door, but it gets hung up in the gravel.

Salo grabs a hold of my door, too. "I have heard many horrific tales of what goes on behind the center door." He leverages a foot against the cave wall. "On the count of three. One, two, three…"

TASK COMPLETE:

Enter the West, North, East, or South-East dungeon.

For completing the task you earned 100 experience points

NEW TASK:

Take down The Monster Allocation Chamber force shield.

Use Hawkwinds Cadence to take down the chamber's force shield.

CHAPTER 17

I top off my lantern with oil and hold it out to Bella. She ignites it with a flick of her thumb. "Standard marching order, team."

We step around boulders, duck stalactites, and follow a constantly winding path downward for over an hour to an open iron door set in the cave's rocky hall. The ominous darkness presses upon us as if to remind us of the little time we have left. Beyond the iron door, we find a perfectly square room with a stone cut floor and walls. In the middle, a rusty iron spiral staircase leads down into darkness.

I've sent my Jareth avatar along this route more times than I can count, but everything looks and feels different in person. There are more threats, more dangers, than when navigating the pixelated screen.

I wrap a hand around the center post and dip the lantern into the stairwell. A cold stale air rises from the depths. "It looks sketchy." I place my foot on the first step gently to see if it will hold my weight. The cross-piece creaks and buckles, but holds. "We're good." I take the next step, and my boot falls through along with half my leg.

Salo reaches out and catches my hand. "Sketchy."

"Step lightly everyone." I hold firmly onto the railing and adjust my footing. "Keep to the edges where the wood is more reinforced."

We descend the staircase for what seems like endless turns. Spiraling our way down into a small oval stone chamber. A single bricked hallway leads into further darkness.

Biff comes off the last step and leans against the wall. "That was the longest flight of steps ever." He taps his peg on the floor and massages his knee.

"Hang in there, Biff." I check my Grimoire. "Just a little under three hours until midnight. We have no time to rest."

"I told you we should have left him," Hans says.

Salo bends over next to one of the walls and picks up a large bone. "This is not from an animal." He peels off a strip of rotten meat. "My guess is it came from a full-grown Minotaur."

I'd never encountered a Minotaur during my previous expeditions to Setan's lair. It's as if the game has gotten harder, as if it knows we're here and wants to thwart us from saving it.

That will *not* happen on my watch.

I direct the lantern down the hallway and strain to see ahead. Running into a Minotaur would be bad. Running into whatever killed it would be worse. From experience, I know it's best to make it to the monster allocation center with no labyrinth encounters. The tight corridors make combat very dangerous.

We follow the hallway for thirty minutes and come to a four-way intersection.

"Okay Bella," I say. "I know the route through this labyrinth like the back of my hand, but keep your eye on me, this real-life version is crazy. If I make a wrong turn, don't hesitate to knock me upside the head."

"I'll knock you upside the head." Hans peers down each of the halls and looks at me bug-eyed. "Keep your mind in the game."

I square up to the tunnel on the right, raise my right hand, and point straight ahead. "Follow me." I lead the party down to another four-way intersection where I turn right and stop just before walking into what looks like a bottomless pit. "Oops." I hold my arms out to block my party from advancing into the abyss. "That was supposed to be a left."

"I really hate being to fool who follows," Hans grumbles. "Are you sure you know the way?"

"Yes," I blow out a breath. "I am sure." We turn around and continue. The corridor curves to the right, then zigzags left and right several dozen times before a long hallway ends at a T-intersection.

Biff rests a hand on the wall and lowers his head. "You are positive we are on the correct path, right?"

It's disorienting walking a route I've navigated so many times with a mouse and keyboard. "These directions are etched in my head. We're good." I pivot to the right, stop, and pivot left. "This way."

We continue down a long straightaway that ends with a right turn, left turn, then down a steep set of stairs. A chill zips down my spine. Before taking the last step, I freeze and motion for the party to stop. Something is wrong here.

I crouch down and look over the rectangle vestibule before me, scattered with broken white stone chunks. An arched entryway leads into the large room, dimly lit by flickering torches.

I've never seen this room before.

I look back at the team and lower my voice. "This area is not in the game." Did I take a wrong turn? Impossible. I'd descended into this section of the maze more times than I'd cooked a bowl of mac n' cheese.

Bella crouches next to me. "I don't recognize it either. It is weird that it is lit." She points ahead. "There is something going on outside the entryway. The floor looks like it is moving."

"Slim." I gesture him forward. "You, Biff, and Salo take the left wall. Bella, you and Hans are with me to the right." I douse my lantern's flame and return it to my pack. "Quietly."

We slink along the walls, kneel, and peek around the side. One short step takes you down into a large square room jam-packed with a variety of wandering cats. Some are big. Some small. Some solid. Others are multi-patterned in color. They move slowly, winding in and out of each other in random directions, and cover the floor completely. A noisy meow-purr hum mixed with periodic shrieks, growls, and hisses fills the room.

"Why is there a clowder of house cats in a dungeon labyrinth?" I recognize some familiar breeds like a coatless Sphynx, an elongated Siamese, and a spotted Bengal.

"My—um—Kurht was a big, big cat guy," Bella says. "Look at them. They are all so cute." A fat belly cat with a squashed face, torn off tail, and missing patches of rotted pumpkin colored fur waddles by and hisses in our direction. "Except that one."

"Why are you cowards hiding?" Hans steps from behind the wall to the center of the archway. "Cats are harmless. There's a door on the other side. Let's get going."

Salo leaves his spot on the wall and leans over the step. "Don't be so sure. Things are not always what they seem in a dungeon." He rubs his eyes with both hands and sniffs. "These felines look evil and suspicious to me."

Skookum squeals and ducks under Slims hat. "Skook agrees with you, Salo." He adjusts the cock of his headwear. "I've never seen anything like this before."

Biff sits down on the step. "Feeding cats brings wealth and good fortune. Does anyone have a treat for them?" Several cats rub against his peg leg as they continue with the flow. "Here, kitty, kitty." He extends his fingers toward a fluffy white Ragamuffin.

The feline sniffs, and then rubs its head against Biff's fingers.

"Awww." Bella kneels next to Biff. "Looks like you found a friend. If a cat gives you a lick, it means she accepts you as a member of her family and establishes territory by marking you with her scent."

Biff pets Fluffy on the back of her head and then under the chin. "This one is very cute."

"*Meow.*" The cat's eyes briefly flash red as it licks Biff's finger.

"She likes me." He grins. "Oh—wait." His finger turns white at the tip and then paleness creeps up his arm. A stiff crackling sounds echoes in the chamber. Biff stands and grabs his shoulder. "A stoning!" he cries. "Cut it off, quick."

Bella pops up. "Riff!"

Without a thought, I draw my sword and bring it down on Biff's upper arm. The blade clanks in rebound, hitting the stone with an ineffective spark.

I'm too late. In the blink of an eye, Biff turns into a white stone statue.

A PARTY MEMBER HAS BEEN STONED!
NAME: Biff Thunderpunch... STONED

The Biff stature stares at us all in horror, unblinking. I stare back, trying to process what just happened. Then I look away, trying and failing to remind myself that he's only an NPC. Not real. Not alive. Yeah…just an NPC.

I'm not very successful.

Slim bites his bottom lip and angles his cane toward the cat pit. "Which one did it?"

I hold my sword out and step to the edge. "It was a fluffy white one." I look into the flowing mix of colors and tails, but I've lost track of the culprit. "It's deep in that mess now."

Slim lowers his head, wipes a hand across his forehead, and looks sadly at our new Biff statue. "Biff always had bad luck with pussy."

"The worst luck." I rest my hand on the statue's shoulder. "So much for that 'Cats are harmless' comment, Hans."

Hans shakes his head. "I was being sarcastic, Riff. Everyone knows all cats want to kill humans. There was a study."

Slim strokes Skookum. "I can tell you for sure that study was wrong. My connection with Skook makes me familiar with all types of felines. Cats are just fine with humans."

"Sure, Slim." Hans walks to the edge of the cat pit. "Just be sure to keep your little neurotic mongrel away from me." He steps down into the room and slowly walks into the furry sea. "Thanks to Biff, we now know these are Sumxu cats. Don't piss them off or let them lick your bare skin."

A MONSTER HAS BEEN IDENTIFIED: The monster 'Sumxu Cat' has been revealed to you by Hans Talhoffer.

This monster is now known to you and your party.

```
SUMXU CAT
LEVEL: 1 (15XP)                          HIT POINTS: 2
ARMOR CLASS: 10                          FREQUENCY:
Rare
NO. APPEARING: 1 – 100+                  DAMAGE: 1-2
SPECIAL ATTACKS: Claws, Lick
SPECIAL DEFENSES: Acute smell, Climb, Hide, Move silently
INTELLIGENCE: Animal  ALIGNMENT: Neutral          SIZE: S
TYPICAL WEAPONING:
DESCRIPTION: A Sumxu Cat appears very much as does a common housecat.
```

I step towards Hans and point a finger. "You knew about this monster and didn't tell us?" I'm about to player kill this guy for real.

"I thought they were regular cats up until the lick." Hans crosses the room to the door on the other side, opens it, and waves us on. "Time management people. Come over."

"I bet he knew," Bella glairs across the room. "I told you about him."

Slim stands beside Biff's statue, presses his hands together in prayer position, and bows. "There are ways to turn stone back to flesh, Riff." He rests a hand on the statue's shoulder. "There are ways."

The squashed face, fat belly cat reappears, gags, hacks, and retches uncomfortably.

I take a step towards the ugly feline. "What's going on with the Cheshire Cat?"

Slim quickly snaps his hand away from Biff's shoulder. "Oh, no." He shields his eyes with a forearm. "Stand back."

The fat belly cat coughs, heaves, and shoots a tube-shaped, wet and hairy clump from its mouth towards Biff's statue. Upon impact, the statue rumbles and then bursts into small chunks and white powder.

Slim steps away from the debris and shakes his head. "There's no coming back from that." He pounds a fist onto the wall. "Damn."

A PARTY MEMBER HAS BEEN KILLED!
NAME: Biff Thunderpunch... DEAD

I shake the message away as quickly as I can. It always bothers me when I lose party members in the game. And this real-life version is even worse. My stomach churns. "I'm sorry, Slim."

"Hey." Hans waves his arms in a frantic crisscross pattern. "Come on. No time to dally."

"Let's go, guys." Bella glances at Biff sadly. "We have to keep moving."

I crack my knuckles and take a cautious step into the pit. "Single file line. Follow me, slowly."

Bella, Slim, and I all make it to the door across the room and look back. Salo has stalled in the middle amongst a dense group of circling cats.

"Just take it slow, Salo." I say. "Don't move forward until they disperse."

He turns around, takes a step sideways, and stumbles. "Aaa-aaa-aaa." He sniffs and wipes a hand across his nose. "So many tails. This is ridiculous." Cats gravitate toward him, rubbing against his legs and purring a deadly song. He looks frantically around the floor in different directions, then rubs his eyes with his fists. "Aaa-aaa-aaa."

Bella grits her teeth. "Is he going to be okay?"

"I guess Salo is more of a dog guy." I watch him spin in a circle and teeter from side to side. "Be patient, Salo. Wait until that pack around you thins out."

R-e-e-r! A cat launches in the air and falls back down into the swirling feline sea.

"Oops, I stepped on a tail." Salo takes two steps forward and stops. His face turns red. "Aaa-aaa-*choo.*" He tips his head back, pinches his nose, and looks around squinting. "I can't take this anymore. Get out of my way you—" He kicks a small calico with maximum force. It flies through the air, splats into the wall, and smears down leaving a streak of blood.

All the cats in the room freeze, their eyes simultaneously flashing red.

"Run Salo, run!" I yell.

One after another the cats jump on Salo, scratching, clawing, and licking at his face.

He steps forward, trips, and falls to the floor with a gurgling sound.

Bella and I step into the room but are met by a line of the room's biggest members. They hiss at us with arched backs and red eyes.

Hans yanks us both back by our shoulders. "Let the NPC die. He's not worth it."

I pull away and draw my sword. "We can save him."

"Too late." Bella turns from the room.

A black cat with silver glowing eyes stares at us from atop Salo's white prone statue.

A PARTY MEMBER HAS BEEN STONED!

NAME: Salo Fatback… STONED

"Pfft." Hans glances at the statue and turns around. "Now that's just cat-astrophic."

A cacophony of heaving sounds fills the room.

Slim pulls a small metal flask from his belt and dips it towards Salo's statue. "To a certified, stand-up fighter." He takes a swig.

Unsightly clumps of hair surrounded by bile and stomach fluids pelt Salo's statue from all around the room. A few seconds later the statue bursts, sending the black cat halfway to the ceiling before dropping down into a cloud of white powder and scattering tails.

A PARTY MEMBER HAS BEEN KILLED!
NAME: Salo Fatback... DEAD

I try to look through the dusty fog of the cat room. "Damn." My stomach churns worse than before. He's only an NPC, I once again try to remind myself. Not real. Not alive. Man...this sucks.

"Oh." Bella runs a hand across her forehead and blows out a breath. "Look, we have less than an hour before the servers are terminated." She flicks her thumb and a flame appears atop it. "We've got to stay composed."

Bella's right, I need to keep it together. "Okay, team." I relight the lantern with her fire, take a deep breath, and wave what remains of my party into a huddle. "I need everyone to remember everything you have ever learned about this dungeon. We need at least four party members alive to awaken the goblin, which means we can't lose anyone else. We also need at least one party member to be at level five, and that would be me. So, we can't lose me. This cat room was not in the game. I am sure there are going to be more surprises to deal with in this final stretch. So, keep your mind at its highest level of awareness."

Skookum squeals and points her nose back to the cats.

Slim kneels down and lays a hand flat on the ground. "The floor is rumbling. Something's coming our way. I am going to say a squad of six to twelve."

"Six to twelve what?" Bella asks.

"I couldn't tell you." Slim removes his hand from the floor. "They are making good time, though. Maybe Setan's Evon guard."

I turn my attention to the dark stone-lined tunnel ahead. "Let's go in." I draw my sword. "Awareness. Be ready."

After a few steps down the hall, I feel a crunch under my boot, and lift my foot to see a half-smashed bone. Piles of bones line the sidewalls. I look at Bella and Hans. "The scattered bone corridor. We are close now."

The four of us kick aside bones for the next ten minutes, then make it to a flight of stairs. This one leads down into a hazy damp corridor. I wave away the mist, step down, and watch my boot sink into an inch of thick sludge. This stuff looked green on my computer screen in the dorm. Here, in real life, it's an ugly brownish red.

Bella steps down into the sludge behind me. "Yuck. Playing this area of the game at home gives no justice to the smell. It's awful."

Slim puts the tip of his shoe in and yanks it out. "This is going to be murder on my dragon skins."

Hans pushes Slim aside, steps into the mess, slips, and saves himself by dropping a hand down into the sludge. "Scheiße."

I look back and smile. "It's slippery in here."

Hans stands, coughs, gags, and flicks the muck off his hand onto the sidewall. "Smells like someone dumped a bucket of cat piss into a porta-potty."

"Look." I point to a slight green glow flickering far ahead of us. "That's gotta be Setan's door." I take a few steps forward and turn to the party. "Final stretch." I pinch my nose. "Grin and bear it."

It takes ten more precious minutes to trudge through the mess. We finally take a few steps up out of the goop. I scrape my boots mostly clean on a stair edge and focus down the hall. "Just a short distance to the glow."

As we continue, the doorway grows brighter and the mist dissipates. Soon, we step through an open archway into a stone-walled room containing nothing but a large glowing green door.

"This is it." I set down the lantern and inspect the door in front of me. Just like in the game, it is heavy oak with iron bands and has a small square peek-hatch in its upper middle surrounded by the four signature ring knockers. "Setan's door."

Bella lights all four of the room's wall torches and stands next to me. "We're here."

Bella, Hans, and my Grimoire all simultaneously vibrate.

WELCOME TO THE MONSTER ALLOCATION CHAMBER

Now, there is a familiar message.

"Finally." Bella sighs, approaching the door and laying her hands on the iron bands. "That's the message I've been waiting for. Let's get to it."

I step to the door and lay my hand on one of its ice-cold iron bands. "Wow." I can't believe I'm touching the goblin's door.

Suddenly, I'm focused and right back to my dorm room routine. It's time to take inventory before the final battle. We have only four party members left, and we're far from being maxed out on hit points and armor class. Bella has some magic for the smoke, but not much else. Hans has a plethora of spells at his disposal, including what he says is a level-four ringer. Slim, hopefully, can hit for some damage and has Skook to boot. So, this is far from a no-damage run, and a lot less than I am used to having before taking on Setan. I do have something I have never had before though—the Keris.

I drop my pack and kick off my regular boots, trying not to think of Biff as I take his off. "Time for some real kicks." I step into the Bombardment Boots and run in place.

EQUIP CHARACTER *Jareth:* **Bombardment Boots + (1) Charge.**

"Soft and comfy, just like my slippers at home." I place my hand on the square peek-hatch and look back at the party. "It's about to get real."

"Stop fangirling, Riff." Hans points to the door and flicks up his hand. "We have less than an hour."

"Right." Hawkwinds cadence. Here we go. I pound on the door with a fist. Three quick, three slow, and one loud pound. The green glow force shield fades from the door but rises behind us, blocking any retreat.

Slim holds a hand to the rear force shield. "At least we're protected from the oncoming mob."

"Way to be an optimist," I mutter.

TASK COMPLETE: **Take down The Monster Allocation Chamber force shield.**

For completing the task you earned 200 experience points!

NEW TASK: **Kill the Greater Hobgoblin Warlord Setan Kober.**

My Grimoire vibrates wildly. I drop a hand over it to keep it in its sheath. "Whoa, calm down already." Is this some sort of extra info? Having never entered this chamber with a Grimoire before, I have to hope it's a bonus of living out the game. But when I look at Bella to see if her Grimoire is doing the same, she just shrugs. Neither hers nor Hans's Grimoire are reacting.

Maybe it's a captain thing.

I pull my Grimoire from its sheath and flip it open.

INCOMING VIDEO CHAT FROM:

MACK JENKINS

TOUCH HERE TO ANSWER

●

"What the—?" I touch the dot and come face-to-face with Mack on my screen. He is sitting in the server room back in The DCQ Players Den. "Mack, how—"

"I'm contacting you through a Grimoire I got from some kid in the bar." He wipes sweat from his brow and peers intently into the screen. "You have a party of toad-fish men and weird humanoids storming in your direction. On top of that, the servers are about to be shut down and leave you dead. With Anton's help, I opened a developer debug menu that includes a sequence to open a couple of portals in the room you're in right now. One will get you all back home."

"Wait!" Anton appears from behind Mack's shoulder and pushes his way into view. "Riff, you still have time to kill Setan. You can still save the—"

"I'm initiating the cheat." The clatter of Mack's fingers on the keyboard echoes like gunfire in our chamber. "You gotta get out of there, now. Two portals will open, one on either side of the corridor. Jump into the one that shows The DCQ Den." He punches a finger down on the DCQ server keyboard in front of him. "Get through as soon as you can. I don't know how long the portal will hold."

"Wait!" Anton's face fills my screen. "These same portals already exist inside of Setan's chamber. You can get in there, kill the beast, save the game, and still make it home." He moves his head in even closer and looks from side to side. "Where's Bella? Talk to her. She knows. Save the game."

I'm having trouble keeping up. I was so focused on the upcoming battle, it is surreal to be ripped out of the mindset of the game and back into reality. A portal. We could get out of this thing alive.

Mack comes back into view. "Riff, you know that beast is an unbeatable glitch. Get out of there before the game is shut down and you die. Initiating portal cheat now."

Two ocean blue swirls appear on parallel walls. The first one reveals The Stag and Hen Tavern back in Chittor. Hans's brunette lady friend is sitting at a table between two hooded men with her head down.

Hans holds a hand up to the Chittor portal and looks in. "Karalina."

The second portal swirls open on the adjacent wall. Inside Mack and Anton are staring at a flat panel screen in the DCQ Den.

"I should have known never to trust a Compass-Keeper," Slim growls. "We had a deal. You can't just portal out of here. The fight with Setan has to happen. I have a family member in that chamber."

It's a tough call. Slim and I do have a deal. But he didn't give a lick about us until someone he cared about was at stake. And he's an NPC. And I don't want to die. There's really no choice. No game is worth a person's—a *real* person's—life. I take Bella's hand and step to The DCQ Den portal.

She rips her hand from mine. "You have the Keris, Riff. We can do this." Her eyes blaze with a fierce fire. "Anton is right. A portal leading back The

DCQ Den exists inside the chamber, just like I told you before we started this quest. We can save the game."

CHAPTER 18

Does Bella *want* to die? Or could she possibly—just possibly—love this game as much as I do? We stand at a stalemate in front of the portals, frozen in silence. She's waiting for me to decide.

"You know, they love me here." Hans pushes past Bella and I and steps one foot inside the Stag and Hen Tavern portal.

"Wait!" I reach for him. "Why would you stay in the game? You'll die if we don't defeat the goblin."

Hans looks down at his legs, then back up at us. "At home, I'm paralyzed from the waist down. There's no way I'm going back to that, and there's no way in hell I'm fighting that unbeatable glitch goblin. This game is the reality I want. Here, I am a man. No, I'm *the* man. I'm living my life in the cloud."

"But we need you—"

He steps through the portal and disappears.

I reach to grab him, but the Chittor portal swirls closed behind him.

The green force shield lifts from behind us and envelops the goblin's door once more. We need four party members to keep that shield neutralized, and we're down to three.

"That's not good." Slim gestures behind us. "There are monsters on the way with nothing to stop them. And we're backed up against a dead-end."

"Damn it." My party is falling apart. And so is my plan.

> NEW TASK: **Take down The Monster Allocation Chamber force shield.**
>
> *Use Hawkwinds Cadence to take down the chambers force shield.*

I lean my back against the wall and slide to floor. "There is no way to get in and save the game without Hans," I groan.

Bella clasps her hands. "That evil son of a—"

"Hey." Mack's voice cracks through my Grimoire. "Take the portal before it closes. Riff, get out of there now!"

Bella skids to the glowing green door, raises a fist, and knocks. Three quick, three slow, and one loud pound. The force shield doesn't so much as flicker. "Damn you, Hans." She looks at me with glassy eyes and clenched fists. "There's got to be another way in."

"There isn't." I stand back up and move toward The DCQ Den portal.

Bella runs to me and wraps her arms around me in a squeezing hug. "Please, don't give up. I can't explain right now, but we have to get in that room. There is more at stake here than just a game, Riff. Trust me, please. We must get in there and kill Setan."

The look in Bella's eyes reminds me of myself pleading with the school counsel to let me keep my scholarship—only ten times more desperate. What she's asking for means the world to her.

"I want to save the game too." I move a piece of stray hair out of her eyes. "But without four party members, it's impossible."

Or is it?

Slim takes a defensive stance at the room's rear archway and looks down the hall. "You need to do something fast or prepare for the onslaught coming this way."

I hold up my Grimoire and look at Mack sitting in The DCQ Den portal. "Mack, I need you in here. Let's show this goblin how the brothers Jenkins get down."

Mack's lips tighten. "You want me in there? To fight the glitch?"

"We need four questers to open this door." He has to do this for me. After all the free rent and, at times, free Chinese food I've bought him. "This is your chance to be one of the few gamers to experience full immersion virtual reality. We are walking on the moon here, Mack. This is team Jenkins. I need you in here."

"Go on." Anton points a finger at the portal. "I'll take care of things on this end. Bella knows what she's talking about. There will be portals on the other side of the door you can use to get back here. I'm sure of it."

"I. Could. *Die.*" Nonetheless, Mack drops his Grimoire into a gaming station cradle and turns to the portal. I grin at him as he approaches, and he grins back. "I haven't used my DCQ character for a long time," he says. "Lucky for you I'm a sucker for a damsel in distress." He jumps into the portal and appears in front of me on shaky legs.

I wrap my arms around him and give him a gigantic bear hug as the portal swirls to a close. "It's the return of the Mack," I say. "I knew I could count on you."

"Bro, why I continue to put my neck on the line for you is beyond my capacity." He stumbles a bit when I release him, but steadies himself against the wall. He's handling the teleportation far better than I did.

Bella gives Mack a hug, then stands back with a smile. "I—"

"Your name is Madmartigan." Mack holds a palm to his forehead and blinks. "I like this version of you way better than your avatar." He looks down at his leather armor, and careens into a wall as his Grimoire buzzes from its sheath at his belt. "This is weird," he mutters, pulling it out.

"You have zero time to get used to this," I say, zoning back in on the mission. "How did you get into The DCQ Den?"

Mack flips over his Grimoire and runs a finger across the back. "Unit number six of six is how. A square kid came into the Spirit & Game with this after you left." He sheathes the Grimoire and smiles. "He was too scared to enter the den, so I talked him into giving me his Grimoire and coin. I had to see what was up after you were gone for so long. Besides, I was out of drink tickets. And once I got in the server room, Anton gave me a rundown."

Slim pushes past all three of us to goblin's door and raises a fist. "You all talk way too much." He gives the Hawkwinds Cadence knock and the force shield lowers, rising at the rear entrance once again. "Much better." He nods, glancing at the shield with relief in his eyes. "We're safe from whatever is coming behind us. For now."

I look over my new party. "Mack." I hand him my dagger. "Acquaint yourself with this quick."

He grips the weapon and works his wrist left and right. "Nice! Instant thief abilities. I should be good."

"Bella,"—I turn to her—"nuke the goblin with the best spell you have, but be ready. Once I get a critical hit on him, he is sure to evoke the killer smoke. Dissipating the smoke is your highest priority."

She cracks her knuckles. "I'm ready."

"Slim, you know a lot about Setan, so give him your best shot. If Skookum has something nasty for him, that's all good too."

Slim raises his cane. "Oh, the beast is about to have a big problem coming his way." Skookum digs into Slim's shoulder, steadies herself, and eyes the door, unblinking.

"Here we go then." I look down at my Bombardment Boots. "I hope the charge in these things has what it takes." The Keris vibrates, nearly popping out of its sheath. I snatch it into my hand and take a few thrusts, dipping from left to right as a pulse runs up my arm, invigorating my body.

NEW PRIMARY WEAPON: **Keris Of Knaud + (4) Charge.** *Distinguished Hack.*

"How does it feel?" Bella asks.

I flip the blade up in the air, spin, and then catch it on the way down. "Feels like supernatural power and extraordinary ability. I'm ready." But still need one last status check.

NAME: Jareth Goblinmasher   *AGE:* 22

LEVEL: 5   *EXPERIENCE POINTS:* 7,093

HIT POINTS: *16/48*

ABILITIES: *63*

ARMOR CLASS: *4/40*

Leather Armor, Small Shield, Bombardment Boots + (1)

GOLD COINS: *0*

SILVER PENNIES: *18*

SPELLS: *N/A*

PRIMARY WEAPON: *Keris Of Knaud + (4) Charge. Distinguished Hack.*
(Soulbound)

Executioner's Sword

POSSESSIONS: *Grimoire (5 of 6), Map+3, Heavynessless Bag, Perfect Placement Belt, Small Backpack, Flask of Oil, (10) Single Day's Rations, Water Skin, The Routier's Rest Rumor Table Scroll, Emerald Gemstone, *Lute + (7) Charm person. (Soulbound) *Location: Mad Cobblers shop – Cittadella*

RACE: *Human*   **CLASS:** *Fighter*   **ALIGNMENT:** *Good*

TASKS: *Kill the Greater Hobgoblin Warlord Setan Kober.*

00:23:04 hours until DCQ server shut down.

Twenty-three minutes and sixteen hit points to get this done. I glance back at my team. Oddly enough, with two dead and one ditched, I feel more confident about the three questers in front of me than I did about the rest of the team I'd been playing with.

Bella, Slim, Mack...they all *wanted* to be here. And that's how victory starts.

I step to the door and watch the upper left knocker morph into the grotesque head I have seen numerous times on my computer screen in the dorm. "There it is." I wrap my hand around the brass ring in the head's mouth and raise it up, then slam it down with one clobbering boom.

S-w-a-c-k! The peek-hatch immediately snaps open.

"Woah." I jump back and hold my breath.

A bloodshot florescent yellow cat-eye appears behind the hatch grill and eyeballs each one of us. "Provide the password, flee, or fight." The deep croak causes the chamber to rumble.

"Um." Here goes nothing. "One, two, six, four."

The eye narrows. "Muahahahaha, that's not it, boy. But because I'm amused, I'll give you one more try."

I take another step back, picture the goblin's weak spot in my head, and grip the Keris. I already know Setan gives three guesses at the password. At this point I just want to fight. "Can someone here please tell this ugly Norman Osborn-wannabe the password?"

"Bandos." Bella says flatly.

"Gigglegibber." Mack says.

"Grrrach." The eye smashes into the grill and bulges. "Three of you are Compass-Keepers, I see. This smacks of Kurht's work. I am sure he sent you. Enter my chamber, and the lot of you will be decapitated. I'll piss in your eye sockets and smash your skulls into pig slop." He looks past us to the shielded hall. "Your party is not worth my time. I'll have my minions deal with you."

The peek-hatch slams shut and the force shield behind us lowers at the arch.

"Not this again," Slim says.

I look back into the corridor. "How much longer until the mob comes?"

A-a-a-a-a! Evons and Liergarnin spill into the hazy corridor at the end of the hall and raise their weapons. They fall over each other, holler, and grunt at the top of their lungs as they kick up sludge toward us.

Slim steps to the arch and wraps a palm around his cane's head. "Okay, Bella and Mack. I'm gonna need help holding these guys off. Riff, handle that goblin. Quick."

Go time. I grip the Keris. "Deeznuts!" I sprint at the door, jump in the air, and drive both boots into its center. "Bomb baby!"

Boom! The door crashes down and I jump on it as it slides forward, riding it into Setan's cell like it's a snowboard.

When I jump off, he's staring me down from the center of the torch lit room, his legs spread apart. He is a giant humanoid twice my size wearing shaped plate and leather armor. His face is saggy, with pale olive green-skin, brownish matted hair, and pointy ears.

The game developers didn't capture half his ugliness in the on-screen version. This thing is *rancid.*

Setan picks up a long oak haft with a double spiked iron block on its end from a wooden table and raises it above his head. "Grrrach." He swings the hammer my direction in a crossing swoosh.

I duck under the blow, raise my blade, and run forward. "Distinguished"—I thrust my blade down across his knee—"hack!" The Keris cuts down to the goblin's bone and blood spurts everywhere. Didn't cut all the way through, but at least my blade didn't snap.

The beast punches me with its left fist, sending me backward and to the ground. The Keris flies out of my hand and slides across the floor to the rear wall.

THE GREATER HOBGOBLIN WARLORD SETAN KOBER

LEVEL: 6 (6000XP) **HIT POINTS:** 65

ARMOR CLASS: 14 (Half plate) **FREQUENCY:** Error

NO. APPEARING: 1 **DAMAGE:** By weapon

SPECIAL ATTACKS: Rending

SPECIAL DEFENSES: Parry

INTELLIGENCE: High **ALIGNMENT:** Neutral **SIZE:** L

TYPICAL WEAPONING: Longsword, Javelin, Greathammer

DESCRIPTION: A large, black-hearted humanoid with olive green skin, brown matted hair, and pointy ears.

Setan wraps his clammy fingers around my throat and lifts me up. "Time to die Compass-Keeper." He tightens his grip and raises the hammer's iron block. "I sentence you to death by bludgeoning."

"*Jacto Saxum.*" Bella plants herself in the doorway and a jagged basketball-sized rock shoots from beyond the door and slams into the upper right section of the goblin's forehead.

"Grrraaaa." The monster drops me and steps back, clutching his head. "Bwaaaaa."

I scramble to my feet, retrieve the Keris, and place a hand against the rear wall to regain my balance. No deadly smoke yet, so that's an improvement. But what's the quickest path to another stab at that knee?

"*Jacto Saxum. Jacto Saxum.*" Bella steps in the room twirling her fingers at Setan. Two rocks whisk out and hurl towards the creature's cranium.

Setan snatches the first stone in a palm and deflects the second one off with it. He then crushes the rock to bits in his massive fist. "Never a second time."

228

He places one hand on the wooden table and launches it at Bella. "Break you with the rack, wench."

Bella dives out of the way just as the table slams into the doorjamb and shatters into planks.

With Setan distracted, I run forward. *Come on distinguished.* I thrust the Keris back across his blood-soaked knee. "Hack!" This time it slices completely through, cutting muscle and bone, warm blood gushing over my hand.

"Buh-wooo." Setan bellows and slams backward into the chamber's rear wall. "Grrr-ach." He crashes on his rear, causing the whole room to shudder at the impact. "The expansion will never come to life, questing scum." He swoops the hammer around and snaps his wrist sending it upward where a spike lodges into the ceiling above his head. "Die Compass-Keeper."

Dark smoke billows down from where the hammer's spike pierces the ceiling. It completely envelops the goblin and continues to fill the room, rolling my direction.

I step to the rear wall, and glance back through the door. Mack and Slim are double-teaming the last standing monster in the room, a large Evon, while stepping over numerous dead bodies on the floor. "Bella, it's time!" I call.

She stumbles to the doorjamb from the right. She's out of breath, but she drops to a knee and raises a hand, chanting, "*Patet in dregs aer.*" A bolt flashes from her finger into the dark smoke. "*Discutio vapos, discutio vapos, discutio vapos.*"

The cloud flashes white and collapses in on itself, leaving the room clear of everything but a pile of tattered rags where the goblin last sat.

"You did it." I almost don't believe it. I help her up and look into her eyes. "We killed Setan."

She nods her head and points to the back of the room. Six evenly-spaced iron jail-cell doors appear along the rear wall.

229

"What the—" My Retina display interrupts my view.

TASK COMPLETE: **Kill the Greater Hobgoblin Warlord Setan Kober**

The Greater Hobgoblin Warlord Setan Kober has been killed! For killing the monster each survivor earned 1500 experience points.

Liergarnin (2) has been killed! For killing the monsters each survivor earned 100 experience points.

Evon (4) has been killed! For killing the monsters each survivor earned 240 experience points.

A WEAPONS STATUS HAS CHANGED: Your weapon 'The Keris of Knaud + (4) Charge' has been changed to 'The Keris of Knaud + (2) Charge'

IN-GAME MODERATOR (» - MOD) MODE UNLOCKED!
You have been granted access to technical details and special tools. (»)

You were hit for 8 damage. Status: 8/48

NEW TASK: **Enter The Kingdom of Broxington.**
The DCQ expansion 'The Kingdom of Broxington' is now open for play! Enter at your own risk.

PARTY STATUS: Multiple members' status has changed.

REORDER THE PARTY: **Yes/No?**

Slim limps into the room. He has a bloody slash in his trousers running from hip to knee. "You got him." He stands over the pile of rags. And blinks once. Twice.

"Someone got you." I move his direction. "Are you okay?"

He nods and waves me off. "It's nothing, and well worth seeing Setan killed. I'll be fine."

Mack follows Slim into the room and hands me my pack. "You should have seen me out there, Riff!" He slaps me on the back. "I ended three of those Evon monsters. I leveled up too. There's a player sheet in my vision. This is amazing!" He wipes both sides of his dagger on his pants, leaving a smear of blood, then sheathes it and looks around the chamber. "What happened in here?"

I toss the pack over my shoulder. "Well." I step to the pile of rags and flatten it out, feeling a small solid lump under one pile. "I just whooped ol' boy up, that's what happened. I told you there was a way to kill the greater goblin."

Mack twists a lock of his hair. "I guess I'll eat my words then. You'll get no more glitch talk from me."

"What do we have here?" I dig under the rags and pull out a Grimoire. "How did he get this?" I check the back. "It says unit one of six."

Bella takes the Grimoire from my hand. "This was not Setan's." She runs to the first cell door on the right and looks between the bars. "He stole it." She moves to the next cell, grips the bars and looks inside. "Hello?" She steps back and raises a hand. "*Aperire cincinno.*"

The cell door swings open, and she runs in.

Skookum hops across the floor, dives between the bars of the first cell, and disappears into the darkness.

Slim pulls a small twisted pick from his belt and fast limps after Skook to the first cell door. He works the tool into the lock, twists it, and swings the door open.

The three cell doors to the left slowly twist and morph into colorful portal swirls.

I tap Mack's shoulder and step in close to inspect them. "Bella and Anton were right about portals being in here. But what's the extra one?"

The first portal shows The Stag and Hen Tavern in Chittor. Inside, Hans stands with his brunette lady friend. They both raise drinks in a circle of smiling NPCs.

I barely resist the temptation to jump through and strangle him.

The next portal shows The DCQ Den at the Spirit & Game. Anton is pushing a man in a black sport coat away from the DCQ world server.

"Look." I point into the swirl. "What the hell is going on in there?"

"Trouble." Mack steps in close. "Let's get home before this thing closes up."

The third portal opens even wider and clearer than the other two. It reminds me of the difference between an old tube style TV, and a high definition, crystal clear 4K Ultra HD one. Inside, a narrow dirt path leads down a hill into a lushly forested valley.

I step to the green valley portal and stare in. "Mack, this has got to be—"

"—the DCQ expansion world," says a deep voice behind me.

I turn to see a scruffy-faced man wearing a robe and slumped cone hat. "That is The Kingdom of Broxington."

I step forward and look at him. "I recognize you from the back of my DCQ instruction manual. You're the Dungeon Crawl Quest developer. Kurht. You're not dead."

Bella hugs Kurht. "No, he's not dead. Riff, this is my dad."

The man holds an open hand my way. "I'm Kurht Knaud, and you must be Riff 'Jareth Goblinmasher' Jenkins. Thank you all for getting me out of that cell."

I shake Kurht's hand and turn to Bella. "Your *dad* is the DCQ developer? Why didn't you tell me?"

"Not everyone I meet appreciates him the way I do." Bella looks up at her father and smiles. "Some hate him because they think he created a glitch-ridden game, others because they believe he is a sloppy programmer. There is so much bad blood surrounding DCQ in the gamer community that I just couldn't take the chance. I was afraid you wouldn't help me."

Mack winks at me and shakes Kurht's hand. "I'm Riff's brother, Mack. It is hard to believe how some gamers act. For me, it's a pleasure to meet a fellow programmer. I'm the one who found your debug menu, by the way."

Slim limps our way with a sniffer on each shoulder. "Hey everybody, I want you to meet a business associate, and close family member of mine." He scratches the sniffer on his right shoulder under its chin. It is identical to Skookum in color, but skinny, soiled, and without the spade tipped tail. "Meet Mustella, Skook's half-sister. She's hungry and needs a bath, but other than that, she's all good." A huge smile crosses his face. "Thank you team Goblinmasher."

"Thank you, Slim," Bella says. "And you too, Skookum. Both of you fought well in the chamber back there."

"I remember you from the tavern back in Chittor." Kurht shakes Slim's hand and pets Mustella on the top of her head. "Your sniffer here was great company as a cell neighbor. She has some amazing stories of your quests. The one about how you killed the three-headed cockatrice kept me in good spirits for days. With a little more time, I'm sure we would have concocted a way out of here."

"She's very clever," Slim says. "And talkative. I'm glad to have her back."

"I have something for your injury." Kurht wraps his hands around Slim's leg. "*Medicor summus seco.*" The wounded area flashes and he removes his hands. "Thank you for fighting alongside my daughter."

Slim stretches his leg. "It's always a pleasure to get healed by a great wizard."

The room rumbles, drops an inch, and shifts back and forth with a shake.

"Time to make our move out of here," Kurht says. "The expansion world portal is about to fuse with the chamber. Once it does, the new world will officially be open for all to play."

I shake Slim's hand and pull him in for a hug. "Thanks for everything, player." I rip my bag from my belt and put it in his hand. "There are a few silver pennies in here, and a gem that should get you off to a good start."

SUBTRACT: 18 silver pennies to Gregarious Slim. New silver penny balance: 0

SUBTRACT: 1 Emerald Gemstone to Gregarious Slim.

SUBTRACT: 1 Heavynessless Bag to Gregarious Slim.

He struts to the expansion portal entrance. "Thank you, Riff. My sniffers and I are about to be the first questers in the new world. Just wait till they get a load of us." He removes his hat and plops it down on my head. "Don't stop playing that guitar."

ADD POSSESSION: **Brim of Profound Musicianship**

Wearing this hat enhances the ability to play all musical instruments.

Mack gives Slim a fist bump and pats the sniffers. "I hate to cut this goodbye short. But, uh,"— he points into The DCQ Den portal—"Anton told me this was going to happen."

I look into the portal and watch the man wearing the black sport coat grab Anton by the collar and toss him to the server room floor. "Who is that?" I blurt.

"That's a Blizivision Studio exec," Mack says. "We need to get in there before he shuts the server down, and we die."

"What?" Kurht steps to the portal. "I'll kill that greedy Blizivision bastard."

"Clearly nasty Compass-Keeper business." Slim shakes his head. "You all handle that. I'll see you in the new world." He steps into The Kingdom of Broxington portal.

As he disappears, I can't help but be jealous. I really wanted to be the first one in there. *Warm it up for me Slim, I will be joining you as soon as I can.*

The room seems to drop out from under us, shaking and rumbling.

"Let's go." Kurht grabs Bella's hand. "We all need to step through at the same time."

I take the spot alongside Bella and ready my feet. Mack stands next to me and nods. "Yeah, let's go."

Kurht looks down the line. "On the count of three." He stares into the portal. "One, two, three."

LEAVING THE WORLD OF DUNGEON CRAWL QUEST.
Saving character and game progress. Please wait...

CHAPTER 19

I step into the portal and am enveloped in complete darkness. This better work.

BAM! A door blasts open in front of me. The DCQ Players Den. I look down and pat my chest. I have my normal clothes back. We're home.

Kurht charges ahead into the dimly lit room "Not today!" He throws a right cross into the jaw of the man wearing the black sport coat.

The man falls back into the server rack, shaking his head. "What the hell, man?"

Anton slowly gets up from the floor. "Kurht, you're alive!"

"And kicking." Kurht raises both fists, ready to pound the sport coat guy again, if need be. "I want everyone to meet my back-stabbing, ex-program and design partner, Asheron Paragon."

"Kurht." The man's eyes grow wide. "I—you—so glad to see you again, old friend."

"Old friend?" Rage flashes across Kurht's face. "No." He shakes his head. "A friend doesn't trick someone into signing a horrible contract and force them to release a game before it is done. That's why I had to create Setan. To ensure only the best gamer would be able to enter the unfinished area called The Kingdom of Broxington."

Asheron is only half-listening. He keeps glancing at his watch. Maybe he's hoping to escape, but if I can defeat Setan, I'm certainly not letting him past me.

"An old friend," Kurht goes on, "wouldn't have reprogrammed Setan to imprison me while I was on my final beta-test run inside the game, so he could let the game fail and the contract terminate." Kurht turns to the rest of us. "With no contract, and me dead, this sniveling trogg was going to take all the credit and riches for my full-immersion technology."

Asheron glances down at his watch. "No *was* about it." His lip curls. "You're too late, Kurht. Blizivision will be shutting down your servers at midnight. The contract is iron clad, and the shutdown is automatic if subscription numbers are not above a quarter million. Can you say Warhammer Online? You're nothing but a failed MMO ho. All things DCQ default to me in three minutes."

"Maybe not." Bella holds out her Grimoire to Kurht. "Daddy, look. Opening the expansion has boosted subscriptions numbers. They're rising fast. We're already over two-hundred-thousand."

What is she looking at? I don't remember seeing data like that on any of my screens. I pop open my Grimoire.

●

New stuff, including a subscriber count. DCQ is in the midst of a massive comeback. Subscription numbers climb by the second.

"No." Asheron reaches into his suit jacket, pulls out a Grimoire, and flips it open. "These can't be legitimate numbers. They can't be."

Kurht smacks Asheron's Grimoire out of his hand, wraps his fingers around his neck, and presses him against the server rack. "There are over five million DCQ accounts, you dirty son of a bitch. I had an automatic advertising blast set up to go live when the expansion launched. We're coming back like *Return of the Jedi*."

For a minute, I'm afraid Kurht is going to kill his old partner in front of our eyes, but then I realize he's not squeezing—just holding the guy there until midnight hits and it's all over, either way.

Mack sits down at a game station and inserts his Grimoire. "Two minutes to go. I'm about to re-up my damn self."

Bella sits at a station next to Mack and holds her Grimoire up next to his monitor. "It's going to be close. If the game is still playable after midnight, we did it."

Kurht is still staring down Asheron. "Keep me updated."

I pick up Asheron's fallen Grimoire and check the back.

Unit 2 of 6

I glare at Asheron. "You know there's still a real player inside the game. If this thing goes dark, his blood is on your hands."

"Sixty seconds till midnight," Mack says. "Less than a hundred subscriptions to go."

I clutch my Grimoire and watch the numbers tick. Tock. Tick. Tock.

So close.

"Thirty seconds," Mack says, tension now in his voice.

With every click of the seconds I picture gamers everywhere getting a notification about the new DCQ expansion. I picture them crawling out of bed, turning on their monitors, and giving DCQ another chance—the chance it deserves.

"Five...four...three...two..."

The subscriber number rolls past 250,001 just before midnight strikes. I lean over Mack's chair and check his screen. "The game is still live." I release a gust of air. "I haven't seen this many users logged on since the North Cave expansion launched."

Bella jumps up and gives a whoop so loud it echoes in my skull. "We did it. We saved the game."

And Hans. And Kurht.

239

"Yes sir." Anton steps to the wall near The DCQ Den door and pounds a fist on its upper corner. The door pops open letting in the boisterous sound of music and lively bar chatter. "Time for him to go." He gestures to Asheron.

Kurht releases his nemesis, spins him toward the door, and kicks him in the butt. "If I see you again, you're dead."

Asheron shoots out of the door with a hand on his rear.

"I'll make sure this trash gets to the street." Anton follows Asheron into the bar and closes the door behind him.

Kurht views his Grimoire with a smile. "Very nice. We are at an all-time subscription high, thanks to you questers." He drops the Grimoire in a trouser pocket and looks the server rack up and down.

I wave Mack over and stand alongside Kurht. Somehow, I was just inside this thing. "So, what's the secret? How do you pull off the full immersion? It's incredible."

"You gotta have vision." He hooks his thumbs in his pockets, beaming. "Others utilize senses and fool the brain into believing that the 'virtual' is the 'actual'. Not in my system. I take you in there for real. No clumsy goggles strapped to your head or brain-machine interface helmets needed. My link between man and machine is comfortable and totally non-invasive. I have found a seamless way to interact with computers using the Grimoire."

He looks at Mack and me, then taps the side of his head. "Get your brain right. I'm going to go deep on you. The Grimoire combines the end user's character with their real DNA. That's what happens when you touch the red dot. After that, syncing the Grimoire into one of my game stations transports the player into the game world."

He takes in a deep breath and hold up two fingers. "Two things. First, is the phenomenon of human consciousness and dreams. Second, there are forces of nature going on here that even I can't fully explain."

Bella gently lays her palm on the server's glass box containing the green glowing stone. "You can explain a little, Daddy."

Kurht puts his palm on the glass next to Bella's and kisses her on the forehead. "This is one of several fragments from a meteor that entered Earth's atmosphere and exploded over Chelyabinsk, Russia. Anton acquired it from his mother who was somehow able to hide it away from the Russian Council of Ministers. This hunk of rock is actually an artifact with some really powerful elements. A small sliver of it resides in each Grimoire."

Kurht rubs his chin. "I am afraid to think of what those Russian hackers could do if they were able to make the fragment-to-computer connection the way I have."

Mack moves closer to the glass box. "They might find a way to hack into election mainframes or something."

Kurht shakes his head. "Enough about science and ancient alien artifacts. If I tell you any more, I will have to kill you."

"Really, Dad." Bella sighs.

"This has to be one of the most amazing feats in engineering history," I say.

"I've just scratched the surface." Kurht pounds on the wall opening the door. "And I'd say it's high time for a celebratory drink. You two helped save my life in more ways than one." He puts one hand on Mack's shoulder and one on mine. "And don't worry about a designated driver. A ride home with Uber Black is on me."

"Right on," I say, but as nice as that sounded, a small part of me couldn't help but think walking through a beast-infested forest while in mismatched boots sounded even better. I already missed living the game.

"But our dorm is all the way in San Diego," Mack says. "And what about my car?"

"Don't worry." Kurht bounces into the hallway. "I have unlimited gold business status with Uber, Mack. And I'll have one of my people bring your car down to you tomorrow, washed and waxed. Nothing is going to stop tonight's celebration. Plus, I want to hear all about how you found the debug menu. You know I only baked that portal in so I can test later parts of the game without playing through the whole story. You're good, Mack."

Kurht goes behind the bar while Bella, Mack, and I plop down on stools in front of him. The room is packed with people from front to back, and all the gaming stations are filled. The DCQ one has a crowd six deep behind it. They raise hands, cheer, and point at the screen.

My stomach twists. The entire world is exploring The Kingdom of Broxington without me, and I made it accessible to them. But my time will come. They may have their screens on, but I had been in the real DCQ world.

Anton returns and holds a ringing cell phone out to Kurht. "It's for you."

Kurht takes the phone and looks at the front. "I missed having this." He scratches the back of his head.

Bella rolls her eyes. "The passcode is one, two, six, four, Dad."

"Thank you, baby." He taps his screen four times, looks down at it and smirks. "I got to take this call. Give me a minute, guys." He walks to the far end of the bar with the phone to his ear.

"One, two, six, four are the pommel numbers." I say low.

"He always forgets his passcode," Bella smiles. "Someone started a rumor that the numbers had something to do with a lottery win. Can you believe some fools thought that was true?"

"Hardly." I blow out a breath and look over at Bella. She is wearing a striped tank top, red skirt, heels, and she looks great. No skimpy leather needed. "So, now I get to meet the real you." I smile at her. "You're even prettier in real life."

She smiles back. "I'm glad to be out of that leather armor and studded tassel thing."

A waitress sets a tray down next to us and leans over the bar. "I need the order for table sixteen, Sid. The tips are good tonight."

A young bartender loads several drinks onto the tray. "You're set."

She weaves into the crowd and points to waving hands. "I got you next. And then you all." The entire interaction feels a bit like one I'd find in a DCQ tavern. Perhaps that is Kurht's intent—to bring a bit of the game world to ours as much as he can.

The young bartender looks at Anton and puts several drinking glasses into a small sink. "We need more staff, Mr. Turishanov. This place is crazy tonight. Did you know we have a line outside?"

"Excuse me my, dude," says a voice behind me. "Aren't you Jareth Goblinmasher?"

Bella looks over her shoulder, then spins on her stool to face the new arrival. "I know you." She tucks hair behind her ear. "You're Ant-bot, the YouTuber."

Mack and I turn around. "Hey, I heard you played here. And yes, I'm Jareth."

He adjusts the clunky, purple-tinted goggles on his forehead. "I've been live streaming commentary on your play through, and my views are off the chart. This has gotta be the best way to launch an expansion I've ever seen. Look around. We've turned this whole midnight promotion thing you're doing into a DCQ expansion launch party."

"You've been live streaming us this whole time?" I ask. "For the last two days?"

"Huh?" Ant-bot looks puzzled.

Anton taps my shoulder from behind the bar. "Time moves slower in the game, Riff."

Oh yeah. It was only midnight here on the same night I'd arrived.

A smooth faced guy with a half-filled mug of beer pulls on Ant-bot's sleeve. "Check it out." He points to the DCQ game station. "You gotta see this new dungeon."

Ant-bot looks at us and holds two fingers up in a peace sign. "I'm a big fan of your questing party. DCQ is back and I love it." He pushes his way into the DCQ game station crowd. "Let me see that dungeon, yo!"

Bella watches him for a moment then turns back to the bar. "That was really Ant-bot. I watch his stuff all the time."

"I know, right?" I spin back to the bar and look over the bottles behind it. My drink just might have to be champagne. "We really did it."

Anton tosses three coasters on the bar. "You name it, you got it. No drink tickets needed for the trio that saved my partner's life and my business. You all got lifetime bottomless cups here."

"All good." Mack points to a curvy crystalline glass decanter on the bar's top shelf. "I'll take a triple Hennessy, Paradis Imperial."

Bella points to a dragon topped tap handle. "I would like an ice cold Southfarthing Frogmorton Ginger Beer, please."

I've always wanted to try Southfarthing. "That sounds refreshing. I'll have the same, Anton."

Bella licks her lips. "Did you know the Spirit & Game is the only U.S. bar with Southfarthing? The only other place you can get it is The Green Dragon Inn on the Hobbiton movie set in New Zealand. Don't laugh, but I think it would be a nice place for a vacation. It's on my bucket list."

Okay, that's it. I'm really starting to fall for this girl. She wants to visit Hobbiton just as much as I do. "You know I've done some research on the Hobbit movie set myself. It does sound cool."

Anton drops two frosty glasses and a snifter on the counter in front on us. "I can use a drink myself." He pours a shot of clear liquid. "*Za zdorovie.*"

Kurht returns to us with a drink already in hand. "That means 'To your health' in Russian, and I agree it's time to celebrate." He raises his glass.

I can't believe I'm about to have a drink with the DCQ creator. I gotta make this good. "It's times like these I like to quote Bilbo Baggins." I raise my glass. "I don't know half of you half as well as I should like, and I like less than half of you half as well as you deserve."

Mack swirls his glass and raises it to ours. "Man, you gotta stop. Tonight, we drink for my main man, Tupac, Prince, and my girl Aaliyah."

"Really, Mack?" Bella shakes her head and puts her glass to mine. "This drink is to the memory of our fallen comrades, Salo Fatback, and the colossal Biff Thunderpunch. Great questers that will always remain in our hearts."

Anton looks over the crowded room and clanks his glass with ours. "To Dungeon Crawl Quest." He swallows the liquid, drops the glass to the counter, and flips open his Grimoire. "Subscription numbers have now exceeded 260,000. The Spirit & Game is going to be in business for a long time."

Kurht finishes his drink, rests an elbow on the bar, and rubs his chin. "Before I went into the game for that final, fateful beta-test, I sent out three packages. One to you Riff, another to Hans, and a third to a kid named Freddie."

"Freddie is the guy who gave me his Grimoire," Mack interjects. "He was a nice guy. Scary, but nice."

Kurht acknowledges Mack with a tilt of his head. "Glad he made that call or we all might be dead." A moment of silent victory hangs between us before he continues. "I wanted one of DCQ's top three gamers to be the first into the expansion. Which brings me to the subject of some reward money. That call I got was from the very happy CEO of Blizivision Studios. He congratulated me on being alive, on the newfound popularity of DCQ, and on my lucrative new contract, which came into effect when the game passed the quarter million subscription mark. And it's a good one this time."

Bella drops her empty glass to the bar and looks at her dad with the widest smile "Yes!"

Anton wraps his arm around Kurht's shoulder and nods his head. "Congratulations."

"There's more good news." He drops a napkin and an ink pen in front of me. "I was asked who to forward a certain large reward to. Riff, I need to know where you're going to be tomorrow afternoon. A Blizivision official would like to present you with a large and well-deserved check. Congratulations, Jarreth Goblinmasher. You won the prize money. You solved the goblin chamber puzzle."

CHAPTER 20

Bang, bang, bang!

I kick off a sheet, roll over, and pull my curtain back a crack. Hot sunlight burns my eyes. I let the fabric go, roll back in bed, and look at the ceiling. Dorm sweet dorm. It's good to be home alive. Alive-for-real-alive.

Bang, bang, bang!

Is that my head throbbing or are the police at my front door? I drop my legs over the edge of the bed, look down, and wiggle my toes. Hmm, I'm wearing the same clothes I had on when I left the Spirit & Game, minus the shoes. What time did I get home last night?

Bang, bang, bang!

I grab my head with both hands. And how much did I drink? Memories and details swirl like an unsettling fog. I feel like I should understand the situation better than I do.

Bang, bang, bang!

Okay, this better be good. Real, real, real, good. I slide on my hobbit foot slippers, open my bedroom door, and head into living room. Mack is passed out on the couch with one hand dangling over the side. "Mack." I kick his hand. "Don't you hear the door? Get up, you half dead sloth."

Bang, bang, bang!

"I'm coming! Stop with the knocking already." I fling the door open and rub the sleep from my eyes. A thin Asian man wearing a gray suit with no tie is standing next to a short, well-dressed bald man.

The short man yanks a pink piece of paper off the door and crumples it up. "Are you Riff Jenkins?"

I nod and the movement feels sluggish.

He looks me up and down once, then proceeds to speak in a professional tone. It seems to take some effort to maintain. "Good morning, Mr. Jenkins. I am Dean Williams, and this gentleman is Shigoshi Kojimoto, co-founder and President of Blizivision Studios. He tells me you solved a glitch that plagued a very popular game his company represents."

Shigoshi holds out an envelope. "This is for you Mr. Jenkins. A check."

The prize money. "Thank you, Sir." I take the envelope. It's thick and weighty in my hand. I point the envelope at the Dean. "It was not a glitch. It was a puzzle that needed to be solved."

Dean Williams rests a hand on Shigoshi's shoulder. "Mr. Kojimoto here has not only made a generous donation to our new Virtual Reality Development and Design program, but he has paid the remainder of your housing and tuition."

"I have more good news," Shigoshi says. "Blizivision would like to offer you a job after graduation. If you accept, we will put you in our Full-Immersion VR division. Your first order of business will be as project manager on a new groundbreaking version of the Dungeon Crawl Quest game you are so familiar with. You will be working hand in hand with Dr. Kurht Knaud."

My jaw drops, and the reaction seems to please Shigoshi. "You know," he continues. "Kurht's knowledge on virtually everything regarding the phenomenon of human consciousness, the senses, and their relationship to the

248

workings of the brain and nervous system are quite incredible. He has successfully combined principles of biology and technology. Our plan is to bring the first Virtual Reality Massively Multiplayer Online Role-Playing Game to life. We want you to be a part of this."

"Damn, you all are loud." Mack yawns and looks over my shoulder. "Did someone say something about a VRMMORPG?"

Shigoshi's eyes light up. "Ah, you must be Mack Jenkins. I was told of your hacking skills. A job offer to work on the DCQ team after graduation awaits you, as well. At Blizivision, we have the experience and technology needed to bring clarity and direction to Dr. Knaud's full dive vision. Together, we will transform his ideas into reality. I look forward to having both of you as part of the company."

I tap the envelope on Mack's shoulder. "It's the design team of Riff and Mack Jenkins, baby."

Mack rakes several dreadlocks away from his face. "What type of things will we be doing with Kurht? I don't want to be nobody's flunky. Technical aspects of productivity software development are my specialty."

"Oh, there are no flunkies at Blizivision," Shigoshi says. "One of your key jobs will be to make sure players that enter live to play another day. Full-dive needs to be a safe reality for everybody. Dr. Knaud has not been so forthcoming on this end."

I step in front of Mack. "Don't bore the man with technical aspects. Everyone knows game design and production is where it's at."

Mack nudges around me. "How much does this job pay, though? Where is my envelope?"

Shigoshi bows. "All the information is in your brother's envelope. Take your time with it. Once again, Congratulations, Riff Jenkins. We will be in touch." He turns and walks down the hall.

The Dean holds out both arms. "I'm proud of you two. We'll get together on this early next week." Sure, sure. How convenient of him to forget all our misdeeds now that we brought his department some money. I grin, enjoying my new status as favorite student and rich gamer. The Dean drops his arms and looks at us closely. "Now, go get some rest. You both look like hell."

Mack and I sit on the couch and I finally get to tear open the envelope. The check sits in the center of several folded pieces of paper. I pull it out and hold it up. "Cha Ching."

$25,000.00

"You're gonna be proud to be my brother this weekend," I say. "We are going to party for real with all this."

Bang, bang, bang.

Bang… bang… bang…

BOOM!

"I recognize that knock." Three quick, three slow, and one loud pound. "That sounded like—"

"—Hawkwinds Cadence." Mack sits up and looks at the door. "It's open!"

"Surprise." Bella waltzes in the door. "Hi, guys."

I stand and shake my head clear. "Bella?" So, it wasn't all a dream. She is so fine.

Kurht ducks around her from behind and hops up and down. "Where is the bathroom?"

"Dad." Bella rolls her eyes. "You're so embarrassing."

"Kurht?" Mack stands and points. "The bathroom's right there."

"Bio-break." Kurht steps into the bathroom and closes the door.

Bella runs up to Mack and me for a group hug. "Good to see you two again. Your campus here is so cool, and the people are so nice. I ran into Mileena downstairs, she helped us find your room."

"Oh really?" I scratch my temple. "How, uh, how is Mileena?"

Bella stands back and smiles. "Did you know she recently created a DCQ profile? She's really interested in the game after what happened. As we departed, she noted I should watch out for you, Riff. What's that all about?"

"Oh, um." I shuffle my feet. "Probably just a joke. The people her are friendly jokesters."

Mack looks at me from the corner of his eye and smirks. "Yep, jokesters."

I straighten my shirt and run a hand through my hair. Oh man, I must look a steaming hot mess. "Hey, Mack and I just received job offers from Blizivision. A guy named Mr. Shinobi just left like five minutes ago."

"You mean Mr. Shigoshi Kojimoto?" Bella laughs. "I know all about the deal. I'm part of it too. The three of us are going to be on a design team with my dad. I'm thinking about transferring to your school here for my senior year. We can start the groundwork on the game together as we work toward graduation. I mean, if that be all right with you too?"

"Sounds good to me." Yes, a perfect way to get to know Bella better. Today really is my day.

Kurht walks out of the bathroom waving a hand in front of his nose. "Did you know that your toilet is broken?"

Oh, crap.

"Really, Dad?" Bella pinches her nose.

Kurht closes the bathroom door and shrugs. "What? It was like that when I got in there. I swear."

251

He points a finger at Mack and me and cocks his head. "I need you two to come work with me at Blizivision as soon as possible. Not only do I have about a million ideas in my head for full dive VR, but also a problem has arisen in DCQ. Your friend Hans is causing havoc."

"He's *not* our friend," Bella snaps.

Kurht shrugs. "Figure of speech. Anyway, Hans is using the power of an un-locked Grimoire to become some kind of a super-griefer. This man found a way to automate some actions in order to gain experience and has leveled up to be an overpowered tyrant. He is killing off all the games' most popular players. He even made deals with the temple priests, so players can't re-spawn. Can you believe he started a griefer-guild? It's bad."

"I got an idea," Mack says. "Shut the game down for five minutes and erase that fool."

"That would be murder," Kurht says. "And not only is that illegal, it would be terrible PR for the game. No, we just need him out of there. And to do that, we need to get his Grimoire back. Hans's family and the police have been asking about his whereabouts. He was last seen entering The DCQ Players Den. These people are on me for answers, and it's a problem. The whole thing has got the Blizivision people nervous, and we don't need them pulling the plug."

Bella whisks by me and looks around the room. "Nice slippers, Riff. I really like them."

Kurht holds up an index finger. "I need you all to get back into DCQ and Game Master Hans out of there. Expel him and return him to his family. I need these problems off my back, so we can concentrate on making our mark in game industry history, a true total emersion version of DCQ. I have the ground work ready and have even picked out a code name for the project."

"You already have a code name?" I ask. "Let's hear it."

Kurht gathers Bella in next to him and lifts his chin. "The new version of Dungeon Crawl Quest will be called The Cave Maze."

THE END

THE FINAL CHARACTER SHEET OF RIFF JENKINS

NAME: *Jareth Goblinmasher »*   **AGE:** *22*

LEVEL: *5*   **EXPERIENCE POINTS:** *8,933*

HIT POINTS: *8/48*

ABILITIES: *63*

Strength: 19   Agility: 10   Intelligence: 10   Wisdom: 12   Luck: 12

ARMOR CLASS: *4/40*

Leather Armor, Small Shield, Bombardment Boots + (0)

GOLD COINS: *0*

SILVER PENNIES: *0*

SPELLS: *N/A*

PRIMARY WEAPON: *Keris of Knaud + (2) Distinguished Hack. (Soulbound)*

Executioner's Sword

POSSESSIONS: *Grimoire (5 of 6), Map+3, Perfect Placement Belt, Small Backpack, Flask of Oil, (10) Single Day's Rations, Water Skin, The Routier's Rest Rumor Table Scroll, Brim of Profound Musicianship, *Lute + (7) Charm person. (Soulbound)*Location: Mad Cobblers shop – Cittadella*

RACE: *Human*   **CLASS:** *Fighter*   **ALIGNMENT:** *Good*

TASKS: *Enter The Kingdom of Broxington.*

THE SNAKE & APPLE INN:
ODDS ON TEAMS ENTERING THE WORLD OF DUNGEON CRAWL QUEST

Team: Bibliophile: 5 - 1

From: Nuevos Aires, Patuson

Members: 6

Key personnel: Nadine Brandes (Enchanter)

Ripley Patton (Purveyor of Myth)

Darko 'Paganus' Tomic (Master Artisan)

Craig McKenzie (Consilier de afaceri)

Robert Woodhead (Samurai)

Andrew C. Greenberg (Bishop)

Team: Family Faction: 8 - 1

From: San Diego, CA, USA

Members: 8

Key personnel: Michelle (Queen)

Christopher II (Prince)

La Skyeya (Princess)

Naleesa (Duchess)

C. KaeShawn (K-Dragon)

Lelia (Marchioness)

Angelina (Countess)

Antonio (The Amazing Brick Guy)

Team: Da Noses: 10 - 1

From: California, USA

Members: 6

Key personnel: 40ozChris (Concoctor)

Mackdread (Herbalist)

Porkchop (Barbarian)

Ma$$ (Troubadour)

Shock-G (Satan Couturier)

Edward Ellington Humphries, III (Mack-Minstrel)

Team: Fantastic Science Fantasy Adventures Press: 12 - 1

From: Nottingham, UK

Members: 7

Key personnel: John Palmer (Nobel)

Beeman Beeston (Apiarist)

Master IAM of Zwolle (Compositor)

Baen Tordaw (NY, USA)

Gerald E. Waterton (SD, USA)

Bryler Alire (TO, CA)

Blue Stringyblade (SA, AU)

Team: Upholders Guild: 16 - 1

From: Parts Unknown

Members: Unknown

Key personnel:

All who have entered The Cave Maze.

All who have ported Into The Game.

Odds subject to change.

ABOUT THE AUTHOR

C. A. A. Allen lives in San Diego with his wife and six children. He is a freelance writer, local hip-hop mogul, and fantasy e-book author. He writes for many online entities, and has been published in the San Diego Reader, and CityBeat magazines. He has provided backup vocals and performed as a "Humpty Dancer" for the multi-platinum hip-hop group Digital Underground. When he isn't writing or spending time with his children, Mr. Allen enjoys horse racing, sports, and several different genres of music.

Twitter: @TheCaveMaze

C. A. A. Allen on Facebook: CaveMaze

Into The Game on Facebook: IntoTheGameBook

FANTASTIC SCIENCE
FANTASY ADVENTURES
PRESS